NIGHT STALKER

It was difficult to remember not to hold his breath. Beau breathed shallowly, quietly. It was not distracting that he could hear, or feel, each beat of his heart now. That was just part of the environment. He glanced at the ground before taking his next step, then paused, listening for any sound from the sentry in front.

How far from the corner is he? Beau wondered. It might be necessary to make a circuit of the house to approach from the other side if the sentry was too far away from this corner. *Which way will he be looking?* It was a game of odds and evens, with the stakes as high as they could possibly be.

For an instant, Beau hesitated. Even with the silencer attached, a gunshot from his pistol would not be totally silent. If anyone was awake inside the house, he might recognize the coughing noise for what it was. But the pistol would be a more certain tool for eliminating the sentry.

The knife. If possible. Otherwise, the pistol. Don't take stupid chances.

Beau edged closer to the corner, moving with almost infinite slowness and care. He flattened himself against the wall, listening with impossible concentration. After a few seconds, he heard the scraping of shoe on dirt, soft, as if the unseen person were grinding out a cigarette.

Now, Beau thought . . .

Other Books in the
SEALS STRATEGIC WARFARE *Series by*
Mike Martell

OPERATION NO MAN'S LAND

Coming Soon

SEALS

STRATEGIC WARFARE

OPERATION
HANGMAN

MIKE MARTELL

AVON BOOKS
An Imprint of HarperCollins*Publishers*

This is a work of fiction. Names, characters, places, and incidents are products of the author's imagination or are used fictitiously and are not to be construed as real. Any resemblance to actual events, locales, organizations, or persons, living or dead, is entirely coincidental.

AVON BOOKS
An Imprint of HarperCollins*Publishers*
10 East 53rd Street
New York, New York 10022-5299

Copyright © 2000 by Bill Fawcett & Associates
Library of Congress Catalog Card Number: 99–96447
ISBN: 0-380-80827-7
www.avonbooks.com

First Avon Books paperback printing: July 2000

Avon Trademark Reg. U.S. Pat. Off. and in Other Countries, Marca Registrada, Hecho en U.S.A.
HarperCollins® is a trademark of HarperCollins Publishers Inc.

Printed in the U.S.A.

WCD   10   9   8   7   6   5   4   3   2   1

PROLOGUE

Even by naval standards, the office was spartan. Lieutenant Anthony T. Holman always kept his desk clear of all but whatever he was working on at the moment. The only routine occupants of the desktop were his telephone, an oversized coffee mug, and an ashtray tooled from the casing of a five-inch shell. Although smoking was officially prohibited in the building, Holman continued to smoke, averaging half a pack during the typical work day. The desk was standard, a utilitarian gray metal artifact of more than twenty years' service—far more time than the lieutenant had put in. His chair was slightly newer, but done in the same ubiquitous gray color, as was the single file cabinet in the corner. The only decorations on the walls were a clock and a single framed photograph. Holman's predecessors had always kept a portrait of the current President there. Holman had a picture of the frigate USS *Mahan*, the first ship he had served aboard, before he had volunteered for the SEALs.

Holman answered a knock on his office door

with "Come in," and looked up at the clock. It was 0930 hours.

"Chief Lucan is here, sir," Holman's yeoman said, only opening the door far enough to stick his head through the opening.

"Send him in," Holman said, nodding.

Chief Petty Officer Frank Lucan entered, stood at attention in front of the platoon leader's desk, and saluted—not with any great military precision. Frank had twenty-one years in the U.S. Navy, almost all of it in the SEALs. Five foot seven inches tall, and stocky, with his hair starting to gray, CPO Lucan was not the type to overawe anyone at first glance, unless you noticed his eyes—dark brown, almost black—when he was angry, or working.

"You wanted to see me, Skipper?" Frank asked after Lieutenant Holman returned the casual salute. The two men were physically very different. Lieutenant Holman was tall and broad. He had been a defensive linebacker in college, and he had never allowed himself to get out of shape.

"Sit down, Frank." Holman waited until the chief was seated on one of the two wooden visitors' chairs in the office. "Langley is sending a man over."

Frank nodded. Langley meant Central Intelligence Agency.

"I can't give you details—hell, I don't *know* any details—but it's a big job for a four-man team, and they want our best. The skipper went over this with all the platoon leaders. It works out you, Guisborne, Rhodes, and Jensen. You'll have three weeks of preparatory training, then several weeks on the job."

"Jensen, sir?"

The lieutenant's eyes narrowed a bit. "You've trained with him, Frank. You know he's good. We've got to use him before he goes stale. Wishing you still had McVeigh is useless. He's out of the Teams." Frank had worked with Arnold McVeigh for a dozen years, and a more perfect team mate was beyond Frank's imagination, but McVeigh had asked for a transfer back to the fleet until his retirement. He was an airedale now, serving aboard an aircraft carrier in the Pacific— his sunset cruise.

"Yes, sir. He's good. Just a little green."

"He'll stay green until he gets a chance to prove himself," Holman said.

"Have the others been notified yet, sir?"

Holman shook his head. "You'll do that, after you hear what the Agency man has to say."

"Any idea at all what the mission is about, Lieutenant?"

"Vaguely." Holman paused before he continued. "You've heard of Faud ibn Landin?"

"Of course," Frank said. "Rich terrorist with delusions of grandeur. Thinks he can take on the whole western world by himself."

Holman smiled. "Not quite by himself. That's was the rumble is about. This Landin is trying to unite a bunch of terrorist organizations in the

Middle East under his command. He's dangerous enough alone, with his money and his ability to convince people to take suicidal chances in his holy war. If he can combine the organizations and manpower of all of these other groups, he can play hell with us. The way I understand it, he's trying to set up a large conference of terrorist leaders—sort of a constitutional convention—to finalize things. The Agency wants to spoil it, and they hope to neutralize him—and maybe some of the other bigwigs—while he's distracted. Anything more than that, you'll have to get from the Agency man. He should be here fairly soon."

"You know the spook?" Frank asked. The question was reasonable. The platoon had provided teams for CIA operations fairly often over the past decade.

"The name I was given is Harry Tombs. It doesn't ring a bell."

"Never heard of him," Frank said, shaking his head. "Not that it means much. Hard telling how many names he uses. He might not remember them all himself."

Holman grinned and shook his head. "Don't start out on the wrong foot, Frank. Give the man a chance before you start jabbing needles into him."

Frank snorted. "Only spook I ever had any use for was Casper."

Harry Tombs arrived wearing a blue pinstriped suit with creases that looked as if they had been laminated to stay sharp, thin blue tie, white dress shirt. His shoes were highly polished, his shave perfect. He made the two SEALs look shabby in their camouflage battle dress uniforms. Tombs was slightly under six feet tall and slender. He would have passed without notice on Wall Street, invisible among the brokers and bankers, or in any other collection of urban professionals. All he lacked was the briefcase.

Lieutenant Holman stood when his yeoman brought Tombs in. Chief Lucan had to rise as well, since the boss had. Holman introduced himself and Lucan. "Frank will head the team you're taking," he added.

Lucan and Tombs were already staring at each other, sizing one another up. The looks were as obvious as two fighting cocks waiting to claw each other to pieces.

"Chief," Tombs said softly, nodding a greeting.

Frank returned the nod, slightly less pronounced. "I understand you've got some field work for us."

A fraction of a smile came and went from the intelligence agent's face, so quickly that it might have been missed by an onlooker. "That's right," Tombs said.

"We might as well sit and take a load off," Lieutenant Holman said, glancing between the two. "Mr. Tombs, Frank has been in the Teams for twenty years. He's the best we've got for the kind of operation described."

"This isn't the time for a full briefing," Tombs

said, ignoring the offered chair. "All I can say right now is that we envision a series of quick in-and-out ops at a number of locations in the Red Sea area. Our base will be the battle group on patrol there. At least part of the time."

Frank nodded. He had not expected a minute-by-minute charting of the mission at this stage. That would involve only the men involved. Lieutenant Holman had no "need to know."

"You and your men go on alert status immediately," Tombs said. "Get them together. I'll have transport here for you at one o'clock this afternoon. Nobody says anything to anyone, no goodbyes to sweethearts or buddies. Nobody leaves base or goes to married quarters on base. This is well beyond Top Secret."

"We know the routine, Tombs," Frank said. It came out more harshly than he had intended. He did not see, but could sense, the frown from Lieutenant Holman.

"One o'clock, sharp. Ready to go. Right out front." Tombs gestured toward the front of the building, then walked out of the room.

1: ROOT CANAL

PRE-MISSION

According to the timetable, the anonymous corporate jet should have been twenty-five minutes from landing in Cairo, Egypt, where its passengers were to transfer to a helicopter registered to the same corporation. The flight had started in Naples, Italy. But just before the airplane had reached the Egyptian coast near Alexandria, the copilot had called the man the other four passengers knew as Harry Tombs to the cockpit. Three minutes later, the jet banked left and started to climb.

Chief Petty Officer Frank Lucan snorted softly. He waited thirty seconds to see if the plane returned to its previous course, and when it didn't, he looked around to see if his men had noticed.

Quartermaster's Mate 2nd Class Beau Guisborne was slouched in his seat, leaning against the bulkhead with his eyes closed. That was no certain evidence that he was sleeping. Six four, with long arms and legs, Beau looked deceptively mild. But he was the man in the team the others would least want to meet in a dark alley . . . if they weren't certain he was on their side.

Gunnery Mate 3rd Class Robert Rhodes was working a crossword puzzle, concentrating solely on it, as if nothing else existed in the universe. An even six feet tall and lanky, Rob seemed to fit the nicknames he had picked up ten years earlier when he'd first joined the Teams. Farmer or Farmboy: Rhodes was from Kansas but had never lived or worked on a farm. Apart from the general excellence in weapons he shared with all the members of the team, Rhodes had one extra qualification. He was the best sniper in SEAL Team Six—which had many excellent snipers.

Machinist's Mate 1st Class Ike Jensen had noticed the change in course. He had been staring out the window on the other side of the cabin, then turned to meet the chief's gaze.

"Somebody changed the itinerary," Ike said, just loud enough for Frank to make out the words. At five feet eight inches tall, Ike was nearly as short as the chief.

"That's what it looks like," Frank agreed.

"You suppose they called off the operation?" Ike asked.

Frank shrugged. "If they did, we'll find out soon enough. Don't sweat it." Ike was the rookie on the team. He had been a SEAL less than three years, and had spent more than half of that time going through various training programs, alone and with other members of the platoon.

"Yeah, don't sweat it, kid," Beau said, opening his eyes just a slit. He spoke very slowly, taking care to make each word distinct. That habit had started in boot training, when an instructor had screamed that he couldn't understand Guisborne's thick Creole accent and threatened dire consequences if the recruit didn't start speaking English. Even though the instructor had been forty pounds lighter than Beau, the veteran had intimidated the youngster from New Orleans' French Quarter. "The pay is all the same."

Another ten minutes passed—with the plane remaining firmly on a northerly heading—before they learned anything more. Harry Tombs came back into the cabin from the cockpit, and said, "Listen up."

The four SEALs all looked at the spook standing in the aisle, his hands on seat backs on either side to balance him. Rob Rhodes capped his pen and closed the crossword book around it. Beau straightened up in his seat.

"Something's come up," Tombs said, "something we have to take care of before we get on with our main mission." His shrug looked awkward because of the way he was standing. Short and thin, Tombs would look anonymous in a crowd of three. None of the SEALs had ever seen Tombs in action. He was a manager, a controller. None of the SEALs knew anything of his background. "No one else is close enough to handle this quickly, and the word from back home is that it has to be handled tonight."

Just tell us what we have to do, Frank thought. We can do without the pep talk.

THE BRIEFING

"An American has been kidnapped by one of the radical groups operating in Lebanon. The group that kidnapped him is not one of the major groups we're targeting, but operates locally under the suffrage of Hezbollah. More like a neighborhood gang. The hostage is being held in a coastal village just outside Beirut. We expect that he will be moved tomorrow, early, perhaps before first light. The U.S. does not want another long, drawnout hostage affair in Lebanon, so our orders are to go in and retrieve the hostage tonight."

He paused, but only for an instant. "There are two important constraints. First, this has to be done with total secrecy. No one is to know you've been in and out. Get in, rescue the hostage and neutralize his captors, quietly, if possible, then get out without any hue and cry. The second constraint is that you don't leave the prisoner under the control of the terrorists, no matter what. We want to rescue him, but if that isn't possible, your job is to make certain that he can't be pumped for whatever information he might have."

"One of your people?" Jensen asked. The implications of what Tombs had said about not leaving the hostage alive and in control of the terrorists did not faze him. This was the sort of mission that the team had trained for. Even among the elite SEALs, they were an elite—specialists in counter-terrorist measures.

Tombs stared at Jensen for a moment before he answered. "For now, let's just say that it is someone with knowledge that could compromise our primary mission to undermine the upcoming summit meeting of terrorist organizations in Sudan. His identification, if he still has it, is in the name Carl Smith. There will be photographs of the hostage, maps, and other necessary information waiting for us when we land at Incirlik."

"That's an Air Force base in Turkey, just outside Adana, for any of you who might not know," Frank said in something of a stage whisper.

"Carl Smith?" Rob Rhodes asked, under his breath. "We run out of John Smiths?" No one responded to his remark.

"We'll be met by a Navy helicopter at Incirlik and ferried out to a waiting submarine, which will take you in as close to the beach as its commander deems safe, and wait to retrieve you."

"What's the size of the opposition?" Frank asked.

After a habitual hesitation, Tombs said, "Not large. According to witnesses, there were only three men involved in the snatch. Maybe two or three additional men were already in the house where they took him. We don't expect more than that because both the Lebanese government and the Israelis have been making life too difficult for these splinter groups lately, forcing them into tighter cell operations. And we don't have any information that there might be more assets available. It will be tomorrow, according to what we do know, before they can move the hostage to friendlier ground—to the Bekah valley, at least— perhaps all the way to Syria. Like I said, it was a small local group that got lucky and grabbed more than they were expecting. They'll use them to improve their own standing with the big boys, just as quickly as they can turn him over."

"Anything unusual in the way of weapons?" Rob asked.

Tombs shook his head, not *too* slowly. "Not that we know of. Rifles, pistols, grenades, maybe one or two Russian-made SAMs. The missiles shouldn't be a threat. You won't be going in by air."

THE TARGET FOLDER

There was a full target folder waiting for the team when they landed at Incirlik. It was in a heavy envelope carried inside a briefcase that was handcuffed to the courier who delivered it to Harry Tombs as soon as the five men disembarked from their jet. Tombs signed a receipt and the courier left. Tombs and the SEALs walked a few feet to the helicopter that was waiting for him, ready to take off.

Frank almost allowed himself to be impressed by how thorough the mission briefing papers that accompanied the operational order were on such short notice—especially since he'd assumed it had been coordinated by CIA rather than Naval Intelligence. He was neither bothered nor amused by the code names strewn through the cover document for the target folder. He had long ago decided that those names were chosen by people who had failed psychological screening for any worthwhile occupation in the defense establishment.

There were several photographs of the hostage in the package, along with a detailed physical description and an identification code. There were satellite photographs of the village and the surrounding countryside, right down to the beach where the SEALs would go ashore. There were navigation charts for the area and a topographical map of the land area. There was also a list of the gear available for their use on the submarine, along with a few small cases they carried with them.

Harry Tombs left the Navy men to themselves. He sat off by himself paying only casual attention to them as they started to prepare themselves for the mission.

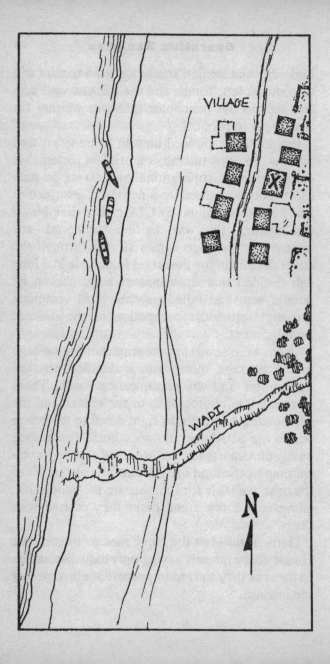

VILLAGE

X

WADI

N

The SEALs studied all of the briefing material on the helicopter, passing the sheets around one at a time. Frank made a few comments as he handed off the papers. "Memorize the map of the village and the terrain down to the water," was the instruction he considered most important. "The house where the hostage is supposedly being held is the one with the red X on it. We can't carry the map with us or call Traveler's Aid." Frank had a special gift with maps. He could study a simple map—like the one that showed the village—for a few minutes and duplicate it from memory, if necessary.

After everyone had had a chance to look over each of the papers in the target folder, the four SEALs moved closer together to study the map together.

"We'll put the boat in here, at the mouth of this dry wadi," Frank said, stabbing at the paper with his finger. "Work up along that wash as close in as we can get."

"Looks like they got this scoped out pretty well," Ike said, as Frank collected the material and stuck it back in the folder. Jensen seemed relieved.

"Assuming it worth a damn," Guisborne said after a grunt. "Maybe it is, maybe ain't."

"Most of the time it is," Frank said, not wanting to spook the team's junior member too much. "And even if it isn't, we'll deal with whatever we find."

THE PREPARATION

The SEALs had only ninety minutes aboard the fast-attack submarine. As soon as it picked them up, fifty miles off the coast of Lebanon, it submerged and started a high-speed run toward the insertion point. Their gear had come aboard with them, in three aluminum crates. The last three weeks had been much the same for Frank and his men—they were always in a rush. The team had been alerted for action, then moved immediately from their barracks at Dam Neck, Virginia, to a facility maintained by Central Intelligence. There had been refresher training on tactics, the usual daily calisthenics and running, weapons practice, and a series of briefings on the coming operation. Then there had been rather circuitous transportation, taking the men to New York and London, and then on to Naples. They had seen little of their surroundings in any of those cities.

Aboard the submarine, the SEALs were given the use of one of the cabins normally occupied by crewmen—the usual residents warned to stay clear while the SEALs were there. Frank and his men changed from their civilian traveling clothes into camouflage BDUs—battle dress uniforms—and boots, put on their black and dark green camouflage make-up, then checked out their weapons and other gear. The BDUs were standard jungle camouflage. At night, that would serve better

than desert camouflage or even all-black clothing.

Although the team wanted this mission to proceed silently, without alarm, they intended to go
in prepared for a fight, which in this case meant
an M16 rifle.

The M16 series of weapons was the first small-
caliber, high-velocity weapon fielded by the U.S.
military. Intended for use by Special Forces, it was
designed to carry light, consisting primarily of
aluminum alloy and plastic parts, with steel used
only where necessary for strength. Early models
were known to cause almost explosive-effect
wounds due to the intentional instability of the
projectile; later designs were more accurate but
less destructive. The light weight of the weapon
and ammunition made it unpopular with traditional military commanders, but the men who
actually carry and fight with them have always
found them dependable—as long as they kept
them clean. And the SEALs made sure they kept
their weapons clean and ready. Being ready

M-16

included a KAC blast suppressor and 100-round C-mag double-drum magazine. If more ammunition was needed, each man had six standard 30-round magazines in pouches on his web belt.

Each SEAL also carried a pistol and knife, as well as three hand grenades—two high explosive, one smoke. The pistols, .45 caliber H&K Mark 23s, were also equipped with suppressors—silencers. Frank and Beau each carried a second knife in a boot. The load of weapons and ammunition was heavy, but no one would carry any unnecessary gear on this mission, no field packs or rations. They had crammed in a quick meal aboard the submarine. That would have to hold them until they returned.

"Just keep cool, kid," Frank advised Ike while the four men were getting ready. "You've never been on an op quite like this. The rest of us have. Remember your training and keep your head. We'll get you back in one piece if you don't screw up."

Jensen swallowed and nodded. He had started to think about what might be coming.

"I hope the intel is right," Rhodes said. "We won't have time to bust into every house in that village looking for our man." Rob and Frank had been together on several snatch operations. One, during Operation Desert Storm, had almost been a disaster. They had been assigned to hit a house in southeastern Iraq to grab a division commander in the elite Republican Guard, and he had not been there, but in the next building over.

He had decided to change beds in the middle of the night.

"In and out and leave nothing behind," Frank said. "If the poop is bad, we still get ourselves out. We run into trouble, we use all the firepower we carry and disappear before the locals can react."

"It's what we do," Guisborne said softly, as much to himself as to the others.

THE MISSION

The few feet of sail that the submarine showed as it deployed the SEAL team were pointed directly at the coast—three nautical miles away. With a new moon and scattered clouds, there was almost no light. That made no difference to the SEALs; they wore night-vision goggles. Frank Lucan and his men got an inflatable rapid penetration boat into the water, then hurriedly climbed aboard. Almost before the craft's small outboard motor came to life, the submarine was back below the surface again, leaving only a few diminishing ripples as evidence that it had ever been there.

All four men stayed as low in the boat as they could, minimizing the silhouette. Beau handled the engine and steering. He had a diver's compass strapped to his left wrist, and held the tiller in his right hand. Frank and Rob were in the prow of the boat, rifles at the ready, though there was little likelihood that they would need them before reaching the coast. Ike was in the middle, doing his best to avoid showing the tension he thought he alone felt. He carried the team's radio, although if there was any need for radio communications before the men were ready to rendezvous with the sub after the mission, it would mean something had gone wrong.

The outboard motor was muffled, the exhaust directed underwater. With the throttle kept near the midpoint, it made very little noise. When the boat got closer to shore, Beau throttled back even farther, making the engine almost completely silent.

It took the team almost as long to cover three miles in the RPB as it had taken the sub to cover fifty miles. For the most part, this was dead time, little for the men to do but watch the water and—eventually—the shore. Time to think, time to worry. But patience was not merely a homey virtue for these men. It was a prerequisite. The Teams had recognized that since their early days in Vietnam, when a team might have to wait in ambush—often in canals, rivers, or rice paddies—for hours until their quarry came within reach.

Only Beau had physical activity to help pass the time. He worked the engine and tiller, watched the compass, and kept an eye on the landmark he had picked out on shore once they got within a mile of the sand. The other three had only to remain alert, watching for unexpected trouble. There was no reason to expect problems going in, but on an operation like this, you had to be ready for anything. Adrenaline helped, but training was a far more important part of the equation. If nothing else, the Teams stressed constant training. It was not just an entrance ritual, abandoned upon graduation from BUD/S, Basic Underwater Demolition School. Training continued as long as a man was in the Teams.

Each man was responsible for a specific area of the perimeter. Rhodes watched to port, Jensen to starboard. At the stern, Beau kept a somewhat less constant watch on the water behind them, glancing back over his shoulder and taking a quick scan as an interruption to his concentration on navigation. And Frank, the team leader, watched ahead.

During the last five hundred yards of the approach, Frank constantly scanned the shore with binoculars, moving his gaze from side to side, working gradually across the beach and up to the olive grove and the first buildings of the village. No people were visible, though he did spot a few goats and donkeys penned up behind mud brick houses. The village was smaller than it had once been—before the years of civil war and repeated Israeli air strikes. The site had been inhabited for at least three thousand years, one generation of buildings built over the ruins of those that had come before. Now, there was an area of rubble and partially destroyed buildings beyond the portion of the village that was still intact and inhabited. In time, these ruins would no doubt be built over again.

What Frank considered important was the fact that the layout he saw with his eyes agreed with the layout visible in the photographs and maps he had studied. So far, at least, the intelligence was good.

Two hundred yards out, Frank lowered his binoculars, then lifted his night-vision goggles. The beach was not totally dark. The sand caught and reflected what little light there was, and the trees and buildings beyond were easy silhouettes. The gentle surf rolling against the sand and rocks seemed almost phosphorescent, the water sparkling before it started to roll back toward its home. Farther north, and more to the east, Frank could see the glowing dome of light in the sky that had to mark Beirut. The city was far enough away for comfort.

A dog barked, well in the distance, its call carrying easily over the water. Beau eased the throttle back another hair, softening the already muted sound of the boat's engine. He had been around small boats his entire life. His father and uncles had been fishermen, working the Louisiana bayous and the nearer stretches of the Gulf of Mexico, and Beau had spent his summers and many weekends helping out. If he had not chosen to enter the Navy, he would undoubtedly have still been fishing for a (meager) living. It had been the uncertainty of the family business that had sent Beau looking for something more certain.

"Ease us over toward that dry creek bed," Frank whispered, turning toward Beau. He gestured to the right. Those were the first words any of the men had uttered since emerging from the submarine seventy minutes earlier.

Beau nodded and moved the tiller to port, edging the boat toward starboard. He glanced back. There was almost no visible trace of a wake behind the boat now. Beau picked up his rifle, balanced it across his legs, and moved the safety to the off position.

Frank leaned back into the boat, turning toward Jensen. "Kid, take a deep breath and let it out real slow. Don't go hyper on us. You know the drill."

Jensen nodded and did as he had been told.

"Take your right hand off your weapon. Flex the fingers," Frank said, and again Jensen obeyed instructions.

"I'll be okay, Chief," Jensen said. "Once we're ashore and moving, I'll be okay." He had been surprised at being asked to join this team—handpicked by the senior chief petty officer in the platoon—and he was eager to prove himself. But three years in the Teams had taught him not to appear *too* eager.

Frank stared at him for a couple of seconds, then nodded once, a short, abrupt gesture. The kid should work out, he thought. Frank would never let the kid know that he had not been his own choice.

Frank turned to the front again and used the binoculars for another complete scan of the shore. The boat was within a hundred yards of the mouth of the dry river bed. By this point, he was nearly lying in the boat, little more than the top of his head visible above the inflated rubber. The camouflaged slouch hat he wore had been crumpled so many times that it presented a most irregular silhouette, and the blotches of camouflage grease-paint on his face would not present a recognizable target at any distance.

He focused on the mission at hand completely now, shutting out everything else. He trusted the men with him to do their jobs. On an op, it was all a man could do to make sure he didn't screw up without worrying about the other guys on the team. Frank thought it was more important for him to concentrate now than it ever had been before. He was staring at his fortieth birthday, coming in less than a month. Frank was no longer quite as . . . sturdy as he had once been. He had slowed down just a step, and his endurance was no longer the same. I've got to use my head to make up the difference, or get out of the Teams, he often told himself. Since he did not want to leave the SEALs, he drove himself in training, and exercised on his own in addition to the usual regimen of calisthenics and running the platoon did at the base. He could still run a marathon, and even if it took him fifteen minutes longer than he had when he was a rookie, he could finish ahead of most of the others in the platoon, even the new

men who had been in diapers when he'd joined
the Navy.

Rob adjusted his position in the boat, anticipating, ready to get out and up onto the beach as
quickly as possible as soon as the bottom of the
boat touched sand. This is a long way from
Kansas, he thought. It was something he would
never *say* again, not where there was any chance
anyone would hear. That was a mistake he had
made for the last time four years earlier, in a bar,
with a couple of dozen other men from the Teams
present. Someone had said, "We're not in Kansas
anymore, Toto," in a squeaky falsetto and someone else had started singing, "We're Off to See
the Wizard," and a half dozen others had joined
in. It had been the wrong thing at the wrong time.
Rob and the two men he had entered the bar with
got out just before the Shore Patrol arrived to
break up the melee Rob had started. In the last
eight years, Rob had been back to the state he
had been born and raised in only three times,
twice for funerals, the other time for his brother's
wedding. If he never went back again, it would
suit him just fine.

Beau eased off a little more on the throttle,
until the boat was barely making headway. He
wasn't certain just how quickly the sea floor rose
here, how steep the incline was, and he did not
want to drive the boat too hard onto the sand.
The bow was aimed directly at the middle of the
indentation of the dry creek bed. Looks good, he
thought—there was no trace of anyone anywhere

around. They would certainly be able to get ashore and across the beach into the cover of the olive grove undetected. After that . . .

He did not finish the thought. He heard the first scraping of sand against the raft and cut the engine completely. The others were already climbing out. Beau was the last. The four men dragged the boat the last thirty feet, out of the water, and up into the rocky bed of the dry creek. At the bow, Frank looped the boat's painter around a rock to keep it secure. The tide had not quite reached its peak yet, and they did not want the boat to float away when it started to ebb.

No one noticed wet boots and trousers. They had spent too many hours, on other occasions, standing or squatting in water up to their shoulders, or necks, for this minimal discomfort to penetrate their concentration. This water, at least, was *warm*.

For perhaps twenty seconds, all four men remained motionless, crouched over, rifles held in both hands, listening, looking—each man staring in a different direction. What little breeze there was came from the west, off the Mediterranean. The smells of land—and habitation—were slow to make themselves known. Frank sniffed at the air. The odor on the air was different from Virginia . . . or Panama, Grenada, or Iraq, or any of the other places he had come ashore over the years. He did not try to identify the components of the smell, beyond the glaringly obvious odor of animal waste.

Finally satisfied with what he saw and heard—or didn't see and hear—Frank made a minimal gesture with his right hand and started moving along the dry creek bed, wadi, toward the village. Landing at its mouth had added almost three hundred yards to the distance they would have to travel each way, but it offered a much better chance of remaining unobserved. Farther north, near the shortest route from shore to village, there were a few fishing boats drawn up on the beach, and where there were boats, there might be people.

For Ike, the transition from boat to foot was almost like an electrical shock, marked by a palpable physical change. It was something he had never truly experienced before. There was a recognition that danger was now imminent, that they were in "Indian country"—as some of the older men in the Teams, with a total disregard for political correctness, still put it. For the few seconds that everyone had stood still, Ike had felt a considerable increase in his tension, a feeling that if he brought a hand near his face, he would get a static shock. The hair on his arms felt as if it were standing at attention, or trying to escape the skin that held it prisoner. He took a deep breath, then blinked once. But as soon as he started moving, following the chief, his tension, his nervousness, seemed to melt away. He could concentrate on doing his job, no doubts left.

There wasn't room.

The four men moved like the well-trained team

they were, scarcely conscious of the movements of one another, but responding as they needed to, instinctively, staying relatively close, dividing the responsibility of watching the terrain around them without needing discussion or orders. Frank led; point was where he felt most at ease, despite the dangers of that position. Rob was next, and a little to Frank's left, covering mainly the left side. Because of that, Ike concentrated mostly—but never exclusively—on the right flank. Beau watched the rear without losing his place in the procession.

They moved in almost total silence, the only sound the occasional crunch of a stone moving underfoot, too soft to be heard more than a few yards away, lost in environmental noises—water washing against the shore behind them, distant animal sounds from livestock in the village and night-flying birds, the rustle of leaves in the olive grove ahead of them.

The beach, and the wadi, climbed quickly away from the water, the gradient generally near twenty-five percent. By the time the land started to level out, the SEALs were sixty yards from the water's edge. The wadi became shallower about the same time. Frank paused again, crouching lower, as soon as he could see the plain above the beach—the olive grove flanking the dry creek bed directly in front, the more distant shapes of the buildings and ruins in the village off to the left.

Frank scanned the olive grove very closely. It

was all too easy to see phantoms among the gnarled trunks and branches, to imagine people—armed men—waiting in ambush. He looked and listened until he was certain that he was seeing only trees and hearing their leaves. The phantoms vanished. The other men stopped almost simultaneously behind their leader, no more than a single step late. They froze in position, waiting, each man scanning his area of the perimeter, overlapping. Finally satisfied, Frank turned just long enough to spot his men behind him. He nodded, the turned back and started moving again.

Once within the grove, the men scrambled out of the wadi one at a time, each man moving to cover behind one of the scraggly trees, kneeling or prone, however he was most comfortable, ready to react instantly to any threat that might appear.

The nearest buildings of the village were less than two hundred yards away. Even Frank could feel his heart rate increasing slightly as they drew closer to the target. Every step they took now, the chance of discovery would increase. If they were spotted before they were ready to break into the house that was supposed to hold the hostage they had come to rescue, the success of the mission—not to mention their lives—might be in extreme danger.

When they started moving again, the four men scurried from shadow to shadow, pausing each time they reached another fragment of cover, staying low, pacing their breathing as best they could. For Frank, the feeling now was almost like the "runner's high" he had heard distance runners talk about, but had never felt himself, even during a marathon—a heady, preternatural awareness, a feeling almost of invulnerability. *Almost.* He never let the feeling take full control of him. Training, experience—and his own nature—would not let him surrender that control. He would not go fey like some ancient Viking warrior. Survival was part of the mission.

For Rob, it was the feeling of being a hunter again. He had hunted pheasant, deer, and various small animals in company with his father, two uncles, and several cousins while he was growing up in Kansas. It was there that he had honed his marksmanship, learning early that he could bring down prey at far greater distances than the others with him would even attempt. By his first year in high school, though, he had started opting out of the fall and winter excursions whenever he could. They had lost their earlier allure. Operating as a SEAL was not nearly the same, but the memories were there, below the surface, adding a slight coloring to his perception of what happened. He had hunted in Kuwait and Iraq, and in other places he dared not talk about.

Beau had memories of hunting as well, but a far different kind. Growing up in New Orleans, there had been gang fights, teenagers hunting teenagers through the streets and alleys. Many of the groups—and most of the enmity—were racist.

Unlike some of his friends, he had never tried to hide or deny his Creole heritage and his mixed ancestry. When necessary, he had fought—as hard and ruthless as he had to be. He had not found it necessary to fight that kind of battle since joining the Navy.

The olive grove did not run all of the way to the buildings in the village. There was clear ground between, ranging from thirty to nearly a hundred yards. Still within the cover of the grove, the four men went to ground again, spread out more than they had been on the move. There were some things that the photographs and maps could never tell them—especially about the presence of lookouts or armed sentries, and whether the animals were restless, liable to make a ruckus at the intrusion of outsiders.

The men took their time with these observations, lying prone, weapons loosely pointed in the direction of the objective, staying nearly motionless. Eyes scanned. Heads turned only minimally. There were both goats and donkeys in pens behind some of the houses, not many, rarely more than two or three animals in each enclosure. A couple of minutes after the SEALs had taken up their positions, a lone dog trotted along the center of the village's lone street, moving away from the intruders, its tail low, intent on whatever goal lay ahead of it.

It was the dog that gave Frank and his companions their first indication of a watcher within the village. The dog started, then took a couple of steps to its left—while looking right—before it resumed its course.

Frank's soft grunt was inaudible, even to the men near him. There was a sentry—at least a person—near the side of the street, outside. That was the easy guess. It was also a shred of evidence that there was something out of the ordinary going on in the village, that the intelligence might be correct about a hostage being held there. What other reason could there be for a watcher there?

Cautiously, Frank crawled over to Beau. The two men looked at each other. Frank pointed into the village, then made a clichéd motion drawing a finger across his throat. Beau understood the order. He nodded, then started moving.

Beau had noticed the change in the dog's movement as well, and had understood what it had to mean. He had already picked a path for himself to the buildings. He stayed low, but did not try to crawl the entire distance. Now that he had some idea where the sentry was, it was easy to keep buildings between him and that point.

It took Beau little more than two minutes to work his way to the second building in the village, next to the house where the hostage was supposedly being held. He came in behind the animal pen, moving very slowly, watching the three goats in it closely, ready to stop moving altogether if any of them started to stir.

At the corner of the building, Beau was very

slow and deliberate about exposing himself. He looked carefully between the two houses, but the sentry was not visible. He had to be either in front of the next house or on the far side of it.

Beau slung his rifle and pulled his knife. This *had* to be done silently, not just because the mission called for stealth. If the sentry had time to raise an alarm, any other guards inside would be alerted—and might kill the hostage rather than risk his rescue. Although Beau could not spare even a second to turn and look for his comrades, he knew where they were *supposed* to go. He trusted that they would be moving into position to support him if necessary.

After a few seconds of standing motionless, listening, a new smell made itself known against the backdrop of animal dung. Tobacco smoke. Beau was unaware of the slight smile that crossed his face when he recognized the aroma. The sentry was obviously not paying full attention to his duties.

Nothing would be gained by waiting longer.

Beau had picked out his path while he was waiting, scanning the narrow passageway between the two houses for any obstructions that might make noise. He knew where to put his feet. He crossed the six-foot gap and pressed against the wall of the house that he assumed held the hostage. Although he moved quickly, it was with extreme care. He was more deliberate about moving toward the front of the house. Beau had his knife in his left hand, away from the building, to avoid any chance of scraping it against the mud bricks.

At this stage, there was a huge chance that things could go wrong, and go wrong *fast*. The sentry might pace down to the corner and look between the houses—too far away for Beau to silence him before he could raise an alarm. Maybe.

It was difficult to remember not to hold his breath. Beau breathed shallowly, quietly. It was not distracting that he could hear, or feel, each beat of his heart now. That was just part of the environment, a metronome. He glanced at the ground before taking each step. He paused between them, listening for any sound from the sentry in front.

How far from the corner is he? Beau wondered. It might be necessary to make a circuit of the house to approach from the other side if the sentry was too far away from this corner. Which way will he be looking? It was a game of odds and evens, with the stakes as high as they could possibly be.

For an instant, Beau hesitated. Even with the silencer attached, a gunshot from his pistol would not be totally silent. If anyone was awake inside the house, he might recognize the coughing noise for what it was. But the pistol would be a more certain tool for eliminating the sentry.

The knife—if possible. Otherwise, the pistol. Don't take stupid chances.

Beau edged closer to the corner, moving with almost infinite slowness and care. He flattened himself against the wall, listening with impossible concentration. After a few seconds, he heard the scraping of shoe on dirt, soft, lasting no more than a few seconds, as if the unseen person were grinding out a cigarette.

Now, Beau thought, as he eased his head closer, glancing past the corner, ready to move in any direction. When he saw the sentry—eight feet away, turned slightly away from him, getting ready to light another cigarette, AK-47 rifle slung on his shoulder, Beau moved quickly. Two long steps and a lunge closed the gap. Beau's right arm went around the sentry's head, his hand covering the man's mouth, pulling back, exposing the man's neck. At the same time, Beau brought his knife around and slit the man's throat, cutting deep enough that he heard the scrape of steel against bone. Blood gushed out over the knife blade and Beau's hand, seeping up his arm under the sleeve of his BDU. Beau held on even when the man went limp, then lowered him carefully to the ground, getting his body on top of the man to still the involuntary thrashing of approaching death. Only when the man stopped moving completely did Beau get back to his feet, looking around to make certain that he had not been discovered.

He needed a few seconds to get his breathing under control. The heady rush of adrenaline that had come during the attack was not ready to fade, but Beau remained alert. He wiped the blade of his knife on the dead man's khaki shirt, then sheathed it and wiped his bloody left hand as best he could before he took his M-16 from his shoulder. He looked around. There was a single window as well as the door in the front of the house. The window was shuttered, as the one he had seen on the rear of the house was. There had been neither window nor door on the side he had come along.

There was no sound audible from inside the house. Nor was there any hint of light around the door or window.

Then Frank was at Beau's side, a hand on his shoulder to get his attention. Frank nodded, an appreciation of the job Beau had done. Beau looked over his shoulder. Ike was at the corner of the building, his attention on the street and the house fronts across the way. Rob would be at the rear of the target house, ready to prevent anyone from escaping through the rear window—and ready to force open the shutter to add his firepower to the operation if that became necessary.

Frank mouthed the word *Ready?* without sound. Beau nodded, sucking in a deep breath while he did. Still, Frank waited, giving his team mate and friend a few more seconds to recover. They had no need for discussion. Although they had no way to know the precise layout of the house's interior, nor any certain knowledge of how many people might be inside—or where—this was a bread-and-butter operation for them, something they had trained at routinely, from the beginning of their varied tenures in Team Six. And they had discussed the specifics of how they would handle this job on the submarine. *No chances* had been the consensus. They would use their rifles to put down any opposition inside. Between noise suppressors on the weapons and the thick mud brick walls, there was every chance that they would not wake people even in the neighboring houses if they didn't give the opposition a chance to fire unsuppressed weapons.

At the corner of the house, Ike kept glancing toward Frank and Beau, waiting for them to enter. As soon as they did, he would move to the doorway behind them, ready to add to the offense, to help pull the hostage out, or to stand off any reinforcements who might attempt to enter the fray—whatever the situation called for. He glanced at the dead man twice, and the second time he had to force himself to look away. He had bled considerably. Now he lay on his back, head tilted at an unnatural angle, the slit throat a second—gaping—mouth frozen in a silent scream.

Frank and Beau took their positions at either side of the door—Beau on the latch side, the right. If they had to break the door down, it would be up to Beau to kick it. He was considerably heavier than the chief.

The two exchanged a final glance. Frank used his left hand to try the handle on the door. The handle turned, and he pushed the door just enough to assure himself that it was not locked.

Frank pulled his hand back just as Beau hurled himself against the door. Beau followed the door into the room, moving across the opening, his rifle looking for targets as Frank crossed behind him to the other side.

Two men had been sleeping on blankets on the floor. The noise of the door slamming against the wall woke them. One almost managed to get his hands on the rifle lying at his side. The other barely got his eyes open. As soon as Beau was certain that neither of these men was the hostage, he took care of both of them, his rifle stuttering out two three-shot bursts. One of the men on the floor managed a long gasp of agony as his body jerked under the impact of the bullets. The other man died in silence, his body moving as if shocked by a defibrillator.

Frank was already moving past those two, toward one of the two doorways at the rear of the room, leading—he assumed—to the only other chambers in the house. He took the one on the right, leaving the other to Beau. There were no doors in these openings, just unadorned curtains to give some privacy to the occupants.

The room Frank had taken proved to be the kitchen, and there was no one in it. A quick scan. Frank saw boxes of ammunition on a small table set against the wall. There were minimal supplies on open shelves above it, a two-burner stove, a small sink. He went back to the doorway. Ike was across the room, watching the street outside.

Beau was moving through the curtain into the final room. Frank hurried to back him up.

Assuming that anyone in this final room might have heard and recognized gunshots, Beau went in low, diving through, under the curtain, and rolled to the left.

A muzzle flashed a staccato light show. The sound of the rifle seemed unbearably loud in the confined room. The slugs went well over Beau's head, and the strobing light at the weapon's muzzle gave him a perfect target. He fired another three-shot burst and the other rifle stopped. It clattered to the floor an instant ahead of the man who had been carrying it.

Frank came into the room, scanning quickly over the barrel of his rifle, his motions a little jerky now as he tried to see the entire room at once. "There," he said, gesturing toward the wall on the left side of the room. "On the bed."

Beau was already getting to his knees. He used the side of the bed to help him get to his feet. The hostage was lying there, eyes open no more than a slit, wrists and ankles tied to the frame of the bed. He showed no reaction to the noise.

Frank was at the man's side quickly, feeling the side of his neck for a pulse. The hostage was alive, but his heart rate was low. "Cut his feet free," Frank said, while drawing his knife to cut the ropes tying the hostage's wrists.

Carl Smith—whatever his real name might have been—showed no sign that he was aware of anything going on around him. Frank took a small flashlight from his belt to get a better look at the hostage's face. It was bruised badly. One eye was swollen shut. Running the light along the man's body, Frank saw more signs that he had taken a considerable beating—blood on clothing that had been ripped several times. His left ankle was also swollen and bruised, at least badly sprained, more likely broken.

"We gonna have ta carry him," Beau noted.

There was a soft whistle from the other room before Frank could answer. He moved to the doorway.

"Company coming," Ike said. He had moved into the house and had the front door partially closed. "About a half dozen men moving this way from the east end of the village. At a jog. They've got weapons."

"Hold on a second, I'll be right there," Frank told him. Then he turned to Beau. "Get Smith out the back window. You go with him. I want you and the Farmer ready to cover Ike and me. We'll slow them down."

He didn't wait for a reply.

Out by the front door, it took Frank four seconds to tell Ike what they were going to do. "Pop out and down. Spray 'em. Then back in and out the back window."

Frank glanced out the door, then muttered, "On three. One, two, three."

He shoved the door open all the way and Ike

went down on his stomach, landing with just his head, shoulders, and rifle outside. Frank stayed over him, in the doorway, firing left-handed. Neither man worried about being conservative with ammunition. So far, very little had been expended. They worked their aim back and forth across the street, getting the range almost instantly.

The split second of surprise was all they needed. At least four of the approaching locals went down hard, hit in the first volley of automatic fire. The others went down, too, but Frank wasn't certain that they had become casualties. In any case, they would be in no great hurry to come closer. And there had been no return fire. Yet.

"Let's go, kid," Frank said. "Pull yourself in while I keep them down."

Ike scrambled backward as quickly as if there had been a viper wanting to get intimate with his ear. Frank loosed another two long bursts at the figures lying in the dirt street, then retreated behind Ike, satisfied that he had scored more hits—needed or not. Jensen went through the glassless window head first, rolling as he hit the ground, coming back to his feet almost gracefully, quickly ready to use his rifle or run, whatever the situation might demand.

Frank was not quite so adventurous in his exit. He hoisted himself up onto the window sill, swung his legs out, and hopped down. "You've been watching too many *kung fu* movies, kid," he said as he moved past Ike. "You and Beau carry Smith down to the boat. The Farmer and I will provide cover."

Jensen and Guisborne slung their rifles and got the still unconscious Carl Smith between them in an upright carry, holding his arms over their shoulders. They started back toward the olive grove and wadi, moving as quickly as they could.

"We'll stick close until we hit the trees," Frank told Rob, once the others had covered the first twenty yards, "then hold back a bit."

"Not too far back, I hope," Rob said. "The locals might head straight for the beach and come around in front of us."

Frank nodded. "Not too far," he agreed.

Even carrying the limp 180-pound man between them, Ike and Beau made good time. Since the locals knew *someone* was around, they were no longer quite so intent on stealth. Speed was more important, and the sooner they were on their boat and well out to sea, the happier they would be. It was likely that their little boat would be able to outrun anything the villagers might have to chase them with.

Rob and Frank leapfrogged each other, one moving while the other kept his attention on the village, watching for any sign of pursuit. The shooting had startled the livestock. The animals were all milling around their pens. There was some bleating and braying. Several dogs were howling.

The two men slid down into the wadi and

turned to look back over the bank, rifles ready for action as they scanned the terrain north of them.

"Maybe we should have blown their boats," Rhodes said. "They might chase us right out to the sub."

"Their funeral if they do," Frank said, and then he was up and moving again. There was no sign of direct pursuit.

By the time he and Rob reached the beach, the others had Smith in the boat and the boat out in the water. Beau already had the engine idling, ready. As soon as the last two members of the team were aboard, he opened the throttle.

"See what you can do for our guest," Frank said, nudging Rob. "We got him this far. Let's try to make sure he's still alive when we deliver him. Ike, arm the pinger and trail it over the side. Make sure the bus knows we're coming."

The submarine rose furtively, scarcely disturbing the surface of the Mediterranean as it came up to retrieve the men and their rubber boat. Carl Smith was hoisted aboard in a basket stretcher and passed below for the pharmacist's mate to treat.

Frank was the last member of the team to slip through the hatch into the submarine. He glanced at his watch on the way down the ladder. It was 0103 hours.

POST-MISSION

Harry Tombs had "borrowed" the submarine's wardroom, where Frank and his men had shed their working gear and taken a couple of minutes to clean up. Then Frank gave a terse report of what they had done. The CIA man sat at the head of the table and listened. He did not make notes.

"You did what you had to do," he said when Frank finished his quick narrative. "A good job."

"What about Smith?" Rob asked. "He gonna be okay?"

"Looks like," Tombs said. "He's still unconscious, or semiconscious. He took one hell of a beating, and apparently he had been drugged at the end, I guess to make sure he didn't try to escape during the night. He'll be airlifted to the *Eisenhower* before dawn, then be taken from the flattop to a good hospital ashore."

"What about us?" Frank asked.

"Vacation's over. Time to get to the work we were sent out to do."

THE REPORT

The four SEALs had gone off to catch a couple of hours of sleep before a helicopter arrived to pick them up. Harry Tombs sat by himself in the executive officer's cabin. The room was dark except for the active matrix screen of his portable computer. Cigarette smoke curled and floated across the glow, thin, wispy clouds that almost made the report he was typing on the screen look three-dimensional. He had already completed the detailed recounting of the mission to rescue Carl Smith, which said exactly what Frank Lucan had told him—almost. All that remained was his summary, his categorization of the effort, and he intended to take great care with every word.

```
In view of the fact that this was not
the mission we planned and trained for
before deployment, and the minimal time
for planning and preparation the SEAL
team and myself did have while enroute
to the operational site, the outstand-
ing success seems all the more signifi-
cant. The SEALs were able to execute my
plan almost flawlessly. I have high
expectations for our eventual success.
```

2: CALLING CARD

PRE-MISSION

The four SEALs sat together for lunch aboard the *Bellman*, a guided missile frigate in the *Theodore Roosevelt*'s battle group, patrolling the Red Sea. It was the second meal aboard the ship for Frank Lucan's team. They had eaten breakfast that morning, then gone to bed. The four men wore camouflage BDUs, which effectively set them apart from the ship's normal complement. Only a few members of *Bellman*'s crew were in the galley, and they gave the SEALs a wide berth. Although no general announcement had been made concerning the "passengers," or the crates of equipment that had been loaded two weeks earlier, scuttlebutt had quickly spread the word that the ship was ferrying "four of those crazy SEAL SOBs and a spook."

Harry Tombs, aka "the spook," rated a seat in the wardroom, but he had chosen to forgo lunch, and had scarcely touched his breakfast that morning. Although the sea was placid and *Bell-*

man was steady in the water, Tombs had been seasick almost from the moment the five men had boarded her just after dawn—to the immediate amusement of his companions.

"You know," Frank said, speaking quietly from habit, "in my twenty years in the Navy, I've spent less than six months total aboard ships. In-and-out crap, like this, mostly." He chuckled. "And maybe three years in small boats, rubber and otherwise."

Beau just snorted. He didn't need to mention that he had done a year aboard a cruiser, his first assignment out of quartermaster school, before he'd volunteered for the Teams. The others knew. The Farmer had served six months on a minesweeper. Ike had gone straight into BUD/S after earning his machinist's rating. That morning had been only the second time he had even *seen* a flattop, and it had appeared even more impressive from the air than the first had tied up at the dock in San Diego.

"You suppose Tombs is going to be able to brief us this afternoon without upchucking a half dozen times?" Rhodes asked. "Man, his face was as green as Astroturf this morning."

"Why would he get seasick on this ship when the sub didn't bother him?" Ike Jensen asked. "I mean, it moved around more than *Bellman*. Here, I can almost forget we're even on a ship."

"Who knows, kid?" Rhodes said. "It's all in the head."

"Yeah. My first wife used to get seasick just

standing on the dock next to a ship," Frank said. Lucan had been married and divorced twice since joining the Navy. He had learned the hard way what some of the men he had trained under had told him: life in the Teams was not a good cement for marriage. Now, he shared an apartment with a woman half his age—for convenience, he said. That arrangement had already lasted longer than either of his marriages.

Beau got up and refilled the pitcher of coffee the four men had been sharing. The last of the ship's crew in the galley had finished eating and left. Two men were wiping tables down now, getting the room ready for the next shift.

At the table, Frank glanced at his watch. They still had ten minutes left before they would need to head toward the briefing for their first scheduled mission of this operation—assuming that the company man who was directing the op was able to proceed. Frank assumed he would be. *I'd make it, no matter what,* Frank thought. *The spook will, too, whatever he feels like.* Frank had never been seasick, but he had known more than a few hangovers, and they had never stopped him.

It was obvious that Harry Tombs was still not feeling well, but he was waiting in the conference room, near *Bellman*'s bridge and CIC, when Frank Lucan led his team in. Tombs was sitting at the head of the table, where the ship's captain would preside over meetings with his department heads, leaning back a little, but holding on to the table with one hand, as if that were all that were keeping him from sliding around the room. There was a thick envelope with TOP SECRET stamped on it lying on the table in front of him. The target folder inside carried an even higher security classification. Tombs looked up as the SEALs filed into the room and moved to take seats around the table, but gave no other indication that he was aware they had come in.

In the passageway outside, Frank had warned his men against laughter or jokes about Tombs's condition. "We got to get along with him the next few weeks, remember. Let's not see how fast we can push him over the edge."

Inside, Frank nearly had to bite his lip to hold back the bad joke that wanted to come out, *"You look like you belong in a tomb, Tombs."* If nothing else, as team leader, he had to set the example. It was absurd, but Harry Tombs looked as if he might have dropped fifteen pounds since Frank had last seen him—that morning shortly after they had been deposited aboard *Bellman* by helicopter. He couldn't have lost that much no matter how many times he knelt to the porcelain god, Frank told himself.

"I'll be okay in a day or two," Tombs said, answering the silence. "I just need a little time to get my sea legs. It won't affect our operations." There was a slightly strangled quality to his voice, as if he were trying to hold back a rising gorge. He stopped talking and took several carefully measured breaths, each slightly deeper and more prolonged than its predecessor. He closed his eyes for an instant. When he had finished the routine, his voice sounded somewhat stronger, or at least, less feeble.

"Most of the terrorist leaders we expect to attend the terror summit in Sudan are already enroute, taking whatever circuitous routes their habitual paranoia suggests."

"Is it still paranoia if everyone *is* out to get you?" Rob asked. That broke through the studied reserve of the others in the team. Ike snickered out loud. Beau cracked a rare smile. Even Frank felt it necessary to cover his face less it, too, show anything.

Harry Tombs chose to ignore the remark. "Our information is that this institutional paranoia will color the summit meeting to an extreme degree. The fact that they're meeting in Sudan, when perhaps only one of the organizations is headquartered there, is part of it. Despite our retaliatory strike on Khartoum after the embassy bombings in Kenya and Tanzania, they feel less insecure in Sudan than in Libya, Lebanon, Syria, Iraq, Iran, Afghanistan, or the various other places they come from. They certainly wouldn't attempt to use Gaza or the West Bank. At least four separate venues have been prepared for the conference itself, all well defended, and the individual leaders and their staffs might have their choice of literally dozens of different locations to stay in when not attending the conference sessions."

"We know all that," Frank said. "It's always

been sort of SOP with these terrorist types. I remember hearing that Arafat, years back, before he became respectable, never slept in the same bed two nights in a row, or switched beds in the middle of the night. Maybe he's still like that. During Desert Shield and Desert Storm, the word we had was that Saddam Hussein sometimes got up in the middle of the night and moved, just so his enemies wouldn't know where the hell to hit. All that really matters to us"— Frank made a gesture to include the other SEALs—"is that our targets are where they're supposed to be when we go in."

"When the time comes for the final operation, we'll hit the right place," Tombs said. "And up until then, we're not looking to bag any of the big shots. We just want to make them a little more paranoid and scramble as much of their security apparats as we can, to make the final show a little more . . . practical."

Beau Guisborne cleared his throat noisily, drawing the attention of the others. "If they be nothin' but crazies, they wouldn't be such bad dudes," he said, a long oration for Beau. "Whatever else they be, they be smart at what they do. We don' forget that without gettin' hurt." His team mates were used to Beau's slow, deliberate way of speaking, but Harry Tombs started to show impatience long before Beau quit talking and waved a hand past his mouth to signal that he was finished.

Tombs hesitated before he spoke again.

"You're right," he conceded. "They're smart, absolutely dedicated to what they're doing, totally ruthless, and perhaps no more cautious than they have to be to survive. In our line of work we have to be cautious as well.

"Let's get on to practical matters," Tombs said after another slight hesitation. "Tonight's operation."

Frank straightened up a little. Yeah, let's get to the job. We can jaw about the philosophy some other time, he thought.

THE BRIEFING

"At approximately sixteen hundred hours, a helicopter bearing the markings of the Egyptian Air Force will land on *Bellman*. Four individuals will get out, ostensibly VIPs come for a tour of the ship. At sixteen forty-five, the four of you will board the helicopter and take off. The bird will land once, for refueling, in southern Egypt. You should be on the ground there no more than fifteen minutes. Your destination is a small oasis in the Libyan Desert, inside Libya, just south of the border between Egypt and Sudan." Tombs broke the seal on the envelope, extracted the target folder, opened that, and started to pass several papers around, one at a time, handing each to Frank first, who looked, then passed them on. The first was a government-issue topological map of the region. The second, of more interest to the

SEALs, was a photograph of the oasis and the area immediately around it. There were several other photographs, of fairly high resolution, that showed three concrete block buildings set apart from the ruins of several mud brick huts in the oasis.

"Depending on the position of *Bellman* when you take off, you'll have between seven hundred fifty and eight hundred miles in the air," Tombs said, while he continued to pass around the briefing sheets. "With the fuel stop, the flight in will run about four and a half hours. You'll jump in high and open your 'chutes as low as possible, aiming for a landing zone just over a mile northwest of the target."

The briefing sheets started to make their second circuit of the SEALs, each man taking a little more time to study them this time, giving the documents more attention than Tombs.

"What's there?" Rhodes asked.

"It's one of a number of depots the Libyan government has established near their borders to funnel terrorists and equipment into other countries in the region—Egypt, Sudan, Chad, and beyond. Their, ah, clients or middlemen come in and get whatever they're being offered. The depot is maintained and guarded by a garrison of about twenty Libyan soldiers. The mission is to go in and shut it down, doing maximum damage to the garrison and any munitions at the site. Choose your weapons with that in mind." Tombs paused before he added, "You are to consider

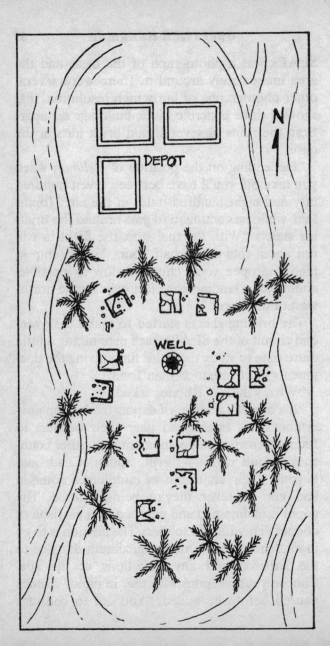

yourselves in a free-fire zone from landing to pickup."

Rhodes and Guisborne glanced at each other. Beau shrugged, minimally. *Free-fire zone*: they were to consider *anyone* they came across to be hostile, a valid target.

"Land transport is limited. The road north is almost imaginary, a series of landmarks subject to change depending on the wind and sand movement. Part of the way it's rock, mostly it's just hard-packed dirt. The way south, across the border, is even less well defined. The Libyans use half-track trucks mostly, and a few six-by-sixes. Nothing moves *fast* on the ground."

"Our pickup will be . . . ?" Frank asked.

"The helicopter that drops you in will circle around and land to pick you up east of the oasis. You'll be in direct radio communication with the pilot and carry a homing beacon you can activate once you find a secure LZ. One additional piece of advice. Don't let yourselves be captured inside Libya. Khadafi might rupture himself with joy. If there's any unforeseen trouble with pickup, head east, toward the Egyptian border."

Only Beau did not look up at Tombs then. Beau did not plan to let anyone capture him, anywhere.

"You should be jumping in just after sunset. That will give you most of the night to get the job done and get out," Tombs said. "Questions?"

There were none. The SEALs continued studying the maps and photos of their target.

"You've got a little more than an hour before

you leave. Assemble your gear and get a meal in"— the CIA man almost gagged at the thought of food—"if you can. It might be a long time until breakfast."

THE PREPARATION

There was little time for anything but the necessities. The SEALs changed into "working" clothes, desert camouflage BDUs. Out in the open, those would be less conspicuous, even at night, than all-black or darker jungle camouflage. None of the men wore standard government-issue footgear. Frank and Beau wore high-topped sneakers dyed totally black. Rob wore civilian hunting boots with deep tread to give him better traction on sand. Ike wore low-cut running shoes.

Next, they drew their weapons. Aboard *Bellman*, they had more choice than they had had the day before. They had not had all of their gear with them then; most of it had been sent ahead. Frank decided to stick with the weapon he had used in Lebanon, an M-16 with the double-drum magazine, though this time the blast suppressor could be left behind. Beau and Rob would carry M-16s with M203 40mm grenade launchers attached under the barrel, and each would wear one or two bandoleers of grenades.

The M203, which replaced the fragile XM-148 grenade launcher back in 1969, was a favorite of the SEALs for its firepower and adaptability.

Mounted beneath an M16, the M203 slides forward for loading with the release latch just above the parent weapon's barrel and a protected trigger just in front of the magazine. To fire the M203, the operator holds onto the magazine of the parent weapon with his firing hand and uses the folding leaf sight on the top of the barrel or the more complex quadrant sight on the barrel's left side. When the target is hit by an M203, all hell breaks loose.

Ike, on the other hand, selected a Remington 870P shotgun, and stuck three boxes of double-ought shells into an ammunition pouch.

"Might have to open a door or two," he said, when Frank gave him a quizzical look.

Frank nodded. "We just might. But if you're going to carry that, better take along a backup weapon."

"I figured on an Uzi and a couple of double magazines."

"Got to say one thing for our spook," Beau

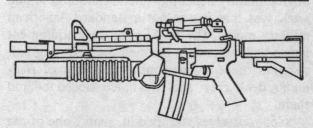

M16 with M203 Launcher

said, as he scanned the several open metal crates. "He give us 'bout anything we could want here."

"Timed explosive charges for the munitions depot?" Rob said, not really a question about what had been made available, but what they should take. "If they got a lot of crap stockpiled, we won't want to be close when it blows. Something incendiary?"

"Just what the doctor ordered," Frank said, gesturing toward one of the crates. "White phosphorus. That'll get things hot enough to cook off anything we're likely to find. A couple of small shaped charges, too, just in case."

The last thing they did was pick up their parachutes and give them a quick check.

THE MISSION

Frank led his men to the helicopter on the landing pad on *Bellman*'s fantail. Frank thought that the waiting chopper was of Russian manufacture, but that was only a guess. It wasn't one of the Soviet military helicopters he had studied. All he *knew* was that it was not a standard American military model. The SEALs set their equipment inside the cabin, then climbed the two-rung ladder into the compartment. A member of *Bellman*'s deck crew slid the hatch closed behind them.

"Get yourselves strapped in, gents," one of the pilots said. Both of the men looking back from the cockpit could easily have passed for Egyptian, but the accent of the pilot who spoke was pure Brooklyn. The two flyers were dressed in nondescript khaki uniforms, without insignia of any kind. "We'll get you in and out safe."

CIA men, Frank thought, contract men, at least. Earlier in his career, that might have made him nervous. There had been stories that circulated in the Teams about operations with contract operatives gone bad, but Frank had never experienced any of those disasters, and had eventually come to have a certain amount of trust in the company men he occasionally worked with, or for—not *absolute* trust, not the trust he would have for a dive buddy, a team mate, but enough to let him concentrate on the job at hand and not worry too much about the outsiders.

As soon as the four SEALs were strapped in, the helicopter took off. The men in back could not hear the talk on the radio between the pilots and *Bellman*.

The helicopter curved away from the frigate and the rest of the task force, settling on a westerly course toward the Egyptian coast, just a couple minutes of flying time away. The passengers made themselves as comfortable as they could in accommodations that had not been designed for comfort. The seats were rudimentary, plastic over metal frames bolted to the deck.

Beau stretched his legs out as far as he could, leaned back, and closed his eyes. He probably would not actually sleep, but he would give every appearance of it. He might not budge for an hour or more. Frank and Rob knew the routine; they had been on other long flights with Guisborne. But if there was any talk among the others, Beau would hear it, and respond, if necessary.

Rob also appeared relaxed, but he kept his eyes open and worked his mouth as if he were whistling, though no sound came out. Ike was more active, watching through one of the small windows. All he needed was a camera to complete the image of the gawking tourist, abroad for the first time, perhaps.

Good, Frank thought. Give the kid something to think about besides what we've got to do. He had found no fault in Jensen's performance the night before, but he was still young, still too prone to nerves beforehand.

Frank also watched the passing scenery—what little of it there was—but more to determine as accurately as he could the helicopter's course. Just before the men had gone out to the helicopter, Harry Tombs had appeared long enough to give Frank the ship's position, both longitude and latitude and in reference to the map. He expected to see the Aswan high dam off to port, and did catch a glimpse of it just before one of the pilots said that it was there. Tombs got that much right, at least, Frank thought, smiling to himself. The helicopter was flying westsouthwest, staying low, less than five hundred feet above ground level. A couple of times during the flight, Frank took out his compass and checked their course.

The flight had been in progress for nearly two and a half hours when one of the pilots came back into the passenger cabin and leaned close to Frank's ear. "We'll be landing to refuel in another ten minutes," he said. "You and your men might want to have your weapons ready, just in case there's been a mistake in the arrangements." He grinned as if that would be the biggest laugh of the year. "We're getting the right identification codes, so I don't *expect* any trouble, but you know how it is."

Frank nodded. "We'll be ready."

"If we do have trouble, we'll have to abort the mission. We'll need to stop here again on the way back, and if that's not going to be possible . . ." He didn't bother to finish that.

"Hell, why didn't we use the Egyptian airbase at Aswan?" Frank asked. "I assume they know we're pulling this caper. That base is secure as hell."

The pilot shook his head. "I'll give you the same answer I got. Deniability. Anything goes wrong, the Egyptian government wants to be able to say it didn't know anything about it."

While the flyer worked his way back into his seat in the cockpit, Frank got the attention of the others. "Lock and load," he said, loud enough for all three to hear. "Just in case the spooks screwed up on the refueling deal. We touch down, unbuckle, and be ready for anything."

"We gonna stick up the gas station?" Beau asked, grinning.

"I guess so, if it comes to that," Frank said.

"I thought we made nice with the Egyptian government," Rob said. "They gonna change sides here?"

"The Egyptians have problems of their own," Ike said, which surprised all his team mates. "Ever since they made peace with Israel, they've had their own extremists to worry about."

"Something like that," Frank said. "Hard telling what kind of 'arrangements' the Company had to make to set up this flight for us. Don't go looking for them to serve bagels and coffee."

Jensen gestured toward the cockpit. The copilot, the one who had come back to warn Frank to be ready for anything, was cocking an Ingram submachine gun. The helicopter had started to descend.

Frank craned his neck to get closer to the window, looking toward the ground. The pilot turned through ninety degrees, giving Frank a fair view of a paved landing strip that showed little sign of usage. There were three buildings in a line set off to the west side of the runway. The runway and buildings were a lighter beige against the dark tan of the sand and rock that occupied most of his view. He also saw one canvas-topped military vehicle, something similar to a U.S. Army two-and-a-half-ton truck, but of European—most likely Russian—manufacture. The helicopter was less than fifty feet off the ground before Frank saw any people below. Three men came out of one of the buildings. One moved toward the truck. The others stood at the edge of the paved runway. Frank was relieved to note that none of the men on the ground were openly armed.

"This is as much the middle of nowhere as any place I've ever been," Frank said, too softly for his team mates to hear over the noise of the helicopter's engine and rotors. This side of the Arctic Circle, he qualified silently. The thought that followed almost brought a smile to his face: the men sent here must have really screwed up the last place they worked.

The helicopter was still fifty feet off the ground, aiming for a black X painted on the paved strip near the buildings, when Frank released his seat belt—and gestured for his team mates to do the same. Frank shifted one leg to give himself better leverage in case they had to move quickly to defend themselves. The others also prepared.

As soon as the aircraft had settled onto the X, the copilot unstrapped and came back through to climb out through the large doorway in the passenger compartment. He carried his submachine gun at his side, muzzle toward the ground next to his feet. Although he had not been invited, Frank got out with him. Rob moved closer to the door but stayed inside the helicopter.

Frank did not move far from the door, hanging back when the copilot moved off to talk with the two men who were waiting. The rotor continued to turn overhead, the aircraft's engine idling. There was still more than enough noise and rushing air to keep Frank from hearing anything of

the conversation, even though the men just clear
of the whirling umbrella of the helicopter's rotors
appeared to be nearly shouting.

The two men talking with the copilot were
fairly nondescript in appearance. Both had dark
hair, dark complexions. They might—or might
not—have been Egyptians. One of them made a
come-on gesture at the truck and it started moving, slowly, toward the helicopter.

If there's going to be any trouble, it'll be soon
now, Frank thought. He concentrated on the faces
of the two men talking with the copilot, but
tracked the movement of the truck as well. The
fingertips on his right hand started to tingle a bit,
almost as if anxious for something to happen.

The truck stopped, then backed through a 180-
degree turn. There was no tailgate or rear flap on
the truck. Frank could see a dozen metal barrels,
and a portable pump. So far, so good, he thought.
But he remained vigilant.

Frank took three steps farther from the side of
the helicopter, scanning as far around as he could
see now. One of the locals was gesturing toward
the rotor, shouting something at the copilot. Now,
Frank could hear just enough to realize that the
man was saying that the engine should be shut off
before the refueling operation started. Frank did
not hear the flyer's reply, but the vigorous shake
of his head was enough. The men argued for
another thirty seconds, then the local shrugged
and turned to the truck.

Refueling took longer than ten minutes, but

that did not bother Frank. They appeared to have made excellent time on the first half of the flight, and a few extra minutes now would help insure that it was after dark when the SEALs parachuted in near their target. The hose feeding the fuel pump had to be switched manually from one barrel to the next, and the copilot had climbed up into the bed of the truck. He sniffed at each barrel as it was opened, as if he thought he might detect any irregularities.

It took six barrels to top off the helicopter's fuel tanks, apparently leaving the other six for the second time, sometime in the night, after the operation was finished. The copilot spoke with the locals for another thirty seconds. The truck moved away. The helicopter's copilot turned and walked toward Frank and the open door.

"You get in. I'll follow," Frank said, when the flyer got to him. The man just nodded.

Frank did not really start to relax until the helicopter was a thousand feet up and a half mile from the refueling stop horizontally. He put the safety on his rifle on, then strapped himself in again. And wiped the palm of his right hand on his trouser leg. It had been sweating. After five minutes—much longer than he really needed to work through the remnants of his adrenaline rush—Frank unbuckled his harness again and got up to move toward the cockpit. He stuck his head up between the two pilots, both of whom glanced his way.

"There's no need to set any speed records on this last stretch," Frank said, speaking loudly enough for them to hear him. "We'd rather not be silhouetted against the setting sun when we jump in." He gestured forward. Already the helicopter appeared to be flying directly toward the sun.

The pilot in the left-hand seat nodded, and throttled back the engine just a hair. "No problem," he replied. "We're going to do a 'lost our way' act as we approach the border anyway, just in case the Libyans have radar pointed our way and working. That'll add a few minutes."

Back in his seat, Frank continued to stare out the window. There was no longer anything to see but sand, rock, and the growing shadows cast by hills and dunes. The helicopter varied its altitude, gradually getting lower. Having been warned of the maneuver, he was unsurprised when the craft turned first toward the south, then reversed course a couple of minutes later, before edging around again to a westerly, then southwesterly heading. Evening had come to the east. In the west, the sun was sinking into the horizon, a red-hot globe being tempered in the sand.

The pilot continued his haphazard-appearing maneuvers, even heading directly east for almost three minutes, before changing course again and heading south before turning *almost* straight toward the drop zone. There would be a last-minute course change—literally—before the helicopter would aim directly at the location where the SEALs would jump. The pilot would increase speed and climb rapidly during that final minute.

"Check your gear!" Frank shouted, so his team mates would hear him. "It won't be long now." Weapons had to be secured, harnesses checked to make certain that nothing would come loose. Frank looked at the altimeter strapped to his wrist. The devices had all been adjusted for the difference between sea level and ground level at their destination. The men checked each other's parachutes, back and forth.

"Make sure the safeties are on on your weapons," Frank reminded the others, checking his own again even though he had specific memories of flipping it after the refueling stop. The habitual caution that made him double-check everything had contributed to Frank Lucan becoming an *old* SEAL.

When the copilot came back into the compartment and said, "Three minutes," Frank nodded. He and his men were ready. He checked his watch. Each of the others did the same. *Three minutes*.

The flyers could communicate with each other through the interphones in their helmets. The copilot stood by the side door of the helicopter, waiting for word from the pilot. Frank remained seated, arms on knees, his wrist turned so he could watch the face of his watch; like the others in his team, he wore the watch with the face on the inside of his wrist. The men all had night-vision goggles, but stowed securely in their packs. They would not wear them during the jump. For that, they had special jump helmets and goggles.

Two minutes. Each SEAL had a different perspective on jumping. Frank had come to enjoy it. For several years he had been part of a civilian skydiving club, going out and jumping every weekend he could—in addition to occasional training and mission jumps in the Teams. Beau accepted the need to jump as part of the job. He was neither averse nor particularly fond of it. Rob had mellowed. At one time, he had been the one who always took it to the edge, holding off to be the last man in any group to open his chute, cutting each dive a little closer, as if tempting fate—or the limits of his own courage. Now, he was content to pull with the rest. Ike was still new enough to parachuting to be nervous at each jump. Since completing jump school, he had made a dozen training jumps with the platoon, but had never jumped in on an operation. This would be only the second time he had jumped from a helicopter; he had been terrified the first time, afraid that he would somehow open his chute too soon and have it chewed to confetti by the rotor. He was breathing deeply now, trying to calm himself, remembering the irrational fear and the way the others had laughed when he'd mentioned it. It was always an effort of willpower for him to launch himself out into open air. But willpower was one quality he had in abundance.

One minute. The copilot gave Frank a signal. Frank nodded. The helicopter was not equipped with any automatic system to tell the SEALs when to jump—no system of lights that the pilot could activate in front. That was why the copilot was in the passenger compartment acting as jumpmaster. The four jumpers were out of their seats now, lined up on the other side of the door that the copilot shoved open. Quickly, they went through one last check of their equipment.

Thirty seconds. Twenty. Ten.

Frank counted the seconds off in his head but continued to watch the copilot, who was getting continuous updates from the pilot. The copilot raised one hand above his head—the other was gripping a handhold on the side of the compartment, *tightly*.

. . . Three, two, one. The copilot brought his hand down sharply. The signal.

Frank used one hand and his feet to launch himself through the doorway, into the air beating down from the rotor. Even after hundreds of jumps, Frank still experienced an inner rush to rival the air hurtling him away from the aircraft— a speed-up of his heart rate, a hot flush to his cheeks, a tightening of muscles. A mile below, the desert was mostly a dark blotch, only dimly illuminated by the early stars. He counted out two seconds before he spread his arms and legs to slow his fall, just a little, to keep from getting too far from the men who had to follow him in. Only then did he start to make out the silhouette of the hills and the oasis, enough to mark the landing zone they would aim for.

Behind Frank, the other three men had piled out of the helicopter as quickly as possible, one almost directly on the shoulders of the man in front of him. This was a work jump, so there would be no fancy acrobatics, no joined formations, but the team would stay as close together as safety permitted. During the freefall, they achieved a fairly consistent echelon formation, each man a little higher and more to the right than the jumper in front of him.

The loose fabric of their BDUs flapped violently, dragging on equipment harnesses, trying the security of each piece of gear. Each man kept an eye on his altimeter, careful not to let his rate of descent get too extreme. As they fell, the men maneuvered to give themselves more room. At eight hundred feet, Frank pulled his ripcord. As his pilot chute, and then the main parafoil—both black for the night jump—opened, Frank seemed to be jerked upward as his companions fell past him, each man opening his own chute in close sequence. The echelon reversed itself, with Frank on top rather than at the bottom.

These were sports parachutes, rectangular canopies designed to give the jumper the greatest possible control over his landing, not the huge hemispheric canopies used by airborne soldiers and aviators. Frank worked his suspension lines to bring the initial swaying under control and started slipping air to move him toward the landing zone. Hanging on a pocket of air, he scanned the rapidly approaching ground, looking for any sign that they had been spotted, that there was opposition waiting for them. It would have taken the worst kind of luck, but that did not mean that the threat could be ignored. At the moment, the SEALs were helpless, and would be until they were on the ground, free of their chutes, weapons in hand.

It was difficult to gauge the exact instant of landing in the dark. Depth perception was limited. Although Frank was prepared, the shock of landing was still unexpected. But his landing was good. He hit with bent knees and rolled, the way he had been taught in jump school—ages before. Before he could come to a stop, Frank had hit the release latch on his chute.

The sand was still hot from the day's exposure to the sun, but there was a hint of coolness to the breeze that caressed cheeks numbed by the faster air of the jump. Frank took a couple of deep breaths, pacing them, slowing his body after the rush of the last minutes. But he got his rifle ready at the same time, quickly checking to make sure that it had suffered no damage in the landing.

He started to gather in the canopy of his parachute, pulling the rig into a small bundle as he moved toward his men. "Everyone okay?" he asked in something of a stage whisper.

There were short affirmatives from each man, a grunt or a single word, soft.

"Let's bury the chutes so they don't know how we got here," Frank said. Burying the rigs took no more than a minute, scooping out depressions in the loose sand and covering them. In time, the desert winds would either uncover the chutes or bury them more completely. Either way would make no difference. The SEALs would be long gone by then, and there were no "Made in the USA" tags on the chutes.

Rob used a portable GPS—Global Positioning Satellite—set to determine their position precisely. "Right on target," he reported. "That way." He pointed in the direction of the oasis. The four men had discarded their jump helmets in favor of soft caps and their night-vision goggles.

The desert was not simply drifting sand dunes from horizon to horizon. There was sand, but there was as much hard stone, and even occasional bare patches of hard, nutrient-starved soil; intermittent stands of starvation grasses, more brown than green, brittle, breaking rather than bending when the wind became too much to resist.

Frank took the point, not worrying about staying on a direct heading but keeping to the lowest areas of ground, cutting down the distance at which they might be spotted. He had no concern about time. They didn't have that far to travel, and they had hours of margin.

The night wind was not excessive, but it provided the primary sounds, blowing itself and sand. The wildlife—and even in an area as bleak and barren as this, there was wildlife—was silent. The only animal any of the SEALs spotted before they reached the oasis was a single bird, a night hunter soaring in lazy circles high overhead.

Although they moved carefully, the four men covered ground quickly, taking no more than twenty minutes to come within sight of the oasis and the buildings it sheltered.

Doesn't look anything like oases in the movies, Ike thought as he scanned it. There's no big pond in the middle and lush trees around it. The fifteen or twenty trees that made up the oasis were scraggly date palms that appeared to be barely surviving. There was some grass, the same miserable excuse they had seen on the walk from the LZ, but in somewhat greater concentration— enough, perhaps, to provide grazing for a single horse or donkey for a few days. In place of an open pond, there was a well, a circle of low stones marking that central feature. Ike and his companions were lying just behind the ridge of a low dune on the west side of the oasis, about two hundred yards from the first trees.

The SEALs took several minutes to study the scene, to make the connection between reality and the photographs and maps they had studied, and—far more important—to search for the guards they assumed must be posted.

Two guards, at least, Frank thought. Maybe even three. Depends how nervous they are.

No guards were immediately apparent. Frank scanned from left to right, then back the other way, more slowly the second time across, looking for any hint of movement in the false-color vista of his night-vision goggles. First of all, he checked the new buildings. Around the bases of the nearest trees. Then the ruins of the older buildings. Ruins: nothing much more than waist-high remained of the old huts. The roofs of the new buildings were slightly above the level that Frank and his companions were at, but he saw no trace of a rifle or face over the low parapets that enclosed them.

Men sleeping in two of the buildings, Frank thought. Supplies and munitions in the third. The briefing had not included any definitive information on which buildings were used for what. There were two trucks parked, off beyond the new buildings, together, their tailgates up against each other, the way tractor-trailer drivers in the States sometimes parked their rigs to deter theft. Some supplies in there, as well, Frank thought. That might mean that they were expecting people in for a pickup. Or it might mean that extra people were already there, waiting for morning before driving off in the trucks.

Small windows were visible on the near sides of two of the new buildings. The angle was wrong for Frank to tell whether there was a similar window in the third building.

Frank slid back away from the ridge. The others followed him back down into the hollow.

"Anyone see guards?" Frank asked, his whisper so faint that the others had to strain to hear him even though they were clustered close together. Three heads shook negatives at their leader.

"Me either," Frank admitted. "Either we're slipping or they're being awful careless. Let's get spread out. Beau, you've got the left. Farmboy, the right. I don't want us spread over more than sixty degrees of arc here. Make sure we've all got clear fields of fire and enough room that we don't start dropping shit on each other. I want grenades through each of the windows to start. On my signal. Farmboy, you put a couple of incendiary grenades on those trucks. Then we deal with whatever comes out of the buildings, trucks, or trees. Blast anything on two legs that moves. Ike, you stick fairly close to me. You've got the up-close stuff. We won't need that at first."

Beau and Rob scrambled away, staying low on the near side of the dune, moving quickly to get into position. Frank and Ike remained where they were until the others were fifty yards away, starting to move up the face of the shallow dune toward their initial firing positions.

"Okay, kid, our turn," Frank whispered.

Ike nodded. He had given up trying to get the others to quit calling him *kid*.

The two men worked their way back up the windward side of the dune and settled in at the ridge, crawling to their positions. They squirmed into the sand about five yards apart. Although the weapon would be useless at this range—just under two hundred yards, Ike had his shotgun at the ready. If he needed the Uzi submachine gun, he could get to it quickly enough. He had it on a sling across his back. It might do *some* damage at this distance, but like the shotgun it was primarily a close-range weapon.

Frank glanced left and right, making certain that the other two men were in position and watching for his signal. He was not worried about their ability to hit small windows with the grenade launchers attached to their M-16s. They had good Bushnell rangefinders, and enough practice with the grenade launchers that it would not take them long to zero in on the targets. Frank checked his rifle. The safety was off. The selector was set so that each pull of the trigger would fire a three-shot burst.

I'd be happier if we could see their sentries, Frank thought. There ought to be two, and maybe a sergeant of the guard to wake up each shift. He shook his head, just a little. Maybe they were off behind the buildings or trucks. There were areas out of sight of any of the SEALs. But if there were guards, they ought to react quickly to the first grenades. That'll be soon enough, Frank thought.

He raised his right arm, glanced to either side again to make sure that Beau and Rob were watching, then brought the arm down quickly. The two men with the grenade launchers triggered their first rounds within two seconds, as quickly as they settled back into firing position.

"Now we see what we've got, kid," Frank said, sighting his rifle at the cab of one of the two trucks. He put two three-round bursts into the cab door, then aimed for the cab of the other truck. He thought it possible that the guards might be sleeping in the trucks. By that time, the first grenades had exploded—both against the walls of the buildings, missing the small windows. But Beau and Rob had reloaded and the next rounds did better. Beau's high explosive grenade went through the window it was aimed at; Rob's exploded on the sill, dividing its shrapnel between the desert and the building's interior.

"Hell of a way to wake up," Ike said, but not loud enough for Frank to hear over the explosions and his own gunfire. Ike did not even notice the difference in the way he felt this time over the mission in Lebanon. True, at the moment he was only a spectator, but his nervousness had almost vanished once he was safely on the ground. Right now, it was almost like watching a war movie in a theater.

Frank moved his rifle fire, breaking the glass in the window on the one remaining building—just so they don't feel neglected, he thought. He kept an eye on the doors. As soon as one of them opened, he would transfer his aim to get anyone trying to escape the destruction inside.

The two men with grenade launchers operated with a smooth rhythm, popping new rounds into their launchers as quickly as possible. Each man had his own system for arranging the types of grenades in their bandoleers—the important consideration was that the shooter knew where the

HE, white phosphorus, and incendiary rounds were so there would be no delays.

"Frank! Under the trucks!"

This time, Ike's shout was loud enough for the team leader to hear. Frank saw the figure crawling away from the truck, toward the trees, or the ruins of the mud brick buildings. One of the sentries. Frank moved his rifle and loosed a three-shot burst, and saw the sentry's body jerk several times as at least two of the bullets hit him high in the back. The man's head came up sharply, then dropped. He stopped moving.

One of the building doors was pulled open. Two men ran out. Frank switched his aim and cut both of them down before they had run five steps. Only then did he notice that neither man carried a weapon. Beau slipped his next grenade—an incendiary—through the open doorway, and a burst of flame erupted inside, spurting back out through the door and window, glaring orange, red, and yellow. Over all of the other sounds, Frank heard screams, almost too high-pitched to be recognizable as human.

Rob dropped four grenades on the trucks before he touched off the ammunition they carried. There would never be any way to tell just what mix the trucks had carried. There were several small explosions, and what appeared to be bullets cooking off, then a massive fireball erupted. The blast sent a concussion wave rolling out, heat and sound that the four SEALs could feel. The ground shook. Sand danced. Debris flew, tracing burning arcs in the night. The fireball itself might have reached fifty yards in diameter and three times that height before consuming itself, leaving smoke and burning trees and grass behind, and a miniature mushroom cloud rising above. Small fires burned on the sand and bare rock where pieces of debris had landed. The building nearest the trucks had the facing wall blown in.

If there were more screams from that building, Frank and his companions did not hear them.

Frank got to his feet, gesturing first for Ike, and then for the other two as he started moving toward the buildings in the oasis. He kept firing as he moved, targeting doors and windows, sparing with his bursts, because there were no visible targets. There was only limited return fire, uncoordinated, poorly aimed. The surviving people in the buildings obviously had no idea where the attack was coming from.

The four SEALs were halfway to the nearest building before several more men tried to escape. Gunfire from two or three rifles in the doorway covered the first man as he ran toward the well and the ruins on the far side of it.

He almost made it. A burst of rifle fire caught him just as he reached the low circle of stones that marked the well. He pitched forward, onto the stones. For an instant it appeared that he would fall into the well, but he did not, slumping to the ground next to it, pulling one of the stones over onto himself. The men who had been attempting to cover him fared no better. Beau dropped a fragmentation grenade right in the doorway.

"Let's finish this off!" Frank shouted, uncertain whether anyone but Ike would hear. It wasn't crucial. They all knew the mission. They went to all three buildings. Frank and Ike took the one in the middle, the one that had suffered least from the initial assault. Beau and Rob split the other two.

The door of the center building was still more or less intact, and closed. "Okay, kid, let's see what you can do with that scattergun," Frank said.

Frank kept his own rifle trained on the door while Ike moved to within ten feet of it and started blasting the hinge side of the door, two rounds near the top, two near the bottom, shattering much of the door itself and knocking the remnants inside. That left four rounds in the weapon. Ike used those, through the doorway, moving his point of aim for each shot. Then he dropped the shotgun and slung his Uzi around, clicking off the safety before he had the weapon in position.

"Go!" Frank said. He went through the doorway and to the right, his rifle on full automatic now. He started spraying the interior before he had a chance to look for targets. By the time Ike came through the doorway, moving to the left, Frank could see that there was no one left alive in the building, and only two corpses, pockmarked

by shotgun pellets and rifle bullets, growing circles of blood merging with each other.

Half of the single room was filled with crates
stacked six feet high. Frank could not read the
Arabic inscriptions on the wood, but he had no
doubt that they had found more munitions.

"We'll come back for this," Frank said, gesturing Ike toward the door again. "Let's make sure
the other buildings are secure."

Frank was a step in front of the youngest member of the team, just moving through the doorway
when a new weapon entered the fight. Frank recognized the deeper pitch of a heavier-caliber
weapon than the M-16s he, Beau, and Rob were
using—just as bullets started cracking against the
concrete blocks at his side. He pushed backward,
shoving Ike out of the line of fire, and took cover
at the side of the door.

"One man," Frank said. He had managed only
a quick glimpse of the lone gunman running
toward the buildings, diving for cover near the
remains of the two trucks, briefly silhouetted by
the dying flames from those vehicles.

"The other sentry?" Ike whispered.

Frank nodded. "You keep him busy from here.
I'll go out the window and work around." He was
interrupted by another burst of gunfire from the
man outside, bullets that hit the doorway and one
of the crates inside. "I don't hear anything from
the others, so they should be trying to work into
position as well."

Ike thought of, but didn't raise, the other possibility, that one or both of their team mates might have been hit. He just slipped a new magazine into his Uzi and got ready to move to the doorway when Frank slid around the edge of the room to get to the window on their right.

Frank had no difficulty getting through the window. There were crates piled in front of it, one lower than the rest, so he climbed out as if on an oversized set of stairs, jumping easily to the ground outside. Beau came out from behind the rear corner of the building on that side and crossed to Frank.

"Got us a hero out there," Beau whispered. "One hero."

"I know," Frank said. "Give me ninety seconds to get around the huts, then draw his attention. The kid will open up when you do. Tell him. Once you've got the hero looking your way, I'll pop him from behind."

Despite the words, neither man assumed that there was indeed only one hostile left to face. Beau kept scanning. And Frank moved as if he suspected that there might be a platoon of Libyan soldiers waiting for him to make a bad move. He stayed low, running clear of the buildings into the minimal cover of the trees—as far from the light of the fires as he could. He saw Rob moving toward him from the third building. Frank gave him a come-along gesture and they ran on, moving for the far side of the oasis, to come in on the remaining shooter from behind.

Beau and Ike started shooting before the other

two were nearly in position. Frank and Rob picked up the pace a little, staying three or four yards apart. There was no need for talk or signs. Frank led and Rob adjusted. They had worked and trained together long enough for that to come naturally. They moved to within eighty yards of the lone guard, crawling the last ten. The flames of the trucks had died almost completely away, leaving only a few wisps of smoke to obscure vision.

When the local soldier lifted up to fire a burst at the two men he was facing, Frank and Rob also raised up, but they had their target clearly in sight. Bullets from both rifles raked the man, jerking his body around for several seconds after he had died—before he could even fall to the ground.

Silence.

Frank whistled to let the others know that the fight was over, then turned to Rob. "Any problems in that hut you hit?"

Rob shook his head. "I guess the explosion of the trucks wiped out everyone. Five bodies, none still kicking. One of the walls had caved in."

"Let's get the job finished. There are crates of munitions in the center building. I don't know yet about the building Beau had. We blow or burn the lot, then get the hell out of here before the cops show up."

For the first third of the hike out to the rendezvous point, the new fires in the oasis were a beacon. Almost routinely, the four SEALs glanced back in that direction. It was unlikely that the fires would draw attention very quickly. The territory was far too isolated. Perhaps a pilot would notice and either come in for a look or radio the news of a fire in the desert, but even if that happened, it would take time for the Libyan military to react. Long enough for us to get the hell away from here, Frank thought after he had spoken with the helicopter pilot and made sure that they weren't going to have to walk all the way back to the Red Sea.

Frank was asleep almost before the helicopter was off the ground. Rob had to shake him awake when they approached the refueling stop. Once more, they treated the stop as potential trouble, guns ready for use. But, again, refueling was accomplished without difficulty. Frank did stay awake after that, all of the way back to *Bellman*.

POST-MISSION

The watch changed aboard ship. Men hurried along companionways to duty stations. Frank and his team mates sat in the armory and cleaned their weapons, even the pistols that had not been taken from their holsters. This was no "prettying up" for an inspection. They were master craftsmen caring for the essential tools of their trade.

Harry Tombs came into the room and closed the door behind him. He stood there, leaning back against the door, while Frank gave his verbal report of the mission. Afterward, Tombs asked few questions. His voice still sounded weak, and Frank thought that the CIA man appeared green yet, still seasick.

"Get some sleep," Tombs advised. "Another busy night coming up."

THE REPORT

Harry Tombs leaned back and looked at the report on the screen of his portable computer. While he proofread the document, he sipped carefully at the green tea that had been all he had been able to keep down since boarding *Bellman*. Alone in his cabin, he even managed a brief smile as he reread the summary at the end of his report.

```
Twenty-one hostile bodies were counted.
It   is   believed   that   no   hostiles
escaped. The team destroyed all three
buildings  at  the  terrorist  depot,  as
well as two military trucks, and a con-
servatively estimated six to eight tons
of   munitions   destined   for   terrorist
organizations  in  East  Africa  and  the
Middle East. No evidence of the iden-
```

tity or origin of the attacking force
was left. Extraction was accomplished
without incident.

Despite his execrable seasickness, the operation was off to a good start.

*The man was so thin that he looked taller than he
was. In general, he was fairly nondescript, middle-
aged with a thin but curly beard, brown with gray
streaks. He was dressed in white silk loose-fitting
trousers and a tunic, the latter held tight by a dark
brown sash wound several times around his waist.
On his head he wore a turban-wrapped tarboosh,
white around a brownish red. Peering through
bifocals (that he never allowed himself to be pho-
tographed wearing), he stared at the message on the
screen of his notebook computer. He might have
been a mid-level clerk in a government office somewhere, or a shopkeeper reviewing his books. He did
not look like the most-wanted terrorist in the
world, with a price of five million U.S. dollars on
his head.*

*Faud ibn Landin growled softly under his
breath, not even conscious of the sound. The e-
mail he was reading was bad news. It had come
encrypted so securely that no intelligence agency
would have any hope of reading the transmission.
The software had been developed by program-
mers in India, and was far more secure than any
encryption software the foolish Americans would
permit to be sold in the United States.*

"We'll have to postpone the meeting, Nasir," Faud said, speaking softly. He looked over the top of his computer screen at the aide who was the only other person in the room. "Shining Star won't come. They've had trouble at home, some business with a group of villagers who claimed to have an important Yankee prisoner." He shrugged, minimally. "And Al-Bahr suggests that we might have had something to do with destroying a load of munitions they were to pick up from the Libyans early this morning. They believe we are involved in some trickery."

"We should head back to Afghanistan immediately," Nasir said, ignoring any other concerns. "I said it was a mistake for you to risk yourself away from where we can protect you fully." Nasir was ibn Landin's chief of security. A dozen hand-picked bodyguards surrounded the building that housed the terrorist leader. Armed heavily, even with shoulder-fired surface-to-air missiles, the bodyguards did not ease Nasir's worries.

Ibn Landin pushed his chair back and stood. The butt of a 9mm pistol was visible now, tucked into the sash around his waist. A second pistol, a .38 caliber revolver, was holstered around the top of his right boot, concealed by his loose-fitting trousers. The other boot held a knife that was made of surgical steel, its blade honed as sharp as any surgeon's scalpel. "This time, I think you are right, at least about returning to the camps for the time being. I'm going to have to talk with these people, calm their worries, before we can go ahead

with the meeting. And I need you to find out everything you can about these two incidents."

"Why not call the meeting off completely?"
Nasir suggested. "You can talk with the others one
at a time, bring them to the camps, or meet them
close by, where the Americans and the Zionists
can't get to you."

"That wouldn't work, Nasir, and I've told you
why. We can't form a complete union unless we
can actually all come together, face to face. Without
that level of cooperation, of trust, we can never
succeed. We need the reality of union, not just a
paper show."

"You already command the devotion of as many
people as the other nine men together. Why do we
need them at all?"

"Precisely because the others have as many
trusted followers as I have, Nasir. We will double
our numbers in one stroke, and once we can show
that level of commitment, we'll draw more people
in. And we'll achieve more equal alliances with
those governments who support us. In a year, we
can be a nation without borders, Nasir, as strong as
any member of the Arab League, and more united
in purpose behind the flag of Jihad. We'll be strong
enough to engineer the destruction of Israel and
force the abject submission of the infidel west."

3: SNOWFLAKE

PRE-MISSION

The four SEALs had the weather deck of *Bellman* pretty much to themselves. Frank had called his men out for calisthenics and a morning run at 0930. Exercises had eaten up the first half hour. Now, he was leading his men in a brisk jog around the ship's open main deck, from the heliport on the fantail to the missile launcher on the foredeck. Seven laps equaled a mile, roughly, and the SEALs were in their twentieth lap of the morning. Their pace was slowing. The coarse black hair on Frank's back and shoulders was matted down with sweat. All four men were sweating profusely. Despite the twenty-knot breeze generated by *Bellman*'s speed southeast along the Red Sea, the temperature was already over a hundred degrees fahrenheit, and there wasn't the slightest hint of a cloud anywhere in the sky.

As the group reached the narrow band of shade on the port side of *Bellman*'s superstructure, Rob stopped running and leaned over, hands on knees, trying to catch his breath. "Enough!" he called out, loud enough that Frank—twenty yards farther on—heard. Beau and Ike stopped running immediately, and moved into the scant shade. Frank took another couple of paces before he slowed to a walk, then turned back toward the others.

"Crazy, runnin' out in this shit," Beau said, when Frank had rejoined the group.

"We've got to keep in shape," Frank said, but he didn't complain about the others quitting. It had been getting to him as well, age and heat added to the normal exertion. It was a little much. "After this, we'll have to get back to doing our workout at first light."

"Not when we don't get back from an op until four in the morning," Rob said. "We're not going to turn into pig fat if we miss a couple of days out here. Anyway, what damned use we gonna be to anyone if we get so dehydrated we can't stand up?"

"I'll try to get some idea what our schedule's going to be when I see the spook," Frank said.

"Yeah, tell him his jobs are screwing up your training regimen," Rob suggested, "and one or the other has to go." Beau and Ike laughed.

"Tell him he can do the running for us," Beau said. "Let him sweat the seasick out." That was good for another laugh. Even Frank could not suppress a grin.

"Okay, you've made your point," Frank said. "But we do need to keep in shape. *Bellman* has some exercise equipment below. Use it."

* * *

After a quick shower and a change of clothes, Frank went to Harry Tombs's cabin. He knocked and Tombs told him to come in.

Tombs was lying on his made bunk, staring at the overhead when Frank entered and closed the door behind him. The CIA man swung around and sat up.

"Something bothering you?" Tombs asked quietly.

"No more'n usual," Frank said. "Just thought I'd check and see how you're doing, and ask what's up next for us." He had already noticed that Tombs looked healthier than he had the day before. There was color in his face again—other than green. "If we don't have any jobs for a day or two, I want to make sure my people don't get out of shape."

"I'm doing better. Sit down," Tombs said, gesturing to the one chair in the small cabin. Frank sat.

For a moment, Tombs just stared at his visitor. He respected the ability of Lucan and the other SEALs, but habit and training dictated separation, a certain studied aloofness. The habit of secrecy was even more deeply ingrained. It would have been a relief to talk about the dispatches he had received that morning, maybe get another perspective on what appeared to be going on, but. . . .

"For now, we continue working, hit the bad guys as hard and as often as we can. Right now, the more shit we throw at them, the better. You get to the point where you feel your men need a day off, let me know."

"We haven't hit anything hairy enough for that yet," Frank said when Tombs paused. "Hell, we've really only started."

Tombs nodded. "We'll have our mission briefing at two this afternoon. For now . . . well, let's just say we've got an ambush to set up and execute.

THE BRIEFING

By 1400 hours, Harry Tombs looked as if he were almost completely recovered from his seasickness. He moved with assurance and his voice was firm again. The SEALs were waiting when he entered the conference room and opened the target folder to start passing the briefing documents around.

"A transfer of funds, expected to consist of bullion and British and German currency, is scheduled to take place between eleven o'clock tonight and three o'clock tomorrow morning," Tombs started. "In part, these funds are to help finance the terrorist activities of a group calling itself Glory of God. More than that, the money is to help pay for security at the summit meeting that ibn Landin has engineered. Glory of God is to route some of the money to at least one and perhaps two other groups. Glory of God has gone by several other names over the past couple years. There's a breakdown of aliases and activities in the folder. Our job is to prevent the transfer and impound the bullion and currency. Make 'em all tighten the purse strings a little."

"Hell, I thought all these terrorists did their money transfers through banks and so forth now," Frank said. "Electronic transfers or numbered accounts. This sounds more like drug money changing hands in South America."

"You're not too far wrong," Tombs said. "Our information is that the money comes from the drug business—opium, to be specific. Ibn Landin may be rich in his own right, but his legitimate sources of income in Saudi Arabia were cut off a long time ago, and he's been forced to diversify. Drugs, kidnapping for ransom, even robbery. Two banks in France and a diamond exchange in Amsterdam that we're sure of. Despite all the money he's poured into terrorist activities over the last decade or more, he's probably worth more now than when he started."

"Hey, you two are way ahead of the rest of us," Rob said. "You been talking this out ahead of time?"

"Not substantively." Tombs paused and looked around the table at each of the SEALs.

"This is the layout," he said. "*Bellman* will separate from the rest of the task force in about three hours and increase speed to put us near the

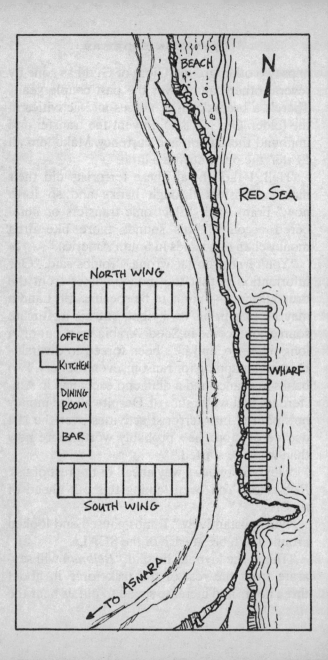

coast of Eritrea just north of the town of Mitsiwa shortly after dark this evening. We will go ashore by rapid penetration boat, and set up our ambush near a small hotel on the outskirts of Mitsiwa, where one group of people is going to turn over several suitcases full of cash and gold to another group of people. We get the money, and do whatever is necessary to the people involved to make certain they can't positively identify us as Americans, then return the way we went in."

"We?" Frank said, staring at Tombs. "The way you say that makes it sound as if you intend going in with us."

"Exactly," Tombs said.

There was silence for a moment. Frank could feel the stares of his team mates, but he continued to look at Tombs. That's all we need, Frank thought.

"I don't think that's the best choice," the chief said. "I mean nothing against you, but you haven't had the specialized training and physical conditioning we've had, and on top of that, you've spent the last two days puking your guts out. The boat we're going to use to get in and out is likely to bounce all over the place, and you couldn't handle *Bellman*. You'll be useless if you're seasick, and worse than that. Having you along could endanger the four of us *and* the mission, just because you want to play James Bond all of a sudden. I wouldn't take anyone in like that, not even one of my own men. We can't count on being able to carry you and wait for you to get done puking every few minutes."

"I'm not asking you to carry me," Tombs said, his voice coldly rigid. "I can take care of myself. I didn't ask your opinion about the manning on this op. And I am the boss here."

"I don't give a damn what you did or didn't ask," Frank said, his tone matching the CIA man's almost perfectly. "The four of us are a team. We've trained and worked together for years. We know what to expect from the rest, what we can and can't do. We know we can count on each other. We don't know diddly-squat about you."

"Deal with it. We don't have photographs of any of the possible couriers available. I've either seen most of the people ibn Landin might trust to transfer so much money, or studied their photographs before. We hit the Wednesday night poker club by mistake, we're all knee deep in the shit. Besides, I'll be handling the glass ear. We might have trouble figuring out what room they're in otherwise."

Frank tried to marshal more objections, but there was that one fact he couldn't get past. Tombs was in command. If he wanted to go along, there was no way Frank could prevent it without breaking more Navy regulations than he wanted to contemplate.

"We will obey orders," Frank said, after the silence had gone on for more than a minute. "But

I'm going to put my objections in writing. I want them on record in case things go wrong because you come along on this."

"Fine. You do that," Tombs said. "Now, can we continue with the briefing?"

There was an icy formality to the rest of the session.

THE PREPARATION

Machinist's Mate Ike Jensen had been free early and so had already kitted up. Now he sat and watched the other members of his team preparing for the mission. It was rather humorous, in a way, and he had to smile. When he had applied for the tests to be a SEAL, even when he was in BUD/S, Ike had wondered what a real SEAL thought about while preparing for the field. He had imagined some sort of psyching up process, maybe the sort of self-hypnosis the ancient Viking Beserkers were said to practice. The memory brought out a full smile. Jensen wondered at it for a moment, then went back to fastening his boots.

The truth was that there was no secret. No ritual, no kata, nothing. Like all SEALs, Ike was a professional who prepared like any professional would to do his job. You review the details, check and recheck your equipment and weapons, wonder where you'll go for break on your next leave.

More than anything he now understood that professionalism made the difference. Frank had been right, he could trust every man on the team to be where he was needed when he was supposed to be there. That's what worried them all about taking the spook. The company man may be in charge, they were used to that, but he wasn't one of them. He hadn't trained as they had, he hadn't passed the test of Hell Week. Simply put, they were a team and the company man wasn't a part of that. Having to include him, to ensure his safety, might cause them to hesitate. But hesitation could mean failure, even death.

Jensen stretched. He was nervous, everyone admitted they were before a tricky mission, and this one had a greater potential for disaster than most. The plan just wasn't precise. They didn't know which building, the number or armaments they might be facing, even the timing was too loose. But looking at his team mates, Ike knew they had the skill and abilities to overcome almost any obstacle. Nervous, that was human, but the young SEAL was also confident in his own abilities and those of his team mates. They were professionals, well prepared for anything they were likely to face. Knowing this helped the Machinist mate retain his air of calm even as the muscles on the back of his neck tensed.

He turned the machine gun over in his hands. The 9mm M10 Ingram is one of the most compact submachine guns in the US military inventory.

The high cyclic rate of fire causes it to empty its 32-round magazine in about two seconds if the trigger is held down. It takes a good deal of training and practice to fire the Ingram in short, effective six-shot bursts, especially since it's a two-handed firing weapon that packs a lot of muscle. But that's what being a SEAL was all about. Control. Discipline. Principle. Ike checked his pack and came up with the sound suppressor that screwed onto the threaded muzzle of the Ingram. It was a reminder of just how dangerous this mission was going to be.

Eventually, Ike put the weapon away and repacked the silencer for the trip in. Then, taking the opportunity while the others finished select-

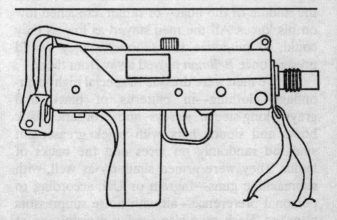

9mm M10 Ingram

ing and checking their weapons, Jensen leaned back against a locker and reviewed the map he had already memorized.

THE MISSION

Bellman had lowered the SEALs' RPB—rapid penetration boat—over the port side, away from the African coast, no more than twenty-five hundred yards from shore. The ship slowed only minimally. The transfer would be done on the fly. Harry Tombs and the SEAL team climbed down a rope ladder into the boat, then cast off the painter holding the RPB to *Bellman*. The SEALs took up the same relative positions they had during the rescue mission in Lebanon. Tombs sat in the middle of the boat—or rather, crouched low on his knees. All the men stayed as low as they could, to minimize the silhouette they would present once *Bellman* moved away from them.

All five men were dressed in special night-camouflage clothing—in patterns of black and grays—long-sleeve jerseys and trousers, black boots and slouch hats, with black greasepaint smeared randomly on faces and the backs of hands. They were armed similarly as well, with submachine guns—Ingram or Uzi, according to personal preference—all with noise suppressors attached. Each man also carried a pistol and at least one knife. The firearms had no easily discovered serial numbers. The clothing had no tags. None of the men carried or wore any identification, military or civilian. If anyone was killed or captured, there would be no way for the local authorities to prove who they were or where they had come from. Not even fingerprints would provide identification. If necessary, files would be extracted from FBI and naval records.

There had been virtually no talking among the five men from the time they'd rendezvoused on *Bellman* before climbing down into their RPB. The SEALs had done their talking before, going over the tactical details of the operation. Frank explained tactics in far more detail than he would have for just his men—staring at Tombs through the simplified instructions. Tombs might be boss of the operation, but Frank Lucan retained tactical control. Once in the boat, silence was a matter of routine discipline, not continuing disgruntlement over the presence of the civilian.

Bellman maintained its speed and heading for several minutes after the RPB cast off, so there would be no reason for observers to mark a specific point where *something* might have happened out of the ordinary. By the time the ship adjusted its course by turning several degrees to port, farther from shore, the small boat was a third of the way to the Eritrean coast even though Beau kept the engine throttled back far enough to minimize the RPB's wake. *Bellman* would continue on course through the Mitsiwa canal before making a slow turn to port to circle the Dahlak Islands to head back northwest to rendezvous with the team.

After sunset, there was little chance of running into any local boats out in the water. Most of the fishermen put out in the pre-dawn twilight and were back in port before midday. The boats that handled freight transportation along the coast also worked almost exclusively during daylight hours. And this was not an area known for pleasure boating. The small number of residents of Mitsiwa wealthy enough to afford recreation of that nature had other things to do with their money—like hiring bodyguards to keep them and their money safe.

It was early enough in the evening that there were still a considerable number of lights on in the town of Mitsiwa, even streetlights. But the number was much smaller than it would have been in any American or European town of comparable size. The one improved highway serving Mitsiwa led west to Asmera, some sixty miles away, but the men in the RPB could see the headlights of few vehicles.

Using binoculars and night-vision goggles, Frank identified the inn that was their destination. The building was single story, of stucco covered brick, whitewashed. The layout was simple, three sides of a hollow square with the courtyard facing the Red Sea. According to the briefing papers, the inn's office, kitchen, dining room, and bar were in the central part of the structure, with guest rooms in either wing. Everything faced the courtyard, with private doors to the guest rooms. There was a smaller addition built onto the back of the central section, with refrigerated storage for the kitchen. Only the public rooms were air conditioned. A small jetty along the shore protruded far enough to let small boats tie up to deliver food and supplies—or an occasional traveler coming in by water.

Several cars were parked in the courtyard.

Beau aimed for a point a couple of hundred yards north of the inn. As the RPB neared shore, Frank could no longer see into the courtyard. He turned to studying the section of coast where the boat would land. The inn was at the very edge of settlement. Along the shore, civilization appeared to come to a sudden halt. Farther inland, there might be hundreds of shanties where refugees and the working poor lived, but not here. There might almost have been a line drawn: town here, wasteland there. All the better for us, Frank thought; I hate to work in a crowd.

Someone had spent considerable time watching the inn, over a period of weeks, if not longer. The patterns of business had been carefully delineated in the briefing papers. There were rarely more than two or three guest rooms occupied overnight. The inn's primary business came from its bar and dining room, from lunchtime through early evening. The supper crowd reached its heaviest between seven and nine in the evening. Business in the bar started tailing off soon after the dining room quit serving at ten and the barman was usually able to shut down for the night by eleven. After he finished cleaning up and left, the only staff left would be a night manager and a single porter, unless the inn had most of its rooms occupied—a rare occurrence—in which case a second porter might be on duty.

The narrow beach just north of the inn was not sand, but primarily rock and gravel—rounded bits of stone that had been tumbled and polished by years of tides and the wash of boat engines. The RPB grounded a few feet short of the beach, and the men hopped out into the water to pull it ashore and into the cover of a scraggly bush that had somehow survived almost at the water's edge.

Beyond that, the ground rose in a sharp bank, about six feet. Water had undercut the land above. Tombs and the four SEALs got down behind that. For a moment, they all watched over the top, looking for any sign of people about—any hint that their approach might have been noticed.

Then, when Frank was sure that the five of them were alone, he moved closer to Tombs and whispered close to his ear. "You might be in charge of the overall operation, but remember this. I'm the team leader, and in tactical control. You do what you're told, and God help you if you fuck up."

Tombs turned to stare at Frank. He waited a

few seconds before he whispered back, "Then lead."

"Until we get in position, you stick close to me. I've got to know where everybody is, and I don't have to see the others for that."

Frank whistled softly to get the attention of his team mates, then made a gesture. Rob was the first man over the top of the embankment. Then Frank nudged Tombs. "Let's go." They clambered up away from the beach and moved a little to the right. At the same time, Ike moved up and to the left. Beau was the last man. He gave the others a ten-yard headstart before he climbed out and followed them.

The team moved in a roughly diamond-shaped formation, with one point too heavy because of the presence of an extra man. They all moved in a crouch, weapons at the ready. But this was one mission where they hoped that there would be little need—if any—for gunfire. If the terrorists transferring money could be caught unaware, put under the gun before they could start using their own weapons, they could be dispatched silently— one way or another.

The goal was to get in and out with as little fuss as possible. If they could finish their mission without disturbing the inn's staff or any other guests, that would make it perfect.

The rocky soil was poor but did manage to support some grass, but nothing larger. The team moved to a position fifty yards from the north wing of the inn and went to ground—flat on their faces—while Tombs used his "glass ear," a listening device that could read conversation from the vibrations talk set up in window glass as well as more directly to eavesdrop on the eight guest rooms on that side of the hostelry. It was still early— it would be another hour before the anticipated earliest time for the transfer specified in the briefing—but it might be possible to find likely guests before then. Frank and Tombs each had binoculars. Tombs might spot a familiar face. If they didn't find anything here, they would move around to the far side of the inn to survey the eight guest rooms on that side. Then come back later, if necessary.

"One way or another, we'll find our targets," Tombs had told the SEALs near the end of the briefing that afternoon.

"If they show up," Frank had replied.

"They'll show up."

Maybe, Frank thought after ten minutes of watching for movement near the windows in the rooms he could see. There was a light burning in only one of those rooms, and no one moved past the window during the time that Frank stared at it. This side or the other, he thought. Should have had two bugs so we could watch both sides at once. And radios to communicate.

"There's someone in that room with the lights," Tombs whispered. "I can pick up snoring. Almost loud enough to hear without the glass ear."

"Just peachy," Frank whispered. "Listen, we're

not going to be sure of anything just sitting here. We need to move around, down near the front, where we can see both sides at once."

"Front of the courtyard?" Tombs asked.

"You said it. Back down by the water. If necessary, we can hide at the edges of the pier." Should have planned on that from the start, Frank thought. If he hadn't got me so riled about going along, I would have. He shook his head, a minimal gesture. Letting emotion get to him had been a major screw up. *Maybe I'm getting too old for this.* Frank waited long enough to give Tombs a chance to object, then signaled to the other men.

"I'll go first," Frank said when the other SEALs came close enough to hear whispered instructions. "We've got to get down where we can see the whole operation at once. Farmer, you nursemaid our spook. Ike, you get on my tail and stay there."

Frank didn't wait for comments or objections. He didn't even look to see how Tombs reacted to *nursemaid* and *spook*. He simply didn't give a damn.

There was no evidence that anyone was looking their way—or that there was anyone around *to* look. But Frank took every precaution he could, short of slithering along on his belly. He moved slowly and steadily, walking in an uncomfortable crouch.

He had his Uzi ready, but if any of them needed guns at this stage of the operation, the night would be a total bust.

They had little more than the length of a football field to go from where they had been to the shore. Frank angled a bit farther from the inn as he moved. Once they were down by the water again, they could move toward the center of the inn with less chance of being discovered by accident. If they had to go into the water, so be it. SEALs would hardly notice it, and if it made Tombs uncomfortable, all the better. Maybe he won't be so damn eager to come along next time, Frank thought.

Frank had covered nearly half the distance to the shore when car headlights came around the seaside corner of the Inn. Twin cones of light swept across the field Frank and his team were crossing. There was scarcely time for the five of them to drop to the ground before the light reached them.

Then the light was gone. The car had turned into the courtyard of the inn. It parked and the engine was shut off. That might be part of our target, Frank thought. He lifted his head, and then got up and started moving again, hurrying now. He wanted to see how many people got out of the car and where they went.

"Damn," he muttered under his breath when he finally got close enough to the water to see into the courtyard. There was no one moving. Whoever had been in the car had already gone in—somewhere.

"Quick, slide along until we can cover all three sides of the courtyard," Frank instructed as the others came down over the embankment behind him. He sent Ike on first, then Tombs and Rob, then moved into the line himself, leaving Beau at the rear again. That was where Guisborne preferred to operate.

For an area generally starved for lumber, the wharf was surprisingly constructed of wood—pilings thicker than telephone poles, eight by eight beams, and heavy planks. Rock had been blasted or dug away to accommodate larger boats than might routinely be assumed to need the wharf. Only right along the shore was there a shallow shelf. The wharf was thirty yards long, and extended ten feet out from the shore. Near the northern end, there was a gap between wharf and shore, as much as five feet right at the end of the dock.

There was nearly four feet of clearance between the water and the bottom of the wharf's decking.

We could have brought the boat right in here and tied up underneath, Ike thought as he edged his way along the ledge toward the southern end of the wharf. Saved ourselves a lot of trouble. His shrug was only mental, and quickly over. He had to concentrate on the next stretch of rocky ledge. It was narrow, slippery, and angled a little toward the water. The gentle swell, rising and falling against him, didn't help. Twice he came close to losing his footing. The second time, it was only a good handhold that kept him from sliding completely off the ledge.

Ike was already wet to the waist. That was no problem, though he was getting uncomfortable with water in his boots. A fall would mean a splash though, and that might draw attention—the one thing the SEALs did not want.

Finally, he reached the end of the wharf. The land jutted out a little just beyond the end of the decking, and he was able to find a position that seemed secure. He looked over the embankment toward the inn. He had a clear view of the doors and windows along two-thirds of the courtyard—all but the south wing—as well as the ends of the wings.

Now, we wait, he thought. He scanned past the inn, toward town and then out over the water. If a boat came up from the south, he would not want to be caught with his head sticking up.

Twenty yards away, Tombs and Rob were at the beginning of the gap between wharf and shore. They could see all of the doors and windows facing the courtyard, though the angle on the north wing was acute enough to make Rob wonder if Tombs's eavesdropping device would be fully effective there. There was barely room for Tombs to get his head up above the level of wharf and shore to use the glass ear. Rob had moved a couple of feet away from the CIA man, where the gap was wide enough to give him a chance to get his weapon up over the edge if he had to use it.

Five yards farther on, Frank's view of the courtyard was the counterpart of what Ike could see.

Frank could not see the windows facing the courtyard from the north wing.

At the north end of the wharf, Beau gave the courtyard little attention. He watched the outer side of the north wing, and the area north of the inn—land and water. This gonna be a dry hole, he thought, unconcerned by the irony of the cliché. Like the others, he was wet to his waist. But even if no one showed up to hand over cash and bullion to someone else, security was important. If they were captured by locals and made to talk, they would be in trouble—and the U.S. government would have a major diplomatic flap. We got home, people steer clear of us like we was dead fish been sitting in the sun for a week, Beau thought.

When the lights went out in the inn's kitchen, Frank looked at his watch. It was 2230 hours, ten-thirty at night. Three minutes later, a man and woman—both dressed in white—came out of the central portion of the inn and went to one of the four cars parked in the courtyard. They got in. The car was balky. Its driver had to try several times before the engine came to life. The vehicle backed all the way out of the courtyard and toward the north, then shifted into forward and drove out past the south wing, turning toward town.

It was nearly an hour later before the lights went out in the bar. One man came out and started walking. He had his hands stuck in the pockets of his khaki shorts and was whistling. Just after he left the courtyard, rounding the corner of the south wing, he stopped and looked toward the shore.

Ike, the nearest SEAL, held his breath and *very* slowly lowered himself a few inches. Only the top half of his head, from the eyes up, had been exposed at the start. When he stopped moving, little more than the top of his hat might have been visible to the man by the corner of the building. If he started toward the shore, Ike would see him before he got too close. And then . . . ? If the man came too close, he would have to be silenced. One way or another.

The others had also lowered themselves, slowly, taking care not to move quickly enough to draw the attention of the man they all assumed to be the inn's bartender. Only Beau stayed up far enough to watch him. He edged farther away from the north end of the wharf, ready to climb ashore and go after the whistler, if necessary. Beau unsnapped the strap on his shoulder holster, drew his pistol, then screwed the silencer in place. The whistling man was seventy yards away, but Beau was confident that he could make the shot if he had to.

After nearly five minutes, the man lit a cigarette, blew one long puff of smoke, then started walking toward town. Beau let out his breath, softly, but he continued watching until the man disappeared from sight, on the dark road into Mitsiwa. Then he removed the silencer from his pistol and put both back where they belonged. It was ten minutes until midnight.

By one o'clock in the morning, Frank was about ready to believe that the rendezvous would not come off. There were no lights on in any of the guest rooms in the south wing. In the center, one light showed in the lobby, but even the light by the entrance had been switched off at midnight. Frank could still see light shining out of one guest room on the north wing, but that was where Tombs had said there was a man snoring, hours before.

Frank did remember that the briefing had indicated that the rendezvous might take place anytime between 2300 and 0300 hours, but every minute that went by seemed to make it less likely that anyone would show up. And no way for anyone to tell us if new intel has come in, he thought. Harry Tombs was the SEALs' only link to the intelligence apparatus providing information for this entire series of operations. If something happened to him, Frank could do nothing but take his men back to *Bellman* and notify his superiors in Virginia.

It was 0115 hours. Frank took out his binoculars and scanned as much of the sea as he could. *Bellman* was out there, somewhere, waiting for a message from the SEALs to set up retrieval. There was traffic on the Red Sea, but most of the lights Frank could see were well out, near the horizon. And more beyond that, he thought. Most com-

mercial shipping would steer east of the Dahlak
Islands. Even the rest of *Roosevelt*'s battle group
would be out there, somewhere, staying as near
the center of the deep water and as far from
potentially hostile land as possible.

Frank started to slide along the ledge toward
Harry and Rob. His legs were cold and stiff after
standing in water so long. The Red Sea might be
relatively warm, but it was at least ten degrees
below normal body temperature, and that left
him slightly chilled. Ten years earlier, it might not
have bothered him at all, but he was aware of it
now. He could feel it.

Tombs and Rhodes both noticed Frank coming.

"Doesn't look like your people are going to
show," Frank whispered when he was as close to
the other two as he could get. "Maybe their plans
got changed."

"Maybe," Tombs whispered back, "but it's too
early to give up. That end room on the north.
There's someone in there. Sounds like he's just
pacing back and forth from the window on this
side to the far side of the room. Back and forth,
like he's waiting for someone, or something."

"You got any idea which end of the transfer he
might be?" Frank asked. "If we could be sure it
was the one with the loot, we could hit now and
get out before the other side arrives. That'd do
the job, wouldn't it?"

"If we could be sure," Tombs conceded, "but we
can't. Our information wasn't quite that complete. If we hit the people waiting to get the

money, we might be out of luck. We don't know
what recognition signals they might have."

"Just a thought. You still figure on waiting here
till three o'clock if we have to?"

"If we have to," Tombs said. "Maybe ten or fifteen minutes past, just to be sure. That would still
give us time to get back to the boat and make our
rendezvous with *Bellman* before dawn."

Barely, Frank thought, but he did not say it. He
just nodded, then edged his way back to where he
had been before. Movement helped take the
strain from his knees and ankles.

Beau was the first to hear the sound, not just
because he was nearest, but because it was a
sound he had known since he was a baby—the
sound of a small boat engine throttled well back.
It was coming along the shore from the north. He
slid back under the embankment at the edge of
the wharf, into the water. After a glance south, to
make certain that none of the others were
exposed enough to give away their position, Beau
turned his attention to the north again, searching
for the boat that was making the noise.

When he did spot it, the boat was no more than
fifty yards away, and within thirty feet of shore.
Maybe close enough to see our boat, Beau
thought. That might mean trouble, whether the
boat carried the people the team was there to
intercept or someone else. If it was a local army
or police patrol. . . .

We might have us an international incident,

Beau thought. He got as low as he could without risking slipping off the underwater shelf. Little more than his head, arms, and submachine gun were above the surface. He held himself motionless then, not even daring to glance south again, to see if the others had heard the approaching boat.

They had. Tombs and Rhodes had ducked under the wharf. CPO Lucan was ready to duck under as well. Where he was, the underwater ledge extended under the planking. But he didn't want to go under until he had to. It was more important to watch the boat until he could tell whether it was coming for the dock or going on past.

This must be it, Frank thought. I wish someone had said something about maybe they'd come in by water. But it would have made little difference. The men were where they could see the target, and—Frank hoped—out of sight of the new arrivals.

The boat's engine stopped as the vessel was drifting toward the wharf. Frank made out the sounds of rope being tied to a cleat. Gently, the boat scraped against the rubber fenders hung over the side of the wharf. A second man climbed from the boat onto the wharf. Footsteps moved across the wood decking and out onto the gravel walkway leading toward the courtyard. From his position under the wharf, Frank could see the two men. One of them was carrying a submachine gun. Frank wasn't certain, but he thought it might be an Uzi.

Are there only two? Frank wondered. He didn't question that these men were the people they were after; the submachine gun was evidence enough of that.

Someone needed to check the boat, and quickly, before Tombs or one of his own men started to move. Frank went back toward Rob and Tombs. He didn't dare talk, not when there might be one or more people still in the boat, but he got the message across with hand signals. He took Rob's submachine gun. Rhodes was the man to check the boat.

Rob lowered himself the rest of the way into the water then pushed off gently, swimming in a slow breast stroke, moving as silently as he could. Before he got to the far side of the wharf he took a deep breath, then slipped underwater and propelled himself forward, using his legs now. Visibility was nonexistent, but Rob swam outward until he was certain that he was clear of the boat, then jack-knifed his body around and came to the surface facing back toward the shore. With his mouth just barely out of the water, Rob took several slow breaths while he treaded water and looked at the silhouette of the boat.

The near side of the vessel was ten feet away. The fiberglass hull had between three and four feet of freeboard—clearance above the water. The deck was higher at the prow, lower at the stern. The boat was about twenty-five feet long, and there appeared to be only a low cabin amidships.

At first, Rob saw no sign of movement aboard, so he paddled back farther to give himself a better angle. Even then, it was not movement he saw first, but the flash of a cigarette lighter and the glowing end of the cigarette it lit—before the man turned his head toward shore again.

Good enough, Rob thought; keep looking that way. He started moving toward the boat again, keeping his head just above water, watching. He plotted his moves in advance. There would be one tricky moment—getting from the water into the boat. The second he put weight on the craft, it would tilt in response, and that would alert the man aboard.

There was no room for error. There would be no second chances. Rob knew he had to make the transfer the first time, in one fluid movement, before the man aboard could turn to defend himself or shout a warning.

Rob went underwater, going down until his feet touched bottom, then he pushed himself upward, using his arms and legs to give him more momentum. When he popped out of the water, he grabbed for the gunwale of the boat, pulled himself over the side, and lunged forward as he drew his belt knife, a titanium MPK. The single man on the boat seemed frozen by surprise for a fraction of a second, but that was all the break Rob needed. As the man finally turned, realized what was happening, and started to bring up his Uzi submachine gun, Rob barreled into him—knife first.

His aim was perfect. The blade slid between the man's ribs, straight into his heart, as Rob's body slammed into him, knocking him backwards, half onto the wharf. The body gave one convulsive jerk as death claimed it. Rob pulled his victim back into the boat, pulled the knife from the body, then took a quick look inside the cabin to assure himself that there was no one else present.

Rob looked toward the inn then. The other two men had gone inside, though he had not seen where they had entered. It did not bother him. There would have been four other pairs of eyes watching that. There were lights on now in the nearest room on the south wing of the inn, where it had been dark before. Rob did not go back into the water. He crossed the top of the wharf, staying low, as he aimed for the point where he had left Frank and the spook.

"Off to the left," Frank said, handing Rob's submachine gun back to him. "They're in the first room on the south wing. You and Ike cover the back and this side. Stay low. We'll go in the door and the window on the courtyard side. When we hit, you stick your gun in the window on the end."

Rob nodded, then started moving to the left, running low, almost bent double, until he passed the end of the wharf and Ike. He slid to the ground then, facing the south wing of the inn. Ike hoisted himself out of the water and moved into position a few feet to Rob's side. The two men glanced at each other, nodded back and forth, and Rob started moving at an angle toward a point some yards from the corner of the inn. The two men moved alternately, one getting up and scurrying forward a few yards while the other stayed prone, ready to provide covering fire should that prove necessary.

Within seconds, Tombs and the other SEALs were also moving, their target the door of the end room on the south wing of the inn. Frank had given whispered instructions to his companions before they started moving. They angled first to the south, to put the corner of the south wing between them and the office—in case the night manager might happen to look out.

With lights on in the room the SEALs were going to hit, there was little chance that the people inside would see them even if they did look out. And they were more likely watching each other. Frank had been on enough operations against drug smugglers to know that they were more paranoid about the people they did business with than they were about the law.

It took less than a minute for everyone to get into position. Frank and Tombs flanked the window on the courtyard side of the room. Beau was ready to hit the door. His initial job was mostly to distract the people inside. He would give the door a kick near the handle, then duck to the side, out of the way. As soon as Beau hit the door, Tombs, Lucan, and Rhodes would have the muzzles of their submachine guns in the open windows of the room. After that . . .

Frank nodded. Beau kicked the wooden door as hard as he could, splintering wood. Then he dove to the side.

An instant of surprise. That was all that was needed. The barrels of three submachine guns stuck in two windows. Harry Tombs called out, "Don't move or you're dead," in Arabic.

The four men inside froze in position. One man who had started to raise a submachine gun dropped it. Maybe they think we're local cops who can be fixed, Frank thought. He had not known that Tombs spoke Arabic, but it did not surprise him. There must have been *some* reason why Tombs had been chosen to head this operation. Frank could understand a couple hundred words of the language, if it was spoken slowly, but he had scarcely caught what Tombs had said.

"These are the ones," Tombs said.

Frank nodded, then gestured to Beau, who had gotten back to his feet. The door swung open easily now, and the latch and bolt fell to the floor. Tombs moved around to the door. Inside, he and Beau flanked the doorway, their weapons covering the four men they had surprised.

"On the floor," Tombs instructed in Arabic.

The room was not large enough for the men to

spread out. They were close together, touching, when they obeyed. Harry Tombs moved around them, to the double bed against the wall, and flipped open one of the two suitcases lying there. That erased any doubt he might have had that they had found the right men. The suitcase contained stacks of high denomination bank notes— German marks, British pounds, and others, and several plastic tubes of one-ounce gold coins. Tombs opened one. The coins were krugerands. He sifted through the stacks of bills for a moment, checking to make sure that there were no explosives in the case, then he shut the lid and zipped it. Then he looked in the second case and found a repeat—currency and gold.

Tombs picked the second case up. It was satisfyingly heavy. The spy smiled, briefly, then passed the case to Frank, and gestured toward the door before he picked up the second case and passed it to Beau.

Frank moved toward the door, backing away, keeping his eyes on the four men on the floor. Beau stepped to the side to give his boss room to get past without getting between him and the prone men, then started to follow.

Before Frank or Beau realized what was going on, Tombs had drawn his pistol from under his belt. The 9mm Russian weapon had a silencer attached. Tombs fired four times, killing each of the men on the floor with a single shot to the back of the head. The pistol coughed with each shot, but even with the silencer the noise seemed enough to guarantee that it would be heard.

"Let's get out of here," Tombs said.

POST-MISSION

"I don't give a damn *who* those men were, what Tombs did was nothing short of murder," Beau said, the anger obvious in his voice even though he was doing little more than whispering. It was the first chance the four SEALs had found to be alone since the killings. The debriefing session had been short and one-sided, with Harry Tombs doing virtually all of the talking. The money had been counted out. Tombs and Frank had each signed two copies of the inventory, and then the suitcases had been turned over to the captain of *Bellman* for safekeeping.

"He never did say whether he recognized any of those people," Rob Rhodes said. "We can't even say for certain that he killed the right targets." For Rob, the question was more practical than a matter of conscience.

"Men meeting in an out-of-the-way place like that in the middle of the night to transfer close to two million bucks, you can be damned sure they were up to no good, whether they were the specific people we were after or not," Frank said. "Look, there's not a damn thing we can do about Tombs. He's in charge of this operation. We get back to Dam Neck, I'll have a talk with the skipper, see what he has to say. But don't expect it to go any farther than that. This is a company operation."

"If the locals had caught us, they'd have executed us as common murderers," Beau said. "And they'd have the right of it, as much as anybody."

"They didn't catch us. They were never likely to catch us," Frank said.

"Don't it bother you none?" Beau demanded.

Frank took a deep breath. "Hell, yes, it bothers me. But I've seen stuff as bad before. Worse. We do our job. Nobody ever told us we had to like what we were doing. Hell, man, this is a war where the other side doesn't play by any rules but their own. What do you want to do, read them their rights? We don't know that all the folks *we*'ve wasted deserved what they got."

"It ain't the same," Beau said, shaking his head vigorously. "We don't lay 'em down and pop 'em off the way Tombs did, execution style—ain't that what they call it?"

Ike sat apart from the others, glad that no one was paying attention to him. After the team had returned to *Bellman*, before the debriefing, Ike had gone to the head and puked—his body's reaction to what he had witnessed. Now, he felt as if he might have to vomit again.

THE REPORT

The boat rides, going and coming, had been as miserable as Harry Tombs had expected, but he had been careful to avoid showing any discomfort. I won't give Lucan the pleasure, he had told himself—over and over. Tombs had focused on the immediate needs. He held that focus until he completed his report on the mission. He was happy—as happy as he could be in the field.

His report had been as detailed as always, and strictly accurate. He did not attempt to hide the fact that he had executed four men; that would be more cause for censure from Langley than the fact of the killings. Two of the faces had been familiar from briefings, men long sought by the Agency. No tears would be shed for them on that side of the Atlantic.

The count of bank notes and gold coins had been in the main body of the report. But Tombs returned to them in his personal summary at the end.

```
Currency and bullion coins worth, as of
the latest quotes available, approxi-
mately one million eight hundred and
thirty-six thousand dollars ($1,836,000)
were impounded. At this point in time,
that is sufficient to create hardship
among the terrorists the money was
intended for. Between that and the fact
```

that we were not seen and left no iden-
tifiable evidence—meaning that neither
ibn Landin nor the intended recipients
of the money will *know* who intercepted
the shipment and killed the couriers—I
believe it is safe to say that even if
we accomplish nothing else on this mission, we have achieved signal success.

Tombs encrypted the report after going back
through it, line by line, one more time, changing a
word here and there. He transmitted the report,
waited for acknowledgment of its receipt, then
wiped the copy on his computer's hard drive.

When he went to bed, he slept better than he
had since leaving London.

4: GRASSHOPPER

PRE-MISSION

Harry Tombs had given the SEALs no explanation for the order to stand down six hours after their return from Mitsiwa. He did not tell them whether it was temporary or permanent. They had no orders to head for home, or anywhere else. They would remain on *Bellman* and await further orders. Beyond some inevitable initial speculation about the meaning of the stand-down, the SEALs were content to take their time off—except for their daily exercises and runs.

For Tombs, the two days that had passed since the order to halt operations had not been idle. He had been in contact with his headquarters in Langley, Virginia, several times each day. Besides the computer link, he had participated in two lengthy radio conferences.

When Tombs received the initial order to halt operations, there had been no immediate explanation, just a promise of additional information as soon as possible. Ninety minutes later, he had been told that the "situation" had become "fluid," that the terrorist summit was not going to take place as planned, that several of the expected participants had started heading back toward their home bases, or to other safe areas.

It was the next day before the analysts at Langley had been able to inform him that the summit meeting had not been cancelled, only postponed for "at least seven, and perhaps as many as fourteen days." There were still no additional operational orders.

The battle group centered on *Roosevelt* steamed out of the Red Sea, through the Gulf of Aden, and turned south, paralleling the coast of Somalia, always staying at least fifty miles from shore. The battle group's orders were to go as far south as the capital, Mogadishu, before turning north again. In addition to normal reconnaissance flights, *Roosevelt*'s air group conducted training exercises that extended almost to the coast—well within sight of people in the Somali capital. That was, almost, standard practice. The Department of Defense did not want to let Somalia forget about them, and the possibility that U.S. military forces might one day return. The unexpressed addendum was: *to even the score*.

The SEALs had finished their exercises and a brisk morning jog, then showered and had breakfast before 0800. They had still been at the table, drinking coffee, and discussing how they might while away another idle day, when a yeoman came in to tell Frank that his team was "expected" for a meeting at 0815.

"Well, I guess Tombs finally has something to tell us," Frank said after the yeoman left. "Either we go back to work or we go home."

"I hope it's home," Beau said. "Anythin' to get away from that spook." Guisborne had not spoken of the events of the last mission since the stand-down order, but he had never spoken of the CIA man since except disparagingly.

"I don't much care which," Rob said. "Either is better than getting calluses on our butts."

Ike remained silent. He had found very little to say about anything over the past two days. He was almost *afraid* to talk, uncertain what might come out if he started. For the first time in longer than he could remember, Ike had been having nightmares.

THE BRIEFING

"Here's the situation," Harry Tombs said, when he reached the conference room five minutes after the SEALs. "Our work has been having an effect, so much so that ibn Landin was forced to reschedule the summit meeting he's worked the last eighteen months to set up. Some of the people coming got too suspicious when things started happening while they were enroute. We've picked up whispers that some of the groups suspect that ibn Landin himself might be behind recent events, trying to weaken or destroy them rather than just set up a grand alliance with himself at the head." Tombs no longer showed any sign of his earlier seasickness. His appetite had returned, and he had regained the weight he had lost during his first couple of days aboard *Bellman*. He had also regained his reassurance and his voice was as strong as ever.

"The stand-down was to give our people time to track down the next moves, to find out if the meeting was indeed going to be rescheduled, or if it would be cancelled altogether. A lot of operatives have put in a lot of work. Our latest information, somewhat tentative, is that the meeting has simply been pushed back ten days, and will still be held in one of the locations that have been prepared in Sudan. At least three of the groups, including ibn Landin's own organization, are sending additional security assets to Sudan to guarantee the safety of their principals." He smiled. "No one seems entirely willing to leave security to anyone else.

"Tonight, we go back to work." Tombs opened a folder and started the usual process of passing around the orders, maps, and other information.

"This mission has dual purposes. It is related to the rest of our operations, but it is also partially payback, a reminder. The latest warlord in Mogadishu has established a terrorist training

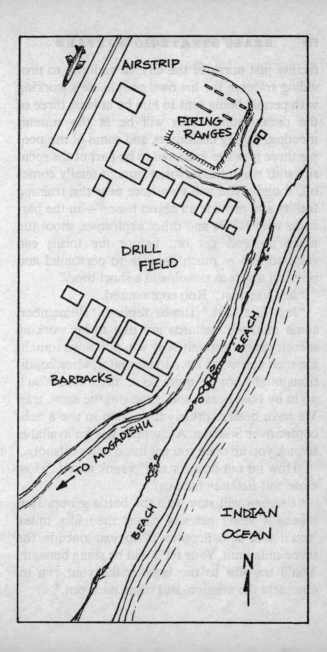

facility just north of the city. In addition to providing training for his own people, he's working with people being sent to him by at least three of the organizations who will be at the summit meeting. Paying customers, and some of the people there now are expected to be part of the security staff when the terrorist summit finally comes off. Tonight, you will go ashore near this training facility and provide an object lesson—hit the barracks with RPGs and other explosives, shoot the place up, and get out before the locals can respond. Do as much damage to personnel and physical assets as possible in a short time."

"Just like that," Rob commented.

"Just like that," Tombs replied. "Remember, some of those bastards are due to be working security at the summit. Any you put down tonight are men you won't have to face later, when conditions might not be quite so . . . favorable. You'll go in by boat again, and come out the same way. We have been expressly forbidden to use a helicopter over Somalia. A chopper will be available to pick you up once you get three miles offshore."

"How far out do we start?" Frank asked. "How close will *Bellman* take us?"

"*Bellman* will stay with the battle group. That means it won't get any closer than fifty miles. You'll ride a helicopter in to just outside the three-mile limit. Your RPB will be slung beneath. You'll transfer to the boat, make your run in, complete the mission, and come back out."

THE PREPARATION

"You know what that means, don't you," Beau said, after Tombs left the room. "We're all the way on our own this time. Things go bad, won't nobody be coming to get us out."

"We've been there before," Frank said. "We go in, do our job, and make sure nothing goes bad. We get ourselves out, even if we have to swim back to the chopper."

"These folks got gunboats, don't they? We gonna take diving gear so they can't pop us in the water?" Beau asked.

"Good point," Frank said. "Now, let's see about the rest of our gear. We want to make noise and raise as much hell as we can. M-16s with C-Mac magazines, grenade launchers, as much ammo as we can carry."

"How 'bout a few Claymores to slow the enemy down?" Rob suggested.

Intended to defend a position against "human-wave" attacks, the Claymore mine is, for all intents and purposes a giant, explosion-driven shotgun. The curved body of the mine holds slightly over one pound of plastic explosive in its rear portion; the front is filled with 700 steel fragmentation balls. The blast of a Claymore drives out its fragmentation at velocities of 3,000 feet per second, creating a curtain of steel shot fifty meters wide and 2 meters tall at 150 meters in front of the weapon. It is guaranteed to cause serious damage to anyone within 16 meters of the weapon who isn't under cover. A series of Claymores can be connected with detonating cord so that all the mines detonate at the same time. Which might be just what the SEALs needed on this run.

Frank nodded his agreement to bring them along. "Now spread that map out again," he said. "We need to be damned careful about where we land and set up." He took the most recent recon photos from the target folder again as well.

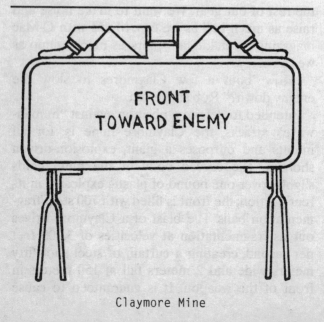

Claymore Mine

THE MISSION

Face masks, air tanks and regulators, and swim fins were lashed in place in the boat under the helicopter, along with two extra cases of 40mm grenades and a half dozen Claymore mines.

Quietly, when Rob had a few seconds alone with Frank during the process of loading their equipment, he said, "I notice the spook didn't invite himself along this time. I guess he doesn't like the odds. There may be several hundred armed men around that camp. Not like having four poor bastards he could off to get his jollies."

"Don't you start on me, too," Frank said. "You don't have to love the bastard, but we do have to work with him."

"Just tell him to keep his ass on this ship after this. He gets himself fragged on an op, some folks might think one of us did it."

"As long as they're not right," Frank said, and then he walked away from the Farmer. Jeez, Frank thought, I hope the spook doesn't want to come along again. Let us just get this over with and get away from him.

Frank did a final check of the gear stowed in the boat, and checked the connections between it and the helicopter, along with the helicopter's pilot and crew chief. The rigging job looked sound. This time, the helicopter was a U.S. Navy craft, sent over from *Roosevelt* for this job. Frank spent two minutes checking the arrangements for insertion and extraction with the pilot while his men got aboard, ready for take-off. All four SEALs had armed themselves the same way this time—M16s with M203 grenade launchers under the barrel. No one bothered with suppressors for the rifles or the pistols they also wore. Each man wore two bandoleers filled with grenades, and the extra crates in the RPB meant that they would be going in with nearly fifteen dozen rounds— almost certainly far more than they would get to use.

Once Frank was in place, the pilot looked back to him. Frank gave him a thumbs-up gesture and the pilot nodded. Thirty seconds later, the helicopter was in the air. They circled around clockwise, approaching *Roosevelt* before turning west. As soon as the helicopter was clear of *Bellman* again, the pilot dropped his craft almost to the water, leaving less than ten feet of clearance over the crests of the gentle swells.

At first, Ike Jensen stared out at the water, but the nearness of it combined with the aircraft's speed started to make his stomach queasy, so he turned away, looking at his team mates instead. The night-vision goggles he was wearing gave a strange cast to skin colors and everything else, but the almost-bizarre imagery was nothing new. Chief Lucan's face revealed nothing. It rarely did. He wore a poker face like a master . . . and Ike had seen the chief playing cards. It was impossible to guess what he was holding from his look or body language. Beau Guisborne had his "game face" on, a fierce scowl, but Ike thought there was more to it than concentration this time. Beau was clearly still angry about what had happened at Mitsiwa. Rob was something of a puzzle to Ike. There was nothing new in that, either. Rhodes could be the most easygoing guy in the platoon, or a hardnose who might turn violent at what seemed like little provocation. Now, he looked nearly comatose, staring vacantly at the bulkhead across from him, as if he had no idea—and less interest—where he might be or where he might be going.

For himself, Ike had spent most of the past several hours trying to insure that he could focus on the night's work without thinking back to the four men who had been killed where they lay the last time the team had gone out. It was hard. Violence was nothing new to Ike Jensen. He had seen a lot of it in the SEALs, especially since the team's foray into Lebanon, but the execution-style killing of those four men—drug smugglers and terrorists though they might be—was still eating at him.

When the helicopter suddenly slowed down and banked through a turn to starboard, Ike looked up, sensing that it was almost time for them to drop the boat and transfer to it. This ride was nothing compared to the long haul they had made to hit the depot in southeastern Libya.

It took three men to make the boat drop—to do it smoothly to minimize the chance of losing any of the gear the RPB carried. Frank helped the copilot and crew chief. The pilot hovered with the Red Sea no more than eight feet below the boat, doing everything he could to hold the helicopter rock steady while the others hit the releases for the straps that held the SEALs' rapid penetration boat in place. As the boat fell free, the helicopter did lift a few feet before the pilot could make his adjustments.

Two ropes were lowered from the starboard door of the helicopter. Beau and Frank were the first men down into the boat, fighting gravity and the downdraft of the rotor to make an easy descent. As soon as they were down, Rob and Ike slid out the door and onto the ropes. Ike was thankful for something to concentrate on fully. The first time he had tried going down a rope into the water, he had fallen. Since then, he had focused on each movement of his hands, and on keeping the rope between his legs to keep his speed minimal. He made the slowest descent of the team, but he stayed dry.

The helicopter moved a few dozen yards away from the boat to minimize the wash from the rotor, and climbed fifty feet higher, then hovered until Beau had the RPB's engine started and the boat headed toward the shore, three and a quarter miles away. The pilot threw the SEALs a salute before turning the helicopter and starting back toward *Bellman*—where it would wait a signal from the team for pickup.

Even with the diving gear, Claymore mines, and extra crates of grenades, the RPB rode only a little lower than usual in the water. Away from the turbulence caused by the helicopter, the Red Sea was almost glassy smooth, only an almost imperceptible swell. Beau checked his compass heading and opened the throttle to start them toward shore. There was still a narrow band of reddish orange, blending into purple and black, along the western horizon. Before the boat got close enough to shore for its passengers to worry seriously about being seen, night would be complete. The black boat and men in night camouflage would be virtually invisible ... they way they liked it.

Ike went back over the operation plan in his mind, trying to "see" the map and photographs they had studied. The training camp was built around a rectangular drill field that was slightly larger that a football field. The barracks were on the left, looking in from the sea. Offices, mess hall, and training buildings were on the right. According to the briefing documents, an old shanty town had been bulldozed to make room for the camp. Farther north were firing ranges and some of the other ancillary requirements for training soldiers. There was also a small airstrip and, off to the side of it, the derelict fuselage of an old Boeing 727—used to train terrorists in hijacking procedures and countermeasures, Harry Tombs had said.

According to the briefing, the camp itself was not particularly well guarded. The trainees stood guard duty but, like American military trainees, without ammunition for their weapons. The real security was provided by the warlord's soldiers, and they were mobile, riding around in old Land Rovers—some dating back to when Britain was still a colonial power in parts of East Africa. Each vehicle would have three or four soldiers, and they would have a machine gun mounted on the vehicle as well as their own rifles and pistols.

"There aren't very many patrols," Tombs had told the SEALs, "usually one vehicle patrolling the beach and the approaches to the camp, especially at night. They put out more manpower only when their boss gets an itch that something might be up."

"The approach of an American carrier battle group might get him itching awful hard," Frank had suggested. Tombs had shrugged.

Ike had been a teenager when the United States had gone into Mogadishu. He could recall news accounts of the men who had been lost, or tortured, the anger that had been expressed back home—but never translated into effective retaliatory action.

We'll get a little of that back tonight, he thought.

The coast was still a mile away when Frank urgently signaled for Beau to cut the throttle. Frank had kept busy scanning the shore with binoculars. What he had seen was the beam of a small searchlight scanning the beach and the waterline.

"One of their patrols," Frank whispered, turning to face the rear of the RPB, after Beau throttled down until the engine was just barely ticking over. Beau shut the engine down completely then. Better than most, he knew just how far sound could travel over water.

All four men crouched low in the boat. Ike moved his rifle into a more comfortable position, even though it would be foolish to think of firing at this range—Rob might be able to hit a target at a mile, though not with the M-16 he was carrying, but none of the others were sharpshooters of Rob's caliber—even if they dared make noise before they got to land. But the action helped ease Ike's tension, knowing he *could* defend himself, if necessary.

The searchlight moved slowly, back and forth, bouncing erratically as the vehicle carrying it continued northeast along the shore. Frank kept his binoculars trained on the source of the light, and on the vague forms he could see around it. The question in his mind was whether the vehicle would go so far then turn around and come back along the beach, or if it would make a circle of the training camp. Either way, he thought, we're going to have to deal with those people before we get out of there.

The next five minutes dragged for all the SEALs. The patrol vehicle on shore continued to move to their right. Then the searchlight went out. The vehicle made a U-turn and sped back toward the southwest. Frank waited until the

vehicle was out of sight, between the training
camp and Mogadishu, before he signaled to Beau
to start the engine again. He didn't need to tell
the others that they would have to be alert for the
return of that patrol vehicle.

Beau did not open the throttle as wide as he had
before. The last mile took as much time as the
first two and a quarter. The other three men had
their rifles at the ready as soon as they were
within five hundred yards of shore, and every eye
in the team was scanning for any hint of opposition—even the trainees without ammunition for
their rifles. An unarmed man could raise the
alarm just as quickly.

The beach was wide, and there was no obvious
place to conceal the boat. Frank still worried a little about that; it had been one of his main concerns during the planning session. They could lose
the boat, and their diving gear, while they were
off attacking the buildings of the training camp.
That patrolling vehicle, and however many men it
carried, was a major threat. It would be a long
three-mile swim without at least flippers, though
every man in the team was capable of making it.

"We'll drag the boat all the way up to the lee of
that rise, by those rocks," Frank told the others
just before it grounded in the minimal surf.
"Move the diving gear away from the boat, just in
case. Take the grenades and mines with us."

They went over the side and grabbed the ropes
to haul the boat along with them. It slid heavily

on the sand and rocks, enough to put a strain on the SEALs. There wasn't even any driftwood or brush around to partially disguise the craft.

We can't wait around to take out the patrol first, Frank decided. That was a no-brainer, but he toyed with the idea for all of thirty seconds. They had no way to know how long it might be before the patrol came along again, if it did, and it might not be possible to take them out silently even then—and the primary target was the training camp. They had to hit that.

Frank and Rob stood guard while Beau and Ike moved the diving gear—to two different spots, one on either side of the boat. Ike moved sand with his feet to at least give a little cover to the two sets of gear he had carried. *Just maybe, it might be enough.* In any commotion, the guards might not notice—or might think they had found everything if they uncovered one stash. Two sets of gear, two air tanks, would not be as good as four, but they would be better than none.

"We'll set up two of the mines to cover the boat and our gear," Frank decided. It was almost the flash of inspiration he had been hoping for. He pointed out where he wanted them. "String trip-wires. That Rover comes along, there's damn little chance they'll be looking for booby traps, let alone see the wires in time to avoid them."

Beau and Rob rigged the land mines, setting them in the deeper shadow under the rise that marked the landward end of the beach. All four men checked for landmarks to be certain that they would not trip their own mines on the way back to the sea. Then Frank spent a couple of minutes with the binoculars, looking for any hint of anyone walking a sentry post at the near end of the training camp. There was one man standing near the closest barrack, smoking a cigarette, looking toward the city. Across the field, Frank saw a man turn the corner, behind the buildings on that side.

"Okay, let's move," Frank said, when he was satisfied. "Stay low. We don't need to get closer than fifty yards from the parade ground. We can cover the entire compound from there."

Ike and Frank grabbed the handles on one crate of grenades. Beau and Rob shared the other. They climbed the rise and started at a slow jog toward the eastern end of the drill field, running almost doubled over. As they ran, they kept watch for any sign that either sentry might be looking their way.

This part of Somalia appeared to be in another period of drought. The grass and shrubbery between the training camp and the beach all seemed to be dead. Some of the grass crunched underfoot. The few trees all seemed to be bare. There was hardly a leaf in place.

Be nice to know how long the current class has been here, Ike thought as he struggled to keep pace with the chief. The newer they are, the less trouble they might cause. All we'd really have to worry about is the cadre, and whatever other trained soldiers are near.

The thoughts were too much of a distraction. He tripped and almost fell. Frank had to slow up for an instant, and gave him a quick look. Then they moved on again.

The two pairs of SEALs moved gradually apart. When they went to ground, it would help to have ten or fifteen yards separation between them. Or more. Seventy yards from the end of the drill field, Frank gestured to the others and they went prone. He had lost sight of the sentry who had been smoking, and he wanted to spot him again before they moved on to their final positions. And the other man—where had *he* gotten to?

It took five minutes before Frank located both men. On the left, the sentry had moved behind the barracks. It wasn't until he came back around the corner that he was visible again. On the other side, the sentry had come up between two of the buildings. He was leaning against the corner of one of them, staring toward the barracks across the way.

There must be at least two more, farther along the line, Frank thought. He looked but saw no one else. Then he glanced at his watch. It was 2230. I hope they don't get relieved until on the hour, Frank thought. Not now, before we're set. He leaned toward Ike. "Now we crawl," Frank whispered. "Keep the box between us like before."

It was almost as awkward as a three-legged race, crawling and moving the crate of grenades a foot or two at a time, but they managed. Once Beau and Rob saw what the others were doing, they started moving the same way. The SEALs needed ten minutes to cover the last twenty yards. Then they settled in, opened the crates of grenades, and loaded the launchers under the barrels of their rifles. No one needed to be instructed to use the crated projectiles first. The grenades in their bandoleers would be saved. They would have those for last, even to use on the run if they had to move. The crates could be abandoned.

The mix of rounds they had was in a nine-nine-two ratio—nine high explosive, nine incendiary, and two smoke. Unlike most of the buildings in the city, the training camp had been built of wood. Those buildings would burn quickly once they were ignited.

Each man started out with HE. Although nothing had been said, the first volley was aimed at the two sentries that had been spotted, two grenades toward each of them. The explosions came in a span of less than two seconds, and each sentry was bracketed. Neither man was seen afterward.

The SEALs moved quickly into a steady rhythm. Each man could load and fire ten or eleven grenades a minute, still allowing himself time to aim each shot. They worked each of the buildings flanking the parade ground, mixing HE with incendiary rounds. Fifty grenades had been fired before any of the SEALs saw men coming out of two of the barracks—still struggling to get into their clothes, carrying rifles but not making any attempt to use them. Frank thought it likely that they did not have ammunition for them. That would almost certainly be locked away in the camp's armory—whichever building held that.

It wouldn't make much difference. Two minutes after the attack started, every building around the field was burning. Men were still coming out of the barracks. Two came out screaming, their clothing—and skin—burning. One man got almost halfway across the parade ground, streaming flame behind him, before he finally collapsed and started to roll, still screaming his agony and fear. Fire spread from the man as the grass caught. Tinder dry, flames moved outward from the source, racing through all of the available fuel.

With armed men visible, each SEAL occasionally took a break from launching grenades to spray rifle fire at the visible targets. As the flames grew in the buildings, the area surrounding them got lighter, casting a haze of orange and red over everything. The crackling of dry wood burning was soon audible as well, between the explosions. There was no breeze at all. The flames and smoke rose in pillars. Around the buildings, more grass fires started.

As the SEALs neared the bottoms of the crates, they started launching smoke grenades into the killing ground as well—green and red as well as white, trying to sow as much confusion as possible.

Frank turned his head to the right and whistled sharply. As soon as the others looked toward him, he made a gesture. It was time to get away. Less than five minutes had passed since the first grenades had exploded. Every building in the training camp was fully involved in flames. There was virtually no chance that any of them could be saved—if the locals even bothered to try.

"No telling how many soldiers might be heading this way," Frank said as the men started to run back toward their boat. There was little need for the SEALs to worry about concealment, or crawling. Speed was more important. The men in the training camp were no immediate threat, and there was no sign yet of the warlord's regular soldiery. There were almost certainly at least a thousand of them billeted within two or three miles of the training camp. The patrol they had seen earlier—and perhaps several others—would be hurrying toward the flames. It would take more time though for additional troops to respond.

How much time, Frank didn't even want to guess.

Ike was still thinking of the Land Rover and its occupants. As best he could, he scanned toward his right, looking for headlights or the searchlight mounted on the vehicle. How many of them? he wondered.

Although the run to the sea seemed to last an eternity, it actually took the four men little more than a minute. They jumped the embankment,

down to the cover behind it. Every one of them
needed a few seconds to catch his breath.

Not one gunshot had come anywhere near
them. It seemed probable that none had been
fired.

"Let's go!" Frank said, shouted, as soon as he
had air to spare for talk. "Get the gear into the
boat and let's get out of here before that patrol
shows up. We don't want to fight them if we don't
have to."

While the others moved the diving gear back
into the boat, Frank used his binoculars to survey
the damage they had done . . . and to look for
hostile troops approaching. There were no lights
coming toward them yet. "Maybe we'll get out
clean yet," Frank mumbled as he moved to help
the others drag their boat back to the water.

The RPB did not seem to be as heavy now, and
it was not just the absence of the mines, the crates
of grenades, and the few rounds missing from
bandoleers and rifles that made the difference.
Each of the SEALs was operating on a full load
of adrenaline, both from the action and their concern that they might have a less one-sided fight in
front of them before they could get far enough
from shore to be safe.

Ike found it hard not to keep looking over his
shoulder toward the city, along the tracks the
patrol vehicle had left on earlier runs.

The four men were moving on wet sand, near
the waterline, when headlights came into view,

the sound of the car's engine a growing growl as it raced along the beach. Four hundred yards. Three fifty.

"We're going to have to hit 'em," Frank shouted. "Get the boat in the water, then we'll use up some of the grenades we've got left."

The last dozen yards of beach seemed interminable. As soon as there was enough water to float the RPB, the SEALs dropped it and turned. They all had grenades in their launchers, and the Land Rover was in range, no more than one hundred and fifty yards away, racing forward at more than forty miles per hour. Its searchlight was moving back and forth, but along the side toward the training camp. Frank had an instant to realize that they had not been spotted yet before he gave the command to open fire.

The patrol car swerved to the left before the grenades exploded. It was moving too quickly to be an easy target in any case. A machine gun started firing, bullets dotting the sand in an arc that only slowly started to reach toward the SEALs. Frank and his men replied with automatic rifle fire and grenades, with the emphasis on the former. The few seconds it took to reload the grenade launchers were hard to spare.

The vehicle swerved again, this time to the right, until it was headed directly at the SEALs. It hit the trip wires and both Claymore mines were detonated, rocking the vehicle over to the right. The headlights and searchlight all went out. The gunfire from inside the car stopped. The vehicle kept moving forward as the SEALs emptied their rifles' magazines into it. Beau and Rob had to jump aside, out of the path of the vehicle. It kept going, into the sea, until water caused the engine to stop. The four men inside were either dead or too badly wounded to stop the car or continue the fight.

"Move it!" Frank said. "Into the boat."

They dragged the RPG into waist-deep water before they climbed aboard. Beau got the engine started and quickly ran the throttle all the way open. The faster they got away from the shore, the less likely they were to have any additional trouble. And the RPG could move quickly.

The other SEALs had each reloaded their rifles, including putting a high explosive grenade into the launcher. As soon as the boat was a hundred yards off-shore, Frank signaled *Bellman* to send the helicopter, then keyed the transponder that would let the pilot home in on the boat without difficulty.

POST-MISSION

"It'll be morning before we get a complete damage assessment on that camp," Harry Tombs said, when the SEALs were settled at the table in the conference room. The team had come straight to the debriefing after securing their weapons. No one had even started to wipe the camouflage smears from their faces. The smells of gunpowder and fire were still on their clothing. "But it looks like you really did a number on them. The pilots in the air cap over the task force said they could see the flames from more than sixty miles out."

"A lot of that might be grass and bushes," Frank said. "The ground was bone dry. But we got all of the buildings flanking that parade ground, all of the training camp buildings. They were fully involved before we withdrew. Damn little chance they'll be able to save anything of them. My guess is that casualties were extensive. We may never know how many. I don't think a lot of them made it out of the barracks." Frank went on to give Tombs a full report. He was sparing of words, and the details of movement and so forth were inconsequential, so he omitted those. "Figure the facility is a total loss," Frank said. He shrugged. "That part doesn't mean much. They were just wooden buildings. They can be replaced in less than a week."

Tombs matched Frank's shrug. "The physical plant is minor. The terrorists you took out, trainees and cadre, are another thing. You did good. Your written report can wait for morning, Chief. Anyone else have anything they want to contribute?"

No one spoke. Tombs nodded. "Get cleaned up, grab a meal, and hit the sack. You've earned your sleep."

Tombs remained seated. He watched the four SEALs get up and leave the room. None of them appeared to be moving very sprightly. Are they just tired, or is the job starting to wear on them? Tombs wondered. How much more can we get out of them before we have to send them home?

Harry Tombs finished encrypting the report and the various addenda to it, including his suggestions for orbital reconnaissance to confirm the destruction and casualties. Later, he would submit his more detailed report, with the written debriefing statements of all four SEALs. As soon as he transferred the file to *Bellman*'s communications officer and watched while the message was transmitted, he could get to bed himself.

They keep on making me look good, and if they don't burn out too soon, I should be up for a promotion when we get done with this job, Harry thought as he headed back to his cabin. He was feeling very pleased with himself.

5: BANANA BOAT

PRE-MISSION

There had been no briefing scheduled for this morning. After the Mogadishu operation, Frank and his men had looked forward to a chance to sleep in. But the four SEALs were wakened before 0600 by a chief petty officer from *Bellman*'s crew and told they had fifteen minutes to report to the conference room near the bridge.

"Now what?" Rob asked as he scrambled for a fresh uniform.

"I don't know a damn thing more than you do," Frank replied after the *Bellman* chief left the compartment. "We'll find out what's up when we get there."

But they did not learn much more then. "I hope none of you left anything behind you might need in the next thirty-six hours," Harry Tombs said, when they reached the conference room. "There isn't time to go back and get it."

"What's going on?" Frank asked.

"You'll get your mission briefing later. Right

now, we need to get on deck to transfer to another ride. You don't need any of your gear. The necessary will be available when we get there. Let's go."

"You're going with us?" Beau asked, his voice a deeper than usual growl. Instead of his usual civilian clothing, Tombs was wearing khaki shirt and trousers—a Naval officer's uniform without insignia.

"Just part way," Tombs said, meeting Guisborne's stare.

Harry Tombs had led the way out to the main deck of *Bellman*, on the starboard side. He carried a thick briefcase with his laptop computer and a few necessary papers.

All four SEALs were more or less startled by what they saw. Ike was dumbfounded. Fifty yards off the starboard beam of *Bellman*, a submarine was just coming to the surface—of a type Jensen had never seen. There was a large structure sitting on the submarine's deck aft of the sail.

"What the hell is that?" Ike asked, stopping where he was.

Behind him, waiting to go through the hatchway, Rob said, "Dry Deck Shelter. Must be one of the Sturgeon-class subs. Looks like we're going to get wet this time out." He gave Jensen a not-too-gentle shove.

"That's *Pompano*," Frank said. "One of the converted jobs."

Tombs and the SEALs climbed down a Jacobs ladder to a waiting boat. The boat sped across to the submarine and its passengers were helped aboard and hurried inside. As soon as the hatch was closed behind them, the sub's crew started through its pre-dive procedure.

"We don't like being where we might be seen," the lieutenant (j.g.) who met them said. "We're rather too obvious."

THE BRIEFING

Ten hours later, Ike still felt a little dazed by it all. With the other members of the team, he had been inside the DDS on the afterdeck, seen the swimmer delivery vehicles (SDVs) it carried, and met several members of the sub's normal SDV team. There was common ground. The men of the SDVTs were all BUD/S graduates, just like the SEALs.

Finally, at 1645 hours, it was time to find out what was going on. The briefing was held in the SDV hangar. Besides Tombs and the four SEALs, two members of the SDV team were present, the j.g. who had met Team Wolf when it came aboard, Lubinski, and a chief petty officer, O'Brian, an old acquaintance of Lucan and Rhodes.

"We'll get through the obvious first," Tombs said, looking at the four SEALs of Team Wolf. "You've already guessed that you'll be riding an SDV on your next operation. Chief O'Brian will piloting, Lieutenant Lubinski will be the navigator. I know you've all trained with the SDVs, but

Lieutenant Lubinski will go over the details anyway in a few minutes.

"We've been steaming at a steady thirty knots, skirting the coast as closely as the skipper was comfortable with. We've rounded the northeast tip of Somalia and are heading across the Gulf of Aden now. We will be just outside the port at Aden about two thirty a.m. At that point, an SDV will be launched. Lieutenant Lubinski and Chief O'Brian will transport the four of you into the harbor. You will locate a boat known as the *Spirit of God*, attach mines to its hull, giving yourselves enough time to get back to the SDV and well started on your way back to this boat before the mines blow.

"The target vessel is basically an oceangoing cabin cruiser, sixty-four-feet long with twin diesel engines, fuel tanks to give it a range of approximately five thousand miles. Normally, it carries a crew of four. At present, we believe there are at least ten people aboard."

"Who?" Frank asked.

"I'm getting to that," Tombs said, trying not to show annoyance at the interruption. "The boat is registered in Muscat to a company that is a known front for Faud ibn Landin's terrorist activities. It is currently carrying at least two high members of his inner circle—and there is an outside chance that ibn Landin himself might be aboard—along with several bodyguards, in addition to the normal crew. The boat docked in Aden when the terrorist summit was postponed."

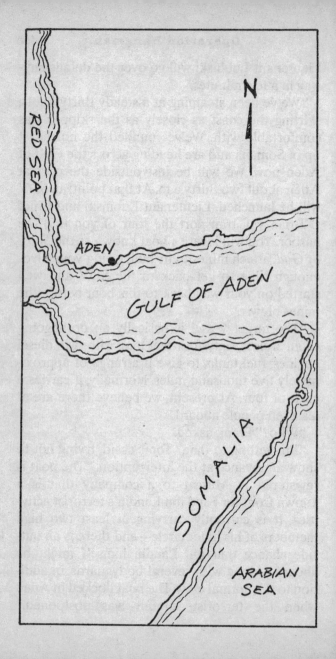

Tombs stopped and hesitated, as if debating with himself what to tell the others.

"There is a specific reason for targeting that boat right now, instead of later, the way we had originally planned," he said, speaking slowly. He glanced at his watch. "Just under twenty-three hours ago, terrorists answering to ibn Landin ran a truck loaded with more than three tons of explosives against the barrier in front of our embassy in South Africa, just as many employees were leaving at the end of their day's work. Altogether, there are more than a hundred dead, twice that many injured—not just embassy personnel but civilians who just happened to be in the wrong place at the wrong time. So we hit ibn Landin close. His boat. Two of his top aides.

"It is important, vital, that you get in and out without being detected. Ibn Landin will get the message without our leaving a calling card. Covert activity on the Arabian peninsula would be politically embarrassing just now if it became known that we were involved. Not only would the government of Yemen yell its head off in the U.N., but the Saudis would be . . . seriously miffed, and that is something we need to avoid."

"A question," Lieutenant Lubinski said. He waited until Tombs nodded in his direction before he continued. "If it appears that we have been detected before our mission is accomplished, do we abort?"

Tombs hesitated before he answered. "If you are reasonably *certain* that your SDV has been spotted by the harbor patrol or local naval or coast units, yes. You will abort immediately and return to *Pompano*."

"What if we're detected after the mines have been attached and the timers activated?" Frank asked.

"Don't be," Tombs said.

THE PREPARATION

After the briefing, and Lubinski's run-through of the use of the SDV, the four SEALs went through the diving gear available to select what they would use for the operation, testing regulators, putting together masks, fins, suits, and air tanks. Frank and Rob examined the mines they would be carrying to attach to the yacht. The boat's hull was made of a resin-based composite, so traditional magnetic limpet mines were out of the question. These explosives had a special adhesive designed to function underwater. A backing sheet had to be peeled off, then the mine could be pressed against the hull and it would stick. Generally.

Once the gear was ready, the SEALs went to supper. They all ate, but Ike had to force the food in.

"Get some sleep," Frank told his men, when they had finished eating. "We've got until midnight. Then they'll get us up and we'll get ready for the op. This should be an easy one. We get in and out the way we're supposed to, we won't even see anybody, let alone have to do any fighting. Just a beer run, nothing to get excited about."

"Had to go and mention beer, didn't you?" Rob asked. "You've given me the taste, and I'll bet there's not a single can on this tub, or anywhere within five hundred miles."

"Give you something to look forward to, Farmboy," Frank said. "We get to someplace civilized, we're all due a good drunk."

Beau grunted. Ike held in a belch; he didn't much care for the taste of beer. On the rare occasions when he drank at all, he preferred mixed drinks—preferably mixed with something sweet. That always brought ribbing from any team mates who happened to be around . . . but they ribbed Ike about everything. Why should his taste in drinks be any different?

The four men worked their way back to their compartment. It wasn't far. They hadn't ousted any of the submarine's regular crew from bunks this time. They shared quarters with the enlisted men of the SDV team. That team was shorthanded. There were bunks to spare.

Ike took off his shirt and shoes. None of the SEALs took off more, and Frank only took off his shoes. Each man lay on top of the bunk he had been assigned. The compartment's light was extinguished. The other occupants of the room were not present.

Of the four men, Beau was the only one who managed to get to sleep quickly. He could sleep anytime, anywhere.

Frank thought about the upcoming operation. He played parts of the briefing back in his mind, tried to firm up the pictures in his head—the boat that was their target, the in and out . . . and what options they might have if something went wrong. Underwater, danger was never far away, and mistakes could quickly be deadly; the environment was nearly as unforgiving as space. On land, at least, there was usually some room for maneuvering, no matter how badly an op went sour. Even unarmed, you had a chance to get away, make your way to friendly ground, or to someplace where a pickup could be made. Underwater, nothing could be taken for granted, not even the air you breathed.

Rob kept thinking about beer, which led him to thoughts about various liberty ports he had visited during his years in the Navy. He thought that he had certainly seen a good piece of the world since signing on for his first hitch—every major base in the United States, including Pearl Harbor; Panama, Subic Bay; some two dozen other foreign ports. And other places—locations a fleet sailor rarely, if ever, got to see. Beer, other drinks . . . and other enjoyments. And a few good fights. Rob's eyes were closed. He wasn't aware of the smile that worked its way onto his face. There had been some good times. A long ride in an SDV would not be one of them, though. The smile faded, then was replaced by a frown. Rob always felt too confined in a swimmer delivery vehicle. Human sardines, he thought, and for an instant his frown deepened into a full-fledged scowl. Six men packed into a can fifty-two inches high, fifty-two inches wide, and twenty-one feet long.

Ike's difficulty was, as usual, nerves. He worried. It was something he had always been good at. Or bad at. He vacillated on which adjective was best for the "condition." As far back as he could remember, he had always worried about just about everything that might—by the farthest stretch of his very active imagination—possibly affect him. Plan for every contingency, even if the odds against are worse than those for winning the PowerBall jackpot with a single ticket. That way there were fewer surprises. But it cost him a lot of sleep.

Eventually, Ike did sleep. So did Frank, who drifted from planning to slumber without noticing; even in his dreams he continued to think about the night's operation. Only Rob did not succumb, and the almost trancelike reverie he fell into was nearly as resting as sleep.

THE MISSION

There were three separate compartments in the dry deck shelter. The first simply provided the connection with one of the submarine's hatches. The second could function as a pressure chamber for decompression of divers. The third, and largest, was the hangar for the Mark VIII SDV.

Two technicians were in the hangar completing the pre-mission checklist for the SDV. Lieutenant Lubinski and Chief O'Brian led the SEALs through the chambers of the DDS. All six men were in wet suits, with air tanks strapped to their backs. Face masks were pushed up on top of heads, and regulators and hoses hung loose.

The Swimmer Delivery Vehicle (more often than not called a SEAL Delivery Vehicle, these days) is the simplest type of submarine. Called a "wet-sub," its inside is flooded with water and the occupants must wear breathing equipment and protective suits against the cold of the water. The crew of two, pilot and navigator, sit side by side in the forward section. The rear section would hold the four SEALs and their gear. To say the back of an SDV is cramped is a serious understatement. The men were in for a long, cold, dark trip.

"We're going to have a run of about six nautical miles to the target once we launch," Lubinski told the SEALs. "A bit more than an hour to get there. We'll let you out in the harbor's deep water chan-

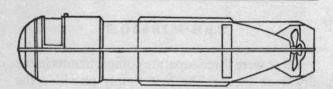

SDV

nel, then get the SDV turned around and wait for you. You'll have ninety minutes to locate the proper boat, do what you have to do, and get back. That's to give us time to get out of the harbor before sunrise. If you can make it in less than ninety minutes, all the better."

"We'll do our best," Frank said. The repetition of details covered in the planning session earlier did not bother him. He liked to know that everyone was working to the same schedule.

The crew of the SDV waited until the SEALs were in the rear compartment. "Get your masks down and check your air connection," Lubinski said. While in the SDV, the SEALs would use the craft's air tanks rather than their own. "Chief, you'd better plug into the radio so we can talk, if we have to."

Frank nodded. Times like this, I'm glad I'm built compact, he thought as he shifted around to get as comfortable as he could. Four men with their gear made the compartment quite confining. It would be a little better once they were wet and near neutral buoyancy, the pseudo weightlessness of the diver. The SDV did not provide a dry environment for crew or passengers.

Lubinski and O'Brian got into their places in the front compartment. The sliding doors on both compartments were closed. After finishing two last items on their checklist, the technicians left the hangar and closed the watertight door between it and the other chambers of the DDS. Only dim red lights were left on inside the hangar, to start the process of night adaptation for the men going out, and to avoid showing light through the hangar door when it was opened.

The six men who were going out the other end were breathing from the SDV's air tanks now. Their face masks were in place. Everything was ready.

Water started flowing into the compartment. The sound of rushing water seemed too loud to Ike, but that was just something else to worry about. The whole thing has to be flooded, he reminded himself. They can't open the door until then. Wouldn't want to get shot out of here on a bubble of air. Opening the large door in the aft end of the compartment too soon might be enough to rip the SDV from the clips that held it in place.

When water first started to seep into the SDV, Ike felt chilled by it. Just hang on, you'll adjust as soon as you're all the way in, he told himself. You know what it's like. It's not like you're in the Arctic. The water is fairly warm around here. Ike talked to himself almost constantly, either aloud or silently. It was something he had always done—at least as far back as he could recall.

The water level rose steadily, soon filling and covering the SDV. It was a couple of minutes more before the sound of rushing water faded. The men in the SDV felt as much as heard the hangar door being opened. Lieutenant Lubinski released the clips holding the vehicle in place.

CPO O'Brian gently opened the throttle on the SDV's electric motor.

With the sliding hatches on the compartments closed, no one inside the SDV could see anything outside. There were no windows, no portholes. They had only the faint green light of instruments in the compartment to let them see *inside*. The SDV was piloted by a Doppler navigation system, with a specialized sonar system to help the pilot avoid obstacles. "Like flyers learning how to fly on instruments only," an instructor had once told Frank—and he had probably told dozens of other SEALs the same thing over the years. "A sub doesn't have windows, and it rarely goes close enough to the surface to use its periscope these days. Hey, underwater at night, the only way portholes would do any good was if the thing used headlights—and how the hell can you sneak up on a target that way?"

Ike looked at the luminous dial of his watch as soon as he felt the SDV start to move. The lieutenant had said that the ride would take a little more than an hour. Ike wanted to be sure he knew when to start expecting the end of the ride. *Are we there yet? Are we there yet?* Ike closed his eyes for an instant. Too many comics, he thought. Too many bad jokes.

Frank found himself wishing there were some way to make transport like this faster. It seemed like wasted time. He had done all the planning, all the thinking ahead, he could reasonably do. Continuing it now—and he couldn't stop himself from doing that—was just spinning his wheels, as likely to hurt as help. After being wakened at midnight, he had taken another long look at the chart of the harbor and the photographs of the yacht they were going after. He worked to memorize the Arabic characters of the boat's name. Harry Tombs had made a point of saying that the name was on the transom in both Arabic and English, *but what if only the Arabic is visible?* Frank had asked himself. Better to be ready. He wouldn't be able to surface and ask a crewman.

Beau gave himself a few seconds to think about how uncomfortable it was with four of them crowded in the compartment. Then he shrugged and put it out of mind. He relaxed, and let himself rest, concerned only with slow, regular breathing. There was nothing else to do.

Rob was unable to put the discomfort out of mind that easily. He was big and the compartment was small. Too small, in his opinion. Riding in an SDV always brought images of coffins to mind, thoughts of trying to escape a casket before the dirt was shoveled in on top. He was not claustrophobic, but he felt cramped. Several times he let a hand drift up near the sliding door on his side of the compartment, fighting the urge to open it, if only a few inches, to give himself at least the sense of having more room. If they're gonna put six grown men in one of these damn things, they could at least make the box bigger, he thought. This is like those damn hippies seeing how many people they could cram into a VW. The ride would have been a lot easier for him if he could have worked a crossword puzzle enroute.

Frank did have one welcome distraction. On the radio link with the SDV crew, he had their occasional comments to listen to. And the lieutenant gave Frank periodic reports on their progress. But the two men up front really did not need to speak to each other all that often.

"There's nothing entering or leaving the harbor," Lubinski reported, once the SDV was close enough for its sonar systems to detect any movement in the channel. "We're not picking up any activity anywhere close."

"That's the way we like it," Frank replied.

A few minutes later, Lubinski reported that they were entering the harbor. "About five minutes until you get out and walk," he added. The joke did not earn a laugh, but the lieutenant had not expected one.

There was just barely enough of a glow in the aft compartment for the other three men to see Frank's gesture, five fingers held up. Ike nodded, though he was directly behind the chief, so Frank could not see him.

Even though the real mission was about to begin, all four men felt a certain amount of relief at the thought of getting out of the SDV and doing their own swimming, stretching muscles that had been confined far too long.

"Your course to the small boats is two-seven-zero magnetic, distance twelve hundred yards,"

Lieutenant Lubinski reported, as CPO O'Brian throttled down the engine near the end of those five minutes.

Frank looked at the compass on his right wrist. "Two-seven-zero, distance twelve hundred yards," he repeated.

"Right. We'll be waiting for you. I'd like to get back to the boat in time for an early breakfast."

"We'll try to accommodate you, Lieutenant," Frank said. He slid open the compartment door at his side and pulled himself out. He paused, body in contact with the SDV, while he put on his flippers and waited for the others to emerge from the vehicle.

Underwater at night, the universe is dark. Even a mere thirty feet below the surface, where the SEALs emerged from the SDV, the moon and stars are at best refracted pinpoints of light marking *up*, and pollution or currents on the surface can hide those. There was plenty of both in the harbor. Visibility was a matter of inches. Allowing divers to stay in visual contact with each other at night, without lights to broadcast their position to others, was an old problem with few good solutions. Frank and his companions wore luminous strips on the forearms of their wet suits, applied stickers that could be ripped off and discarded, if necessary. With the strips in place, the divers could keep tabs on each other as long as they stayed relatively close.

Beau and Rob, the two heaviest members of

the team, carried the mines. Those were specially designed for divers to carry, and included their own air chambers to give the weapons neutral buoyancy. As the divers moved away from the SDV, they shifted into a diamond pattern. Frank swam in the lead. Beau and Rob were to either side, slightly behind and below the team leader. Ike brought up the rear.

Underwater, Beau seemed to be in his natural element. Dry, his motions often seemed languid, even sluggish. On a dive, they were perfect—no wasted movement, no frenzied churning of the water. Long, lazy kicks propelled him forward. Hands and arms were used minimally, mostly for steering. Techniques that most divers had to learn had come naturally to him.

Like the others, Beau occasionally checked his instruments—watch, compass, depth and air gauges. All were important. This dive was planned to stay above the thirty-two-foot mark, to avoid the need for decompression stops at its conclusion. His air tanks gave him two hours of air—a half hour margin of safety, even if this swim lasted the ninety-minute maximum planned, a half hour of air left over when they returned to the SDV and switched back to its air supply. The compass provided the only sure indication of where they had to go, and the course they would have to follow to rendezvous with the SDV. And the watch provided a rough gauge of distance traveled.

Beau kept track of the others. He had to stay

close enough to keep sight of the luminous strips they all wore. Keep track of the formation leader, the other flank, and—perhaps most important—the man bringing up the rear. Don't let the kid drop out of sight; make sure he doesn't straggle. Keeping track of Ike was the most difficult part of that job.

In front, Frank tried to keep the pace moderate, as easy on the team as he could without wasting too much of the limited time they had. Once he estimated that they had covered two-thirds of the distance, he started angling toward the surface. It was time to go up and take a sighting, verify the distance remaining, and try to locate the specific boat they were after.

Near the surface, there was more illumination, a sparkling that still did not present much threat of making the divers visible to anyone above the water. Frank broke water gently, only his head out, using legs and arms to hold position. He gave his eyes time to adjust to the presence of some light, scanning his limited horizon. He turned through a complete circle, noting the position of the two freighters currently docked at the commercial pier, then spotting a half dozen smaller boats tied up some distance away.

The silhouette of the private yacht *Spirit of God* proved easy to spot, about three hundred yards away. None of the other boats even came close to it in size or configuration. Frank looked closer, to see the heads of his team mates, still in formation, as cautious as he was. He pointed at the target and saw an answering nod from each of the others.

Frank took a compass reading, then made a gesture with his right hand, back underwater. He submerged and started angling down, on a heading directly for the target. The other three followed him under.

This time, Frank did not take them as deep. There had been no hint of a patrol boat moving about the harbor. Nothing appeared to be moving on the surface. The team went down only to twenty feet. Frank increased his pace a little. At first it was a subconscious thing, an instinctive feel for covering the last stretch of water as quickly as possible. When Frank realized what he was doing, he slowed back down, but only for a few seconds. We *can* use a little more speed, he decided, and he resumed the slightly faster pace.

Behind him, the others adjusted to his speed.

Only one extraneous thought broke Ike's concentration on this mission. Just after they went underwater again following the target sighting, he thought, *This is what it's supposed to be about.* He had a brief memory of a movie he had seen on television, not a year before—a World War Two movie with James Garner as a Navy frogman on a mission to photograph a Japanese code book; he had been taken close by a submarine whose skipper was reluctant to risk his boat too close to the island that Garner was supposed to infiltrate. The few other SEALs in the dayroom had laughed through much of the movie, deriding it as "hokey."

It was not quite so completely dark now. There was a shimmer to the surface. Ike noticed that Frank was slowly moving higher in the water, until the low man in the team—Ike—was only fifteen feet deep. The second time that Frank went to the surface, the others were even more cautious about exposing themselves, letting no more than the faceplates of their masks rise above the water.

The target was a hundred yards away. It looks a lot bigger now, Ike thought. He had time for nothing else. Frank had slipped back underwater, and the rest of the team had to follow.

It was only by glancing at his watch frequently that Ike could keep track of passing time. Apart from the reminder of a hand moving around the dial, time might have stood absolutely still. Frank went back down close to thirty feet below the surface for the last stretch, and he increased his pace again. The divers were not *racing* toward the target, but they were not out for a lazy swim anymore, either.

When they got close, the hull of the boat was only a darker blur in the water, a place where the surface shimmer ended. The divers moved closer together again, almost within touching distance of each other.

The decision as to where to place the mines had been made during the mission's planning stage. Both would go on the shoreward side of the keel, one close to the boat's main fuel tank, the other just forward of amidship, under the largest cabin. The goal was to get the force of the explosive in the mines as well as fire and explosion from the diesel fuel in the boat's tanks. The timers were set to ninety minutes. The men carrying them came together and activated the devices simultaneously to make certain that the explosions would come at the same time. Then they moved toward the positions where the mines would be located.

One man could peel the backing strip from the adhesive on the mines, but the job was easier with two men working together. Frank and Beau handled the mine that would go against the fuel tank. Ike helped Rob with the other mine, working almost entirely by feel. Visibility had once more been reduced to virtually zero.

Rob placed his mine carefully against the hull and pressed to bond the adhesive. Any force would have translated as sound inside the boat, and there was a faint chance that someone aboard might hear the sound and recognize a potential threat. Rob used both hands then to test the security of the bond. The mine did not come away from the hull.

Ike felt Rob's touch on his shoulder before he saw any movement. Pressure. Rob brought his arm to just in front of Ike's face mask and tapped the watch on his wrist. *Time to go.* Ike nodded, though he knew that Rob would not be able to see the gesture. He turned and paddled out from under the keel of the boat. The other two men met them and the team moved back into its diamond formation.

Frank went back down to thirty feet. Close to the target, he wanted as much water above him as was practical. He also kicked more vigorously going out than coming in. The thought of live mines in the water behind him was enough to insure that. Timers could malfunction. And when those mines went off, Frank did not want to be anywhere near. The concussive force of explosives in water could be brutal, even lethal.

On the way out, there was no need to surface at all. Frank kept a close watch on his compass and stayed precisely on the heading he needed to rendezvous with the SDV. The swim in had taken twenty-seven minutes, allowing for the two times they had surfaced to pinpoint the target. Frank guessed that the return swim would take two minutes less. He was not too concerned about finding the SDV. Its sonar would find the divers.

He wasn't the only one thinking about the live explosives behind them. Ike found it difficult to maintain his proper position at the rear of the diamond. He kept drawing too close to the others and had to consciously will himself to slow down. But, then, two minutes later, he would find that the gap had shrunk again and have to do it all over again.

Twenty-three minutes. Frank saw a green luminous glow ahead of him, then the vague outline of the top of the SDV. He adjusted his course enough to head for the glow, then, when the SDV was almost close enough to touch, angled to the left, toward the open door on the rear compartment of the vehicle.

Frank moved onto the top of the SDV, waiting to make sure that all three of his men got in before he followed. Inside, he switched to the SDV's air supply and plugged in the radio connection again.

"We're all set, Lieutenant. Time to boogie on out," Frank reported. "We're got sixty-one minutes before things go thump in the dark."

The ride back was different than the ride in, psychologically, at least. Each SEAL remained conscious of the explosives they had planted. If everything went as planned—and there was no real reason to believe otherwise—the mines would detonate after the SDV was well out of the harbor, within minutes of rendezvousing with *Pompano*. There would be enough water, and part of the city of Aden, between them and the blast.

Still, Ike was not the only man to feel a tightness between his shoulder blades, an itch, as if anticipating that the explosion would come much sooner, perhaps any second. Ike had to pay conscious attention to keeping his breathing regular—a necessity on any dive. It made for a long ride.

When the explosions did come, none of the SEALs felt anything. Lieutenant Lubinski reported to Frank that the sonar had picked up the explosions, but that was the only way anyone aboard the SDV knew that they had happened.

Eight minutes later, the SDV was moving back into its hangar on *Pompano*'s afterdeck.

POST-MISSION

A quick hot shower, dry clothes, and hot coffee banished the chill the divers had felt on emerging from the water. Cooks were finishing a hot breakfast for the six men sitting in the galley—most of them cupping their mugs in both hands to savor the heat. Scrambled eggs, sausage links, hash brown potatoes, and toast. There was orange juice as well, and as much coffee as the men could drink. There was little talk among them. The isolation of the dive was slower to recede than the chill. They drank coffee, then ate, saying little more than "Pass the salt," or "How 'bout some more coffee?"

But the thaw came. There was, finally, room for small talk in private universes that were again expanding, touching. They did not, could not, talk about the mission. There were other sailors in the galley, cooks and men coming in for breakfast, or just for a cup of coffee after coming off watch.

Ike asked what regular duty was like aboard a Sturgeon-class submarine. Chief O'Brian made a few general remarks. Talk turned to the naval base at San Diego where BUD/S training was conducted, and where the SDV teams were headquartered.

Time passed. It was seven o'clock when Harry Tombs came in.

"Let's move back to the DDS for the debriefing," Tombs said, and he let Lieutenant Lubinski lead the way. They all took fresh cups of hot coffee with them.

Frank's verbal recounting of the operation was even shorter than usual. Not much was necessary beyond *We rode the SDV in, then swam the rest of the way; we planted the mines and activated them; then we swam back to the SDV and rode back here.* Lieutenant Lubinski reported that he had noted no difficulties and that the explosions had been picked up on the SDV's sonar precisely at the time Chief Lucan had told him to expect them. No one else offered any additions.

"We don't have any visual damage assessment yet," Tombs said when the reports were finished. "But we have confirmed that there were two explosions, seconds apart. An aircraft flying quite some distance offshore managed photographs of the immediate aftermath, but those photographs are still being processed.

"Lieutenant, I think you and your chief are finished with us. Thanks for your help."

Lubinski nodded and stood. "Your friendly taxi service," he said. "Nice to have some real work to do once in a while."

After the SDV men left, Tombs said, "We've got a little down time, so you can relax. We don't rendezvous with *Bellman* until just before dawn tomorrow."

* * *

They were back aboard *Bellman* before Tombs
was able to submit his formal after-action report
with its supporting documents. The yacht had
been totally destroyed, its wreckage so mangled
that it would scarcely pose a hazard to other
boats in the harbor.

Too bad you weren't aboard, Tombs thought,
staring at a photograph of ibn Landin on the desk
before him. At least you'll know you've got a
cobra on your ass. I wish I could send you a note,
maybe an e-mail, something simple like "Fuck
you, bugger. We'll get you next time."

Tombs leaned back. No matter what it took, he
was determined to be the man who brought ibn
Landin down.

*Faud ibn Landin appeared impassive as he lis-
tened to the report. His boat, the* Spirit of God, *had
been destroyed in what should have been a safe
harbor. Two of his most trusted commando leaders, as well as their deputies and the boat's crew,
had been killed. As the report came to an end,
Faud recited a prayer in his mind. He took the
extra seconds needed to make certain that his rage
would not be apparent when he spoke.*

*"The deaths are an outrage," he said, and he did
sound calm. "A murderous attack that we will
avenge at the first opportunity. The boat . . . well,
perhaps it was a vanity that I should have out-
grown years ago, part of the trappings of my former life." He always spoke of his life as a*

successful businessman, before finding the light of jihad, *that way.* His *former* life. *"Have we been able to gather any information about who staged the attack, or how? Was it the Americans or the Zionists?"*

Rashish Suleiman, Faud's second in command and designated successor, made an open gesture with both hands. "So far, we have no hard information. No one who survived saw or heard anything. There was an explosion, perhaps two explosions. Then the fuel tank went off as well. Our friends in Aden are pushing for a thorough investigation, but, well, the authorities seem to have little interest in pursuing the matter. One fears that they are merely going through the motions, hoping they do not find anything solid enough to force them toward unwanted diplomatic repercussions. They have gone so far as to release a report suggesting that the explosions might have been due to some mechanical mishap aboard the Spirit of God, *and not the result of a cowardly attack."*

"We must assume, until proven otherwise, that this attack is part of the pattern we have been seeing over the past week." Faud leaned back and looked at the ceiling of the small office. "I must confess that it is slightly possible that we have been stabbed in the back by one of the groups we have been courting, but I don't think it likely, and—for the moment—it makes no difference. That could, at most, account only for the attack on the boat." He paused, thinking. He turned to his second. "We will use this attack to help hearten those whose will

seems weak. It is not impossible that Mossad could mount so many operations in such a short time, but I think it is unlikely. That leaves the Americans. I am surprised that they could strike at Spirit of God so quickly after the bombing of their embassy in South Africa."

"They did have a carrier battle group just off-shore at the time of the attack in Somalia," Rashish said. "And a helicopter from that group approached the three-mile limit twice, before and after the attack on the training camp. That same battle group was close to Eritrea when our agents there were assassinated. And in the Red Sea when the depot in Libya was attacked."

"I believe you are right, Rashish. Of course, it doesn't explain the assault near Beirut, but four out of five is hard to argue. The Americans are afraid of us, my friend. They are afraid of the grand alliance we hope to form, and they're doing everything in their power to stop it."

"All the more reason not to let them succeed," Rashish said.

Faud nodded slowly. "I want you to start by sending the following message to all of the people we hope to have at our summit meeting. 'The American cowards are targeting all of our operations in order to keep us from working together. The recent attacks against us were staged by a special operations group operating primarily from a carrier battle group patrolling the Red Sea and the Indian Ocean. I urge you, for the love of God, to take special precautions in all of your operations, and at all of your locations, through the time of our summit. Union is more important than ever now. We must come together to meet this threat. It is the only way we can be certain of final victory, God willing.'

"You have that, Rashish?" Faud asked.

"Every word, Master." Rashish had not taken notes, but his memory was very nearly eidetic. There was no chance he would forget the message before he could write it down and start it on its ways to the men it was intended for.

"Get the word to our own people as well," Faud said, almost as an afterthought. "I would very much like to have one or more of these Americans as prisoners to show the world. A live prisoner would be worth far more than a dead body." He paused. "Not that we would not like dead bodies as well."

6: BACKSCRATCH

PRE-MISSION

"You're not going to like this one," Harry Tombs said, as soon as the four SEALs had taken their seats in the captain's conference room aboard *Bellman*. "I'm not too happy with it myself, but we weren't given the option to refuse."

Even Beau Guisborne sat up a little straighter in his chair. Tombs had the undivided attention of the SEALs. They had been back aboard *Bellman* less than four hours, time for a second breakfast, showers, and a change of uniform after their time aboard the submarine.

"Tonight's op is a favor to the Egyptian government, payback for their, ah, constructive non-interference with our crossing their airspace to hit that munitions depot in Libya. The target is one of the groups we're after, so the official line is that we further our own interests while helping out friends in the region."

This must really be a beaut, Frank thought. Tombs had never been one to waste a lot of words before getting to the details of the mission.

THE BRIEFING

"I'll be going part of the way with you, as far as the final staging area," Tombs said, "and I'll be there to arrange alternate extraction if . . . well, if there are problems with the primary arrangements. We are going to be cooperating with Egyptian internal security police on this. They are going to provide the vehicle for your final insertion and provide a checkpoint to hold up any pursuit on the way out. In theory."

"What do we do, hijack King Tut's gold?" Rob asked, just to relieve the tension he was beginning to feel.

Tombs gave him a very tired look. "No. The target is one of the groups of fanatical extremists who have been attacking tourists in Egypt over the past several years, blowing up busloads of foreigners and so forth. As far as Cairo is concerned, they're bad for business. Egypt needs all the money it can get, especially from people coming to gawk at King Tut's gold and all the rest of the ancient glories it can no longer hope to duplicate. But the Egyptian government is somewhat limited in its ability to respond. They have to maintain a delicate balancing act to stay in power. There's too long a tradition of assassinating leaders in Egypt."

"All the way back to pharaohs," Beau said under his breath. No one took any notice.

"At ten thirty this morning, we will board a helicopter. You'll be fully armed for a land engagement. Our helicopter will transport us to the Egyptian air force base at Aswan. There we will transfer to an Egyptian helicopter, piloted by their security police, and be taken to the town of Beni Suef, about sixty miles south of Cairo. I'll stay there with the helicopter. The four of you will be taken in a closed van to a police checkpoint just outside the city of El Faiyum in the Faiyum Depression. You will be concealed in a building at the checkpoint. Our information, which comes from the Egyptians, is that a van carrying two members of this terrorist organization make regular runs between El Faiyum and their base north of the city. They come out, make purchases and do whatever business they do, then return. The same vehicle, the same route, almost always the same two men, every day but Friday. The Egyptians will have the route laid out for us. When the vehicle heads back toward their base this evening, the police will stop it at the checkpoint, make the occupants get out—something they do periodically, just to harass them—and escort them into the building, where they will be, ah, detained until they can pose no threat to the op. The four of you will take their places and use the vehicle as your access to the terrorist base. The vehicle is not stopped at the perimeter, again, according to our Egyptian sources.

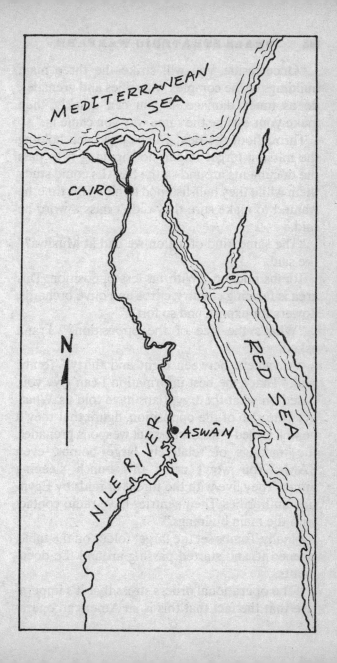

"Once inside, you will strike the three main buildings of the complex with rifles and grenades, do as much damage as you can quickly, then make your escape the same way you came in."

Throughout the talk, Tombs had been holding the mission target folder, not opening it to pass the documents around so the SEALs could study them while they half-listened to him. This time, he wanted to make sure they didn't miss a word he said.

"The same kind of action we had at Mitsiwa?" Ike said.

Tombs nodded. "With far less opposition. This area is farming country, citrus and olive orchards, flowers for export, and so forth."

"What's the size of the opposition?" Frank asked.

"Anywhere between eight and thirty," Tombs said. "That's the best information I can give you, based on what the Egyptians have told us. Whatever the size of the opposition, figure that they'll be well armed—Russian assault weapons, grenades, the makings of relatively large bombs, even SAMs. You won't catch this bunch sleeping either. They live with the threat of raids by Egyptian authorities. Their sentries have radio contact with the main buildings."

Finally, Tombs set the target folder on the table, opened it, and started passing around the documents.

"The operational orders stress that it's imperative that the fact that this is an American operation must not be known. That means don't get captured and don't carry anything that will identify you as American," Tombs said as the order made the rounds of the SEALs. "We have to have full deniability on this, the same way the Egyptian government does. No American weapons at all."

"If something goes wrong, we assume that the Egyptians would rather have us blamed then take the rap themselves?" Frank asked.

"I don't think you would go wrong proceeding on that assumption," Tombs said. "That's one of the reasons I'll be close enough to get something in to pick you up in case there are difficulties and our allies decide to cut their losses and our throats. Just in case," he added after a slight pause. "We'll have assets standing by in the Red Sea and in the Mediterranean. And closer. I can't say more than that."

"Sounds like this could turn into a one-way ticket to Hell," Rob said. He scarcely noted the fact that no one offered to contradict him.

THE PREPARATION

"We've been warned," Frank told his men when they were alone in the armory to select their weapons for the operation. "This could be balls to the wall. My suggestion is, we go in with so much heat that we could take Baghdad all by ourselves. The load gets too heavy, we can always dump the excess, but we can't count on being able to pick up any extras along the way."

"We s'posed to have rides all the way. Don' have to carry the weight alone," Beau said. " 'Sides, we get to the place, we use up all the extra."

"Two radios," Frank said. "I'll carry one. Farmer, you carry the other. I want to be sure we can talk to Tombs when we have to. Two men with M-203s—Beau and Ike, and all the rounds you think you can carry. The Farmboy and I will each wear an extra bandoleer of grenades."

Frank armed himself carefully, ignoring weight for the comfort of having as much firepower as he could possibly carry. An M-16 with the double-drum magazine was his start. He loaded a second double-drum magazine in an ammunition pouch, and eight standard magazines—four pairs that were taped together. He would have taken more of the C-Mag hundred-round magazines, but the team only had eight of them, and he planned to leave two for each of the other men.

"Hey, Tombs said no American weapons," Ike said, when he saw what Frank intended to carry. "There's nothing more American than the M-16."

"You leave Tombs to me, kid," Frank said. "Anybody gets their hands on these weapons, they might find that they came from a shipment that went to the Panama Defense Forces back when Noriega ran things there—and part of that shipment disappeared and was assumed to have found it's way to one of the Colombian drug cartels. A lot of countries use M-16s now; even a few of the terrorist groups we're after favor them over Kalishnikovs. And we don't have any drum magazines for the AK-47s we have."

"We go out with these at the last minute, Tombs won't have time to make us change weapons, not if we put up a fuss," Rob said. He grinned. "Besides, I'm all in favor of anything that pisses the spook off."

"I'm not looking for a fight with him," Frank said. "I'll give him good reasons." A 9mm Glock pistol went in a shoulder harness. Four extra magazines for that went in the pouch with Frank's spare C-Mag. A second pistol, a Walther PPK, went in an ankle holster on his right leg. A boot knife went on the left leg under his BDU, a backup for the knife on his web belt. Finally, Frank took six hand grenades—four high explosive and two smoke. Then he strapped on a bandoleer of grenades for the M-203 launcher.

I must look like hell on two feet, Frank thought, as he moved around a little to judge weight and balance of the load. I'd hate to have to hike twenty miles carrying all this. He looked around. His men were all dressed very similarly. Even Ike had finally quit hesitating and taken one of the M-16s.

"You do realize," Rob said, "the four of us together are packing more mayhem than an entire infantry company did in World War One."

"Anyone for making it a battalion?" Ike asked. The other three all looked at him, surprised that the kid was the one to try that gag.

"Let's not press our luck," Frank said. "You look like you've shrunk two inches from what you're carrying now."

"I can handle it," Ike said. "I'm not carrying much more than you are and I'm a . . ."

"Don't say it, kid," Frank said. "I know what you're thinking, but don't say it." The two grinned at each other.

"We'd better start waddling toward the fantail," Rob said. "Let's just hope we don't overload the chopper."

Climbing a ladderway was an adventure.

Harry Tombs was waiting for them on deck. He was dressed all in khaki— trousers, shirt, and lightweight safari jacket. The SEALs were not surprised to see that the spook was openly armed, carrying an Uzi, with a large-frame automatic pistol in a belt holster. He also carried several spare magazines for the submachine gun.

Tombs looked the others over quickly. His lips seemed to disappear when he noticed the American rifles, pressed tightly together. He didn't speak for thirty seconds or more. Then he took a deep breath and nodded. "That goes directly against orders, but I think I can guess the reasons. Just don't let those weapons fall into the wrong hands. You look like models for 'Blood and Guts' comics. Ordinarily, I'd say you were overdressed, but. . . ." He shook his head and the grin that had been flickering on and off vanished. "Let's just hope you don't need all that shit."

"No argument from us," Frank said. "You're not quite in your banker uniform either."

"I used to be a Boy Scout," Tombs said.

THE MISSION

The Soviet Mil-8 (or Hip, as NATO designated it) was a tough bird. It could carry up to 32 passengers, depending on the internal layout of the seats, and an internal payload of 8,820 pounds. With a normal payload and an altitude of 3,280 feet, it had a range of 298 miles. Even as loaded as they were.

There was really no danger that the five men and their gear would overload the helicopter, but that didn't stop them from joking about it as the aircraft lifted off the fantail of *Bellman* and climbed away from the battle group.

"This bird goes down, we'll be looking for foot-

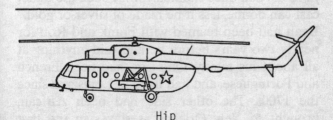

Hip

prints where the Israelites crossed the Red Sea before we can shed all this ballast," Frank said.

"I think we're too far south for that," Ike said. "That must have been up somewhere along the Gulf of Suez. It would have taken a week for them to walk across it here. I don't think even Moses coulda held his arms out that long."

"Yeah, how come he settled on the only patch of land in the Middle East that isn't floating on oil?" Rob asked.

"That would have been too easy," Ike said. "No challenge. Like us using air tanks in a swimming pool."

It wasn't often that the joking in Frank's team turned to religion. Only when things get tense, Frank thought. He still considered himself a Catholic, despite two divorces. The Farmer was Episcopalian: "but I'm not a fanatic about it," Rob said occasionally. Ike was Jewish. Beau . . . the others weren't completely sure what his affiliations might be. Sometimes, he said he had been brought up Catholic. At other times, he talked of a grandmother who was a Voodoo priestess—or something like that. "She give me a powerful juju," he had once claimed. "Ain't been the bullet cast can do me, less it be made of silver or gold." Beau had been teamed with Frank and Rob for nearly two years before he had said anything at all about his family. One side had been French and Portuguese, and had lived in Louisiana since the 1700s. The other side had been African, brought to New Orleans as slaves in the first years of American rule of the city. "We been masters and slaves, but mostly, we been fishermen." Another time he had claimed that one ancestor had been a pirate with Jean Lafitte, and had served at the Battle of New Orleans. The others were never certain how much of Beau's talk they could believe, and when he was just putting them on. It didn't matter.

The helicopter was forced to circle in a holding pattern for five minutes before being given clearance to land at the Egyptian air force base at Aswan. Then, the pilot set the chopper down near one of the concrete bunkers that had been built to protect MiG fighters from Israeli air attacks in the days before the Camp David accord. They landed thirty yards from another helicopter, one bearing markings of the Egyptian air force.

"Everything appears to be normal," the Egyptian officer who met Tombs and the SEALs said in British-accented English. "There has been no deviation from the schedule."

"That's good to know, Colonel," Tombs said. He did not introduce the Egyptian officer to the SEALs.

"I'll be flying you to Beni Suef myself," the Egyptian said. "We are being exceptionally cautious in this, as you know."

Means they don't know who the hell they can trust, Frank thought, but he kept his face expressionless, and his mouth shut.

The Egyptian officer was also good as maintaining a poker face. He showed absolutely no reaction to the quantity of munitions that the five men carried. He merely led the way to the Egyptian helicopter and gestured them aboard.

The Navy flyers would stay with their helicopter.

In the passenger compartment of the Egyptian helicopter, the colonel retrieved a folder from his copilot and gave it to Harry Tombs. "The necessary information," the Egyptian said.

As the helicopter started to lift into the air, Tombs opened the folder and scanned the three sheets of paper inside—details of the route to the terrorist base, a rough map, and information on several of the people believed to be in residence. Tombs passed the papers to Frank, who circulated them among his teammates. Each man studied the map and route with great care. The names meant nothing to them.

The helicopter followed the Nile downstream, north, then northwest, except for a bow to the right near Luxor. The pilot made no attempt to navigate directly cross-county. Nor did he push the Russian-made helicopter too hard. It was a relatively slow flight, rarely getting above 130 miles per hour.

Throughout the flight, Rob did little but stare toward the flight deck, as if he thought he had to watch every move the Egyptians made, just in case they might be up to no good. He scarcely blinked the whole time, and though he never made a threatening move, his hand was never far from his rifle. Beau settled in and closed his eyes, or narrowed them to slits, as if sleeping—his usual in-flight pose. Frank and Ike played tourist, staring out at the monumental temples and ruins they passed. Since the helicopter rarely climbed above five hundred feet altitude, they had good views of most of them.

It was not just the ruins of a civilization that had faded thousands of years before that Frank watched. He did his best to keep track of the helicopter's position. He wanted to know exactly where they were at all times. A precaution. He had studied the maps. Now, he could match what he saw out the window with names on paper. Luxor, Karnak, the Valley of the Kings. It was a few minutes past two thirty when they flew over Asyut dam. About another hour of flying time, Frank thought, unless they decide to get a little more speed out of this egg-beater.

Frank was a little surprised when the helicopter turned ninety degrees to the east, at least thirty miles south of Beni Suef. The unexpected course change made him nervous. He glanced at Tombs to see if the agent had noticed, and might know what was up. But Tombs did not meet Frank's glance. He was looking out the window at his side, showing no apparent interest in anything.

Five minutes later, the helicopter turned north again. Ten minutes after that, he turned to the northwest.

Coming in through the back door, Frank

thought, breathing a little easier. Don't want to be seen coming straight up the river. He couldn't fathom *why*, but it seemed to be the answer to the maneuvering.

They crossed the Nile and landed at the edge of Beni Suef, near a building that flew the Egyptian flag. It was 1545 hours.

"The four of you wait here in the helicopter until they bring the van up," Tombs said as the rotor wound down to a halt. "They'll back it right up to the door and you'll go straight in from here."

Tombs got out with the colonel and his copilot, both of whom very studiously avoided looking at the SEALs, who watched while Tombs and the two Egyptians walked to the nearby building and went inside. There was an old-fashioned delivery van—high-sided and boxy—parked next to the building. The van was white, and showed the effects of long usage, innumerable scrapes and dents, with more than a trace of rust showing.

"I guess that's our ride," Frank whispered.

"Hope it works better than it looks," Rob said. "I haven't seen a contraption like that in years. Like an old milk truck, back when they used to deliver."

"They used to deliver milk?" Ike asked, feigning ignorance. "How long ago was *that*?"

"Never mind, kid," Rob said.

"Stow the crap," Frank said. "We're on the button here." I don't *think* anything will go wrong this soon, he told himself, but it's not too soon to watch for it. He shook his head, a subconscious gesture. They'd have to be crazy to pull anything here, he thought.

The five minutes the SEALs had to wait before anyone came out of the building did no one's nerves any good. Everyone had his weapon in his hands, and more than one pair of eyes checked the selector and safety. When Harry Tombs came out of the building and gestured for the others to join him, Ike was the only one to let out an audible sight of relief, and even that was just barely noticeable.

"Stay alert," Frank warned. He was first out of the helicopter. He kept his eyes on Tombs, looking for any clue that something—anything—might be wrong. The van was not being backed up to the helicopter the way Tombs had said it would be.

"Your driver speaks English, but not very well," Tombs warned when the SEALs got to him. "His name is Sergeant Turhan. The four of you will stay in the back of the van, out of sight, until you get to the checkpoint."

The police sergeant came out. His uniform was starched and pressed, sharp creases in trousers and shirt. The Sam Browne belt that held his pistol holster and two other pouches was polished and looked new. A little shorter than Frank, Turhan was clean-shaven and appeared to be in his late thirties.

"You get in. We go," Sergeant Turhan said, gesturing at the double doors at the rear of the old van. "Get there quick."

Frank opened one of the doors, but stepped aside quickly, out of the way, in case there was a surprise waiting inside. There wasn't. The rear of the van was empty. There were no seats, not even a bench along the side. As he climbed inside, and moved toward the front of the compartment, near the open connection to the driver's compartment, Frank noticed a smell that seemed to be a mix of animal odors and human sweat.

Ike was the next man in. Frank gestured him to a position across from him, also at the front of the cargo area. Frank was right behind the driver's position, on the right. Beau and Rob got in and stayed near the doors at the back.

Harry Tombs stepped into the opening there. "Remember, I'll be right here when you get back," he told the SEALs. "Good hunting." As Tombs closed the doors, Sergeant Turhan hurried around to the front, climbing in behind the steering wheel.

"Quick" was not the word any of the SEALs would have chosen to describe the ride from Beni Suef to the police checkpoint just outside El Faiyum. The distance was little more than twenty-five miles but took the van an hour and fifteen minutes. In town, the streets were dusty—even where they were paved—and crowded with other cars and trucks, bicycles, animal-drawn vehicles, and pedestrians. Twice, before they got out of Beni Suef, the van was actually jostled by people, the vehicle swaying on shock absorbers that had long ago lost any absorbency. Each time that happened, it brought a surge of adrenaline to the SEALs, fearing that some sort of attack might be imminent.

Even on the highway, Sergeant Turhan did not overtax the van's engine. Frank could not read the speedometer but doubted that they ever topped forty miles per hour. Traffic on the highway was heavier than Frank would have expected, and none of it appeared to be moving faster than the van.

Throughout the ride, Turhan seemed unflappable. Nothing they encountered seemed to bother him, nothing out of the ordinary seemed to be happening. Several times the security police sergeant whistled a few bars of some song that none of his passengers could recognize.

The road that the police checkpoint guarded was not one of the main thoroughfares. The road was oiled gravel, barely more than a single lane wide. But there were stop signs aimed in both directions, and a small stone building on the east side of the road. The building was no more than fifteen feet square, and single-storied, with a flat roof. Two police officers stood outside, in the sun, watching for traffic that did not seem to be coming—from either direction.

Sergeant Turhan drove right up in front of the building, coming to a stop between the two officers. They spoke in Arabic, briefly, then Turhan drove around to the north side of the building and parked right up against the wall—the van almost touching the building.

"We are here. We go inside," Turhan said, turning in his seat to look at Frank.

The only door in the building faced the road. There were four windows, two flanking the door, one each on the sides. The white van blocked the view out the north window. Except for a four-by-four-foot toilet, there was only a single room. A counter ran across the middle, facing the door. Two tall stools were behind the counter.

"We wait here," Turhan said, gesturing around the room. "Stay away from windows, please."

Frank nodded, then positioned his men around the room so they could see as much of the surrounding territory as possible. The counter offered no defensive possibilities, only concealment. It was faced and topped with half-inch plywood, held up by a framework of two-by-fours. The walls of the building were sturdy though, and at least a foot thick. Except for the blind side—the bathroom had only a single small window seven feet up—it would not be difficult to defend the building.

"How long will it be?" Frank asked the sergeant, who had propped himself up on one of the stools at the counter.

Turhan shrugged, then glanced at his watch.

"One hour, maybe more, maybe less. We see. They come there." He pointed left, south.

"Their vehicle, what does it look like?" Frank asked.

The police sergeant hesitated, as if he were having difficulty understanding the question. "Small truck. Color like sand." He gestured toward the window facing west.

"A small, tan truck," Frank said, nodding.

Sergeant Turhan grinned and nodded back.

An hour, give or take, Rob thought when Turhan mentioned the time. Rob glanced at his watch. Can't expect much more precision than that. He shrugged. The cops can't control when the bad guys come back. He was not too concerned. The policemen outside were armed with assault rifles and pistols, but Rob had seen no spare magazines. Apparently, the only ammunition they had was what was in their weapons, unless there was more in the police cruiser parked on the other side of the road. And Sergeant Turhan had only a pistol. These guys aren't going to give us any trouble, Rob assured himself.

Although there were no shades or curtains on the windows, there was little chance that the men inside would be spotted by anyone on the outside, as long as no one got too close to the window. There were no lights on inside the building, and the glare of the sun outside was almost as sure a mask as a coat of dark paint.

It was marginally cooler—at least, less hot—

inside the building than in the van. There was no air conditioner, no fan, but the thick walls did provide some insulation.

Waiting was no novelty for any of the SEALs, though it was not the favorite pastime of any of them. Beau remained almost completely motionless, seldom doing so much as blinking. Rob moved in spurts, letting several minutes pass, then stretching arms and legs, just making sure that nothing got stiff. Ike was the most restive. Twice, he started pacing—stopping only when Frank gave him a pointed glance.

Mostly, Frank used the time as constructively as possible. He went back over the directions for getting from where they were to the farm that the terrorists were—apparently—using as a base. He looked at the map, working to commit every detail to memory. Occasionally, he glanced at his watch.

An hour passed; an hour and ten minutes. Only five vehicles had gone through the checkpoint since the arrival of the SEALs. None of those had looked anything like the target vehicle.

"Not so long now, I think," Sergeant Turhan said, when he noticed Frank looking at his watch. "They come soon." He had waited with the SEALs, standing near the door, where he could watch the two officers outside as well as the men in the building—nearly as motionless as a mummy . . . and as expressionless. By turns almost, the SEALs had spent time observing their host, or chaperone. He appeared to be able to go for minutes at a time without blinking, without moving a muscle. But his eyes did move quickly in response to any movement around him.

Half an hour into the wait, Beau had awarded him a minuscule nod of approval, behind his back, deciding that the Egyptian knew his way around, knew his job. He be a good fighter, Beau thought. It was quite an acknowledgment for him to give anyone who had not gone through BUD/S and a host of other training courses. Beau decided that he would rather have Turhan as an ally than an enemy.

After seventy minutes, it was difficult for any of the SEALs to avoid glancing repeatedly at watch and window—the window on the south, the direction the terrorists were expected to come from. Each man *tried* to concentrate on his zone of the perimeter, but no one—not even Frank—succeeded completely.

Seventy-five minutes; eighty.

"Very soon, I think," Turhan said. "They come. They always come."

"Yeah," Frank said, almost inaudibly. Makes no difference to me if they come or don't, he thought. We're not getting paid piecework.

Ike wanted to ask, "How long do we wait?" but didn't, though he had to bite his lower lip to keep the question in. Even without an outsider in the room, it would have been poor form, led to later ribbing by the others. Too impatient, too nervous, still a rookie, still "the Kid." But every minute that passed made it harder to remain silent.

An hour and a half.

"Something coming from the south," Frank said. Although he spoke very softly, everyone in the room heard him. Sergeant Turhan moved away from his post by the door to get a better look out the window to the south.

"I think, yes, them," he said. He went to the door, opened it, and whistled softly. One of the men outside waved a half-hearted salute at the sergeant and nodded.

"We get men out of truck," Turhan said. "Bring them in here."

The truck coming along the road appeared to be doing no more than fifteen miles per hour when it was first spotted, and it slowed down before it got within a hundred yards of the checkpoint. The last thirty yards, the wheels barely seemed to be rotating. Even so, there was a loud squeal as the brakes were applied to bring it to a complete stop, between the two uniformed officers outside.

Frank and his companions could hear a flurry of Arabic through the open window. One of the policemen spoke to the occupants of the truck, then one of them replied at length. There was another exchange before the truck's engine was turned off and both doors on the truck cab opened.

Neither officer had made a threatening move

with his rifle, or moved to draw a pistol. The two men who had been in the truck seemed to accept the demand that they get out, though with poor grace. One of them continued to mutter under his breath.

Sergeant Turhan opened the door with his left hand. He had drawn his pistol with the right, but held the weapon at his side, out of sight.

The three policemen operated smoothly together, as if they had rehearsed the maneuver many times. As the two terrorists reached the door—and got where they might have spotted one or more of the Americans inside—the two assault rifles behind them were suddenly against their backs, and Sergeant Turhan's pistol was aimed at the face of the nearest man. They had no chance to attempt to overpower the police or make an escape. Turhan stood aside and the two men from the truck were prodded inside.

"You go now, quick," Turhan said, turning toward Frank and using his pistol to gesture toward the truck waiting outside. "Men in front wear these." He switched to Arabic and shouted something at the two captives. They both glared at him but took off the loose shirts they were wearing. Turhan took each, then passed them to the nearest SEALs.

"Beau, you and me up front," Frank said, tossing one of the shirts to Guisborne. He quickly put the other one on himself, over his own gear.

Leaving the building, the SEALs had their rifles up, at the ready, turning to left and right to make certain that there was no ambush waiting for them.

The terrorists' truck appeared to be a converted pickup, perhaps forty years old. The back had been modified to turn it into a vehicle like the delivery van. Aluminum sheets had been bolted to the sides of the bed and to each other. A roof had been bolted over them, and a canvas flap hung down on the back, overlapping the original tailgate. A doorway had been cut in the rear of the cab with a torch, to give the people up front access. The old scorch marks where the cutting torch had sheared the metal were still visible. The edges had been pounded over to make it somewhat harder for a person to cut himself on them. But the job was patently amateur.

Frank climbed behind the steering wheel of the right-hand drive truck. Beau went around to the other side, while Rob and Ike climbed in the back. Frank looked back through the cutout to make sure they were in before he put his feet on clutch and brakes and turned the key in the ignition.

"Remember, this thing doesn't have the best brakes in the world," Frank said, as he shifted the truck into first gear. The right-hand drive made that awkward for him. It was the first time he had driven anything on the "wrong" side. "Keep an eye out on the road behind us, but don't be obvious about it. If anyone does come up in back, we don't want them to know you're there."

The truck's muffler appeared to work no better

than the brakes. The engine was loud, and rough. It was in desperate need of a tune-up . . . or a major overhaul. The engine seemed to be getting only a trickle of gas, and acceleration was abysmal.

Gears complained when Frank was finally able to shift the truck into second. "Damn junkyard reject," he muttered.

"James Bond never gets stuck driving crap like this," Beau observed.

"Inspector Clouseau did," Frank observed through gritted teeth. The truck bounced along the road as if it were climbing a flight of stairs. Shock absorbers were also missing, or dead.

"Eight miles of this?" Beau said. It was not really a question. "My teeth be all jarred out."

"We get back on that chopper, I think I'll push Tombs out and let him swim home," Frank said. "Serve him right for sticking us in this pile of rancid camel shit."

After two miles, Frank reached the first turn, off the gravel road onto one that was merely packed dirt, with ruts more than six inches deep. The quality of the ride suffered . . . considerably.

"You trying to shake us to death?" Rob called from the back—shouting to make himself heard over the truck's cacophony.

"We're only doing fifteen, if that," Frank shouted back. "You want to get out and walk, wait for us at the perimeter."

"They could use this in BUD/S, for Hell Week," Rob said. "Shake kids out quicker than anything they got now."

Frank didn't answer. Just then, the truck's steering wheel seemed to develop a will of its own as the rutted road tried to jerk the tires off to the right. The rocky ride deteriorated until Frank was able to wrestle the vehicle back into the ruts.

In the next five minutes, the truck covered less than half a mile, each yard an adventure. Finally, Frank took his foot off the gas pedal and let the truck slow to a stop on its own.

"Maybe we better off driving on the side," Beau suggested. "Looks better than this."

"Can't be worse," Frank said. He had leaned forward resting both forearms on the steering wheel. "That road is a bitch."

"You know, man, you awful pale for an Ay-rab," Beau said. "You want, maybe, I should drive so you can duck if anybody get close?"

Frank lifted his head and turned to look at Beau. "That some kind of racial remark? I'm not all *that* pale."

Beau laughed. "You more pale than me."

"Okay. You drive. That ought to take some of the starch out of you." Frank got out and walked around the truck, scanning the horizon carefully. They were well away from town, out in the areas of orchards and gardens. Just to the right there was a field, several acres in extent, filled with blooming flowers. Ahead and to the left he saw trees. The closest ones were familiar—olive.

"Stay alert," Frank said as he passed the tail-gate. "I don't see anyone, but who the hell knows."

"We shoulda worn helmets," Rob said, softly. "We're getting banged around back here something fierce."

By the time Frank got to the passenger side of the cab, Beau was behind the wheel, and looking across the seat. "Be almost sunset when we get there, way we're goin'," Beau said.

"We sure don't want to stall too long," Frank said as he got into place. "They might get nervous if the truck's too long getting in. Or send someone looking."

Beau snorted. "Bet this heap break down at least once a week. Must be used to it bein' late."

"Wish we'd had a chance to search the two birds who had this truck, see if they had a two-way radio or a phone with them. Let's go." Frank gestured forward.

Driving off to the side of the so-called road did seem to help. There was still some jouncing, but not as much as before. But they did not make any better speed. There was sand over rock, and every time Beau tried to get a little more speed from the truck, the wheels started to lose traction.

"I don't think this speedometer works," Beau said after he had been driving for five minutes.

"Says we goin' twenty-five, and we can't be doin' twenty."

"Fast enough," Frank said. "Faster than we could walk. Watch for a gate. Shouldn't be too far ahead now."

It wasn't—a gate across the road but no fence on either side. That was what the instructions said. A grove of olive trees to the right. Orange trees to the left. The gate was open, and hanging from one hinge. There was a ditch on either side, no more than three feet wide but nearly that deep, so Beau put the truck back on the road and went through the gate.

"Another half mile to the buildings," Frank said. "But we're on the property now. Could be sentries anywhere."

"We ain't gonna just drive up to the front door, are we?"

"No," Frank said. "Get up there where the olive trees come right out to the road and pull off on that side. We'll pop the hood so maybe somebody'll think the engine died. Then we walk the rest of the way."

The sun was low on the horizon, but still mostly above it, casting long shadows in the orchard. Beau pulled off to the right side of the road, parking the truck almost under the branches of the nearest olive tree.

"Out and down," Frank told the men in the back. "Right side. Beau, take the key out of the ignition and stick it under the seat where we can find it when we get back."

Beau grunted. "Maybe we boost something better up there? Maybe they got a Mercedes or something."

The thought was appealing, but Frank shook his head. "Don't want to confuse Sergeant Turhan and his men. But if there are any other vehicles, we don't want to leave them in running condition. No need to let them have something to chase us with."

Beau got out and went around to the front of the truck. He needed a few seconds to find the release on the hood latch, but he eventually got it up. Then he moved into the olive grove with the others who had taken up a quick defensive position, close together, facing out to watch in all directions.

"How far you figure we are from the buildings?" Rob asked.

"Shouldn't be much more than four hundred yards," Frank said. He checked his compass, then pointed a few degrees east of north. "Right about there, I think." He looked through a complete circle. "They figure to have at least a couple of sentries prowling around. We need to see them before they see us. And we want to take them out silently if we do see them."

Frank gave his men two minutes to work out the stiffness of the ride, then started moving through the trees, from cover to cover, angling farther east, away from the road. If they come looking for the men from the truck, he reasoned, they'll concentrate on the area close to the road.

It should take them a bit to think about something going wrong besides the truck. Longer to look for intruders farther off. He hoped.

Before moving away from the truck, Frank and Beau took off the light shirts they had worn over their BDUs. They would have been too obvious against the shadows of the olive grove.

To an onlooker, the movements of the SEALs might have appeared haphazard, as if none of them were taking any notice of the rest, but that was far from the case. Each man remained aware of the relative position of each of the others. They moved, mostly, two at a time, and their formation never strayed far from a rough diamond shape. They were absolutely silent. Twice, Frank held the others up with a hand signal. The first time, he thought he might have caught a hint of movement off in the trees, farther to the right, and he had the others wait until he had assured himself that there was nothing out there but the last shadows before sunset. The second time he held the others up was when he approached a large clearing. This time, he changed direction, turning to the right to go around rather than through the open space.

"Figure they're going to be getting antsy about now," Frank whispered after gathering his team close. The roof of one building was visible, at least a hundred yards away. Unlike most of the buildings they had seen on this trip, this one had a sloped roof with what appeared to be slate shingles. And the gable they could see was either wood or siding meant to look like wood. Unusual. "The truck is late. If they've found it, they know something's wrong, but not what. Anybody spots us now, we might get a half second break before they realize we're not one of their people and start shooting, but don't count on it."

"If they've got everyone out looking for the truck driver and his helper, we might hit empty buildings, have the bogeys on the wrong side of us," Rob said.

Frank nodded. "I thought of that. We get into position, we drop a couple of calling cards on the buildings, then we move, fast, back and to the side, and take the best cover we can. After that . . ." He shrugged, looked around, then said, "Depends on what we can see when the time comes."

It was dark enough for night-vision goggles to help, so the four men put them on. Beau and Ike each slipped an HE grenade into their launchers.

"How close we go before we let them know somebody's here?" Beau asked.

"We get someplace where you've got a clear shot, no closer than we are now," Frank said. "Might even pull back a hundred yards, give them more area to search, give us a better chance to locate them before they locate us."

"This as good a place as any," Beau said. "That clearing. Don' have to worry 'bout the trajectory on the grenades." He gestured. Frank turned to look, then turned back to Beau and nodded.

"Go for it. Farmboy and I will move back thirty

yards. You and the kid put a little distance between you. One grenade each, then you pull back toward us." He waited until everyone nodded.

Better to be doing than not, Frank thought as he moved through the trees. This would be the most awkward time to be discovered, getting into position for the first strike. He kept his focus, searching two thirds of a circle as he moved, trusting Rob to cover the rest. Once the action started, it would be better. Frank always found it almost relaxing to have the first shots out of the way. There was no longer that edge of anticipation, the wait . . . even though there might be more waiting later.

Moving through the olive trees required concentration. So many of the branches were low-hanging that an instant of losing focus might easily result in a collision—annoying at best; at worst possibly dangerous, not just for the injuries that might result but also because the sound of a head hitting a tree might be enough to alert the enemy.

Frank and Rob slid into position—prone, behind tree trunks—almost simultaneously, like dancers who had rehearsed the move together for days. They brought their rifles into firing position and waited.

Thirty yards away, Beau and Ike had both moved, putting a few more yards between them and angling for a good trajectory at the one roof they could see clearly through the trees. Then they looked at each other before glancing back to make sure that the other two were in position.

Beau nodded to Ike. The two men brought their weapons up, took rough aim, and launched the first grenades. Neither man waited to see the results. Before the explosions came, Beau and Ike were trotting back toward Frank and Rob.

Frank gave hand signals telling them to go on past, then angle to their left, farther from the so-called road and the buildings. No additional instructions were needed. The team would maneuver by twos, leapfrogging each other until Frank decided that it was time to move in to resume the attack ... or until they were spotted by the opposition.

The two explosions came close together, but were distinct. All the SEALs could see was the brief glow of the blasts, orange and yellow, appearing, then fading quickly. But they weren't interested in damage assessment yet.

Beau and Ike went to ground ten yards beyond the others. Frank and Rob got up and started moving. We've got their attention, Frank thought. They'll hear that anywhere on the farm. They would look. If the opposition was scattered, at least some of them would start moving toward the explosions. How much time it took the terrorists to decide on, and implement, a coordinated response would determine how successful the SEALs were likely to be. And, Frank thought with some satisfaction, defensive responses were not commonly high on the list of training priorities for people who normally went out and planted bombs to kill unarmed civilians.

Ike's thoughts were similar, but more concise. Give them a taste of their own medicine.

Up, move, down. Keep your eyes open and moving. Look for any trace of enemy movement. It might not be much. Don't wait for confirmation. Even if it's only a bird startled from its perch, go down and signal the others. It might not be a bird, and even a half second lost trying to decide could make the difference. It could make you dead.

Frank had just gotten up to start his next move forward—the third exchange of this maneuver—when several gunshots sounded in the distance. He went flat anyway, even before his mind could come up with, *Just somebody's nerves, shooting at shadows.* Frank glanced around, double-checking the positions of his men. A few seconds to catch his breath and try to determine if there was any activity close enough to be an immediate threat.

When he got up again, Rob got up as well, and they continued on. Another fifty yards this way, Frank through as he dropped to the ground and waited for Beau and Ike to move. Then we'll turn in toward the buildings again and see what we can net.

He had to change those plans though, because on their next move forward Frank and Rob came to the end of the olive grove. They went down under trees in the last row, and Frank gestured for Beau and Ike to stay put.

The buildings were off to the left, all three visible now beyond two acres of blooming roses—flowers that had not been tended recently. Instead of well-trimmed rows, the bushes had been left to spread as they pleased. Nor had flowers been harvested. As many were wilting, losing their petals, as were freshly budded or just opened. It was obvious that the tenants, whoever they actually were, were not actively working the farm.

Frank did not worry that any of his men might start sneezing. None of them had any known allergies to plants.

There was a border, about ten feet wide, between the olive trees and the rose bushes. Along most of it, grass grew a couple of inches deep, the perhaps inadvertent beneficiary of the irrigation still provided for the farm's ignored cash crops.

Just briefly, Frank wondered about the state of the farm. If it was supposed to be a functional front for the terrorist group, it would make sense to keep working it. Leaving it idle would draw attention. If they're not working it, they must not be worried about attention, Frank reasoned. They must think they have adequate protection against interference. Which might be why the Egyptians had requested—demanded—that the SEALs come in and do it for them.

Frank was ready to start his men moving in the direction of the buildings again, within the cover of the trees, when he spotted movement sixty yards away. Three men armed with AK-47s came into view on the grassy border between trees and bushes.

For nearly two minutes, the three men just stood between olives and roses, talking—though Frank could not hear anything they said, and would not have been able to understand much of their Arabic if he could hear. One man seemed to be doing most of the talking, punctuating with wild gestures of his one free arm. He pointed down the lane, then pointed across the field of roses. The other two men left him then, one coming alone the grassy stretch toward where Frank and Rob were hiding. The other moved past the end of the rose field. The third man remained where he had been, in position to watch both of the others—as well as he could see without aid in the deepening twilight.

It's going to be a near thing, Frank thought. He turned on his side and used hand signs to communicate with Rob, to tell the Farmer to take out the sentry when he went past. If the man who had stayed in place saw the activity, Frank would take him out. Then they would worry about the third man . . . and any others the sound of Frank's gunfire might bring. It would have to be gunfire. That man was too far away to take him out silently.

The man coming closer walked slowly, his rifle held at the ready in both hands. He peered into the darkness of the trees, then scanned across the flowers, spending most of his time trying to see into the olive grove.

Rob lay his rifle carefully on the ground and drew the knife from his belt sheath. The matte black blade reflected almost no light. It was just another shadow in the dark under the tree. Maybe he won't come this far, Rob thought as he adjusted his position to make it easier to get up and out when the time came. Maybe he'll turn around and go back before he gets to me. It was a worry, not a hope. If the terrorist turned back, he would still have to be accounted for, and it might not be as easy later; he might have a chance to do some damage of his own first.

Still fifteen yards short of where Rob waited, the man stopped. He spent thirty seconds or more squinting, looking into the dark of the trees. Then he turned and looked back toward the man who had sent him off—a noncom, or the organization's equivalent, Rob thought. Rob nearly held his breath, willing the man to come on, to come within reach. Eventually, the man did start moving closer again, but now he seemed to stop after almost every step, almost as if he suspected that danger was very close.

One of his stops was no more than ten feet from where Frank lay. The chief was absolutely motionless, keeping his gaze down so there would be no chance even of a reflection from the lenses of his night-vision goggles. Frank did not even breathe until the terrorist took another couple of steps away from him . . . and closer to Rob.

Time twisted around itself in the peculiar manner of anticipation and excitement, extending itself in the perception of the SEALs who were nearest the Egyptian with the rifle. Frank became overly aware of the beating of his heart, feeling loud thumps that came too close together. Discovery seemed impossible to avoid. He readied himself for action. If the Egyptian gave any sign that he might have spotted any of the SEALs, Frank would not wait to see if Rob could get to him. He would try to get the man first.

Rob had his arms under him, ready to help propel him to his feet and forward. Two more steps, he thought as the Egyptian came to a stop directly in front of him. Get just a little past me, so I can get you from behind. Advantage could be measure in hundredths of a second. Years of training had given Rob confidence in his abilities . . . and knowledge of his limits. *One more step.*

The Egyptian took that step.

Rob did not look to see where the other Egyptians were, or where they might be looking. He gave no thought to what his own team mates might be doing. As soon as his target moved to the position Rob had marked, he shoved himself up and forward with arms and legs, propelling himself almost like a swimmer at the start of a race.

He hit the Egyptian chest high, carrying him to the ground. Rob's left hand went around the man's head, over the mouth. Rob's right hand, with the knife, came up and across the Egyptian's throat, cutting to the spine, severing throat, veins, and arteries. Hot blood spurted out over Rob's hand and arm. As he rolled to his right, Rob brought the already dead man between him and the Egyptian who had remained at the end of the lane—cover if that man started shooting.

Frank had moved just a fraction of a second after Rob did. He got up on hands and knees and crawled far enough out to give himself a clear shot at the man at the end of the grassy lane. At first, that man showed no sign that he had seen anything out of the ordinary. It was at least twenty seconds after Rob struck before the man at the end of the lane noticed that his companion had gone from sight, and another few seconds before he apparently spotted the body lying in the grass.

He called out, loudly, and took two steps in the direction of the SEALs. Then he turned to his left and gave a shrill whistle. He brought his rifle up and started cautiously along the grassy border then, moving very slowly.

Frank allowed him only two steps. Then he pulled the trigger on his M-16, squeezing off a single shot that caught the Egyptian high in the chest, knocking him backwards and down, dead or near death.

Rob moved back under the trees, retrieving his rifle, then came to Frank and dropped to the ground.

"Let's go," Frank whispered, gesturing to the left. "Time to move in and make some real noise."

"What about the third man here?" Rob asked,

wiping his bloody hand and arm on the ground to get rid of the sticky fluid.

"We see him, we pop him." Then Frank was up and moving.

Although the SEALs moved quickly, ranging deeper into the grove, it was no heedless run. They were careful about noise, rarely making any sound that could be heard more than twenty or thirty yards away, angling closer to the buildings even when they could not see them directly.

In the five minutes they needed to get into a position where they could see all three of the main buildings, they did not see any more of the residents. They heard shouting, at a distance. The survivor of the ambush at the edge of the olive grove had apparently yelled for help.

Let him draw the rest in, Frank thought. His men were a hundred and fifty yards away.

"Hit it," he said, just loud enough for his team to hear him. "Pound those buildings." He stripped off the bandoleer of grenades he was wearing and tossed it toward Ike. Rob passed his string of grenades to Beau. The grenadiers would use those grenades first, then switch to the ones they were carrying.

The division of labor was natural. Two men worked their grenade launchers as rapidly as they could load, aim, and fire. The other two were ready to provide covering fire once the enemy managed to narrow down their positions. Until they had targets, Frank and Rob would hold their fire. Firing blindly now would do nothing but make it easier for the enemy to find them . . . and count their numbers.

Beau and Ike worked in a steady rhythm, the way they practiced on the target range. In little more than a minute, each man launched a dozen grenades, mostly high-explosive, with only a few incendiaries in the mix. Then it was time to move, before the enemy could zero in on them and perhaps return the favor with their own grenades.

Frank led the way, moving toward the left, counterclockwise around the buildings and the clearing that held them. At least one fire had been started in the main house. Flames were coming through the roof and one of the windows on the top story. In the silence after the last explosion from the first barrage of grenades, the SEALs could hear more shouting, as the residents of the complex tried to determine where the attack was coming from, and to locate each other.

Not very well trained, Frank thought. They're just broadcasting their positions. Two men ran across his field of vision. Frank lifted his rifle and sprayed a dozen rounds toward them, certain that at least one of the men went down to stay. The other, he thought, was probably dead as well.

The team moved sixty yards before the two men with the M-203 grenade launchers went back to work. Each man fired another six grenades. This time, they didn't want to give the enemy as much time to respond. Six grenades, then move.

All three buildings had been severely dam-
aged. The main house was burning, fully involved.
The flanking buildings, both smaller and made of
brick or stone, had lost roofs and windows. There
were small fires burning inside each. Ike spotted a
cluster of cars and trucks parked thirty yards
from the houses. On the run, he fired an HE
grenade toward them—his aim good enough
even on the move. The projectile exploded on the
hood of a Mercedes that had to be three decades
old, though Ike didn't realize the age of the car
until later.

When Beau saw what Ike had fired at, he
launched the grenade in his tube at the vehicles
as well. The grenade's detonation was followed
by a secondary blast, as the fuel tank of a large
truck exploded, sending flames out to engulf all
of the vehicles.

For the first time, enemy rifle fire started to
sound close enough to be a concern. The terrorists might be firing blindly, but they had narrowed
down the area where the intruders were. Frank
veered left, farther from the buildings. The fires
were starting to provide too much light for comfort.

Time to get out, Frank thought. Before they get
their act together. "Start using those grenades
where the gunfire's coming from," he called, loud
enough to make sure that Ike and Beau both
heard. "We've done enough damage. Let's get out
while we can."

Frank had only a vague idea of the direction

they needed to head. They had changed course too many times for him to be certain just where the old pickup truck was. He was aware that they had not crossed the dirt road again, so that gave him a general idea. He angled more to the left, not wanting to hit that road too near the buildings.

Beau and Ike each fired off two grenades, angling them high, looking to detonate them above the heads of any pursuers, making it slightly more difficult for anyone to determine just where they were coming from. Both men reloaded their launchers, but put their attention to following Frank through the trees. Rob hung back, but only a few yards, as rearguard.

Three minutes later, there was more gunfire directed at the SEALs, this time from ahead. Some of it came close enough that the enemy had apparently seen *something*. Frank changed course, turning right, but he did not stop or go to cover. Right now, covering ground was more important. The last thing he wanted was for his team to get pinned down long enough for the enemy to bring more forces to bear.

He came out onto the road, driveway, almost before he realized it was there, and kept going. More gunfire sounded. The terrorists were watching the lane. Should have thought of that, Frank thought, spraying bullets along the road as he crossed. He went on into the trees on the far side. The rest of the team got across. Frank waited, dropping for cover for just the few seconds necessary to make sure that none of his men had been killed, or wounded badly enough to need assistance.

"Looks like they found the truck," Rob said. "We'll play hell getting it back if they're sitting on it."

"I sure don't want to walk all the way back to that cop shop," Frank said. "And the boys didn't leave any of the other vehicles up there operable."

There was time for no more. Frank pushed himself to his feet and started moving parallel to the drive, toward the boundary of the farm and the truck they had left behind.

There had been almost constant, though sporadic, gunfire from the time the team had crossed the driveway, but none of it came particularly close as the SEALs worked their way toward the perimeter of the farm. Once they got close to the truck, the SEALs dropped to the ground and crawled in, making virtually no noise at all. They could see three of the terrorists near the truck, using it for cover . . . but uncertain just what side of it they needed to be on for safety. They were moving about, clearly nervous, and out of their element. The men around the truck had no night-vision goggles on, and that put them at an additional disadvantage. The SEALs could see them very plainly.

The SEALs moved to within forty yards of

their targets, spread out so that all of the terrorists were visible to at least one of the Navy men. Frank looked around at his team, then made a gesture, like a child using a hand as a make-believe pistol.

Four shots. Three dead terrorists. The SEALs were up and moving before the last body stopped jerking through his death throes. If there were any other terrorists around, they would have to be taken care of on the fly. Frank intended to get his men in the truck and the truck moving, as quickly as possible.

"Beau, get the hood down. I'll drive," Frank called as they reached the drive. "Rob, Ike—in the back."

No one took it for granted that there was no one lurking in the back of the truck. Ike and Rob went at the flap hanging over the rear as if they *knew* there were hostile guns just inside—weapons first, fingers on triggers. Frank and Ike pulled open the cab doors at the same time, loudly enough to provide a distraction for anyone inside.

The truck was empty.

"Now, long as nobody gimmicked this beast," Beau said as he retrieved the keys and handed them to Frank.

"You ever have any cheerful thoughts?" Frank asked as he inserted the key in the ignition and mentally crossed his fingers.

"Not when I'm workin'."

The starter ground for several seconds as if it would not turn the engine over, but then there was a sputter and, finally, the engine began to run, sluggishly. Frank eased his foot down on the gas pedal and, after another thirty seconds, the engine was running as smoothly as it had during the trip out from the police checkpoint; that is, not very, but enough.

"Hang on!" Frank warned as he made a U-turn in reverse. "I'm going to push this buggy as fast as it'll go."

The truck was rolling toward the gate, gaining speed, when bullets started hitting the tailgate and one side. In the back end, Ike and Rob moved the tarp enough to return fire, spraying the driveway behind them on full automatic, and Ike popped off the grenade in his M-203 launcher.

Driving without lights made the exit even more interesting. Frank's night-vision goggles did not pick out the ruts, bumps, and holes efficiently, and the ancient pickup bounced around like a Ping Pong ball on a sea of mouse traps. Frank felt that he was constantly on the verge of losing control of the vehicle, but that was of less concern than giving any surviving gunmen behind them a chance to catch up. Several times the truck skidded, and once, Frank thought for an instant that it might overturn.

But he pushed the truck for all it was worth until they got to the gravel road, and even then he did not slow down by more than three or four miles per hour. The ride was, however, markedly less rocky.

There was no sign of pursuit. *That cuts down the worries,* Frank thought. *Now we just have to worry that one of them might have used a cell phone to set up an ambush in front of us, and whether Turhan and his cohorts are playing us straight.*

Bright floodlights illuminated the road at the police checkpoint, though the interior of the building was dark. The white van was still parked at the side of the building. Two uniformed officers still stood in front.

"Keep your weapons ready, just in case," Frank warned, as he downshifted to help the pickup's feeble brakes slow the vehicle to a stop. He pulled off the road, just at the edge of the most intense circle of light. "No reason to think our hosts are going to try to screw us, but we don't take chances."

Sergeant Turhan came out of the dark building to stand a couple of paces in front of the door, watching as the SEALs got out of the truck and started across the lighted area toward him. Frank could read no expression on the sergeant's face. *I wonder if he's had any reports yet on what we did?* Frank wondered.

Turhan moved several more steps toward the SEALs. When they were no more than twenty feet apart, his face finally opened up in a grin. "You are back safe. Is good," Turhan said. He gestured toward the white van that had brought the men from Beni Suef. "We go right now. Your people anxious."

Harry Tombs was standing next to the Egyptian helicopter, in the shadows, his Uzi in hand, when the van came into view and headed directly toward the aircraft. The tense look on his face did not ease until he saw all four members of the team get out of the van under their own power, weapons still in hand.

"Any problems?" Tombs asked when Frank reached him.

"Not with the mission. The taxi service left a lot to be desired," Frank replied as he climbed into the helicopter.

POST-MISSION

There had been delays before taking off from Beni Suef and during the transfer to the Navy helicopter at Aswan, and then before they were allowed to land on *Bellman*. Once aboard the Navy chopper, Beau had stretched out on the floor, head on his arms, and gave every appearance of sleeping until the aircraft was descending over *Bellman*.

"We'll go straight to the conference room for the debriefing," Tombs told the SEALs, when the aircraft was finally on *Bellman*'s afterdeck. "Pick your minds before you forget anything."

"Have somebody send in coffee," Rob said. "Lots of it."

"And a masseuse to put our bones back where they belong," Beau said.

The interior companionways of *Bellman* were illuminated only with dim red lights, to help eyes adapt if it was necessary to go out into the night. It was not until they were in the conference room that they had good light.

"What the hell happened to you?" Frank asked Ike, when he saw the youngest member of the team then. There was a lump and a growing black and blue patch over Jensen's left eye.

"Your hara-kiri driving, that's what happened," Ike said.

"Hell, Frank, I thought he'd knocked himself out," Rob said. "There when we were going through the gate. When you almost tipped that truck over. The kid banged his head on the side of the truck and went down heavy. First time I ever heard him cuss so much. He sounded worse than you do on a three-day drunk."

Frank got right in Ike's face, examining the lump and discoloration. "Soon as we get done here, kid, we'll get you to sickbay." He turned to Tombs. "*Roosevelt* has better facilities. Can you set things up to have the doc over there check him out? Make sure he didn't crack his skull or something?"

Tombs nodded. "I'll go talk to the O.D. now, have him set it up."

"Hey, all I need is a coupla aspirin," Ike said,

annoyed because no one seemed interested in what he might want.

"If so, then they'll give you aspirin," Frank said. "We don't take chances we don't have to."

THE REPORT

"Hell of a way to get a day off," Harry Tombs muttered, as he ran the encryption program so he could send his report and its addenda on to Langley. The doctor on Roosevelt had prescribed twenty-four hours' rest for Ike Jensen. Tombs expected that the entire team would be given the extra twenty-four hours. He had made a point of suggesting that in his summary, referring to comments the SEALs had made about the ride and the active nature of the mission.

The summary had been an exercise in carefully worded diplomacy. Tombs smiled, satisfied that he had conveyed just exactly what he had wanted to.

```
. . . Due to the uncertain nature of our
relationship with the security police
of the Egyptian government—and the pos-
sibility that security leaks within
that organization might have endangered
our operation—I felt it essential that
I accompany the SEAL team as far as the
final  staging  area  to  insure  that
extraction would be made as planned—or
```

to obtain alternate methods of extraction if anything went wrong with the
arrangements. I remained with the
Egyptian helicopter at Beni Suef,
armed, with that intent.

"If you don't blow your own horn, nobody else
will do it for you," Tombs whispered.

7: SLEIGHRIDE

PRE-MISSION

Most of the swelling had gone down, but the bruise on Ike's forehead was still vivid. The consensus among his team mates was that it looked worse now than when it was fresh, with its shades of purple and jaundice yellow.

"I'm okay," Ike said, every time one of the others looked at the bruise. He was tired of solicitous questions about how he felt. At first, a little sympathy had been a welcome change from the usual teasing, but the others were carrying it to excess. "You can't use me as an excuse to take another day off." There *was* still some residual pain, and the area was definitely sore to the touch, but Ike was not about to admit that. He did not want to be considered unfit for action, and he worried that the doctor might order him to stand down for another day, or longer; maybe even stick him back in sickbay aboard *Roosevelt* for more tests. "You want more time off, go bash your head against a bulkhead."

The SEALs had gathered early for a 1400 hours briefing. Tombs had passed the word for the briefing four hours earlier, after asking Jensen how he felt. Tombs would not be early for the meeting. The SEALs expected him to walk in the door precisely at 1400.

"Hey, kid, the other night when you saw stars, did they have five points or six?" Rob asked.

"Kiss my ass, Farmboy," Ike replied, an unusually testy remark for him. With his head still aching, he thought that was all the reply Rhodes's gibe deserved.

"Leave him be, Farmer," Frank said. "You were out of line with that." He watched Jensen. Although Ike tried to conceal it, it was clear to Frank that he was still in some pain.

"Sorry, Ike. I didn't mean anything by it," Rob said.

Small victory, Ike thought. He didn't call me *kid* this time. "Yeah, I know, Rob," he said. Watch yourself, he thought. Any other time you wouldn't have jumped all over him for that. He's said worse before, and so have you. "The subject of my head is just starting to bore me stiff."

A minute later, when Harry Tombs walked into the room, the first thing he did was look at Ike Jensen's forehead.

"Don't ask. I'm fine," Ike said before Tombs could speak.

"Never doubted it," Tombs said quietly. "That's why we're here. Time to get back to work."

THE BRIEFING

"Old business first," Tombs said. "We've had word on our last outing. The Egyptian government is quite satisfied with the results, although—publicly—they are voicing outrage at 'another senseless act of terrorism' and promising crackdowns on their domestic terrorists again." Tombs smiled. "The body count is nine dead, including two at the police checkpoint. You were right, Chief. They offed the two men they pulled from the pickup truck. Three other men were taken to the hospital with serious wounds, two from gunshots and one from shrapnel. The survival of all three is officially in doubt. One way or another."

"They gonna send us some of King Tut's gold for our trouble?" Rob asked.

"Dream on, Farmboy," Beau said.

"New business," Tombs said, raising his voice a little to recover everyone's attention. "*Bellman* has been temporarily detached from the battle group and is steaming up the Gulf of Aqaba. The ship is scheduled to make port at Elat in Israel this afternoon, then proceed to the Jordanian city of Aqaba in the morning. Goodwill visits, showing the flag and making nice with everybody. The two ports are only four miles apart at the head of the gulf. There will be brief ceremonies with municipal and national politicians in both ports. Neither will be too time consuming, and you don't have to worry about participating in either. The five of us are definitely persona non grata at the festivities. We might be an embarrassment."

"Do tell," Rob said.

Tombs ignored the interruption. "*Bellman* will remain in Elat until dawn tomorrow morning, then make the short trip to Aqaba. That visit should be concluded by about eleven o'clock, at which time the ship will steam back down the gulf to rejoin the battle group."

"I assume we're not going to just hide in our compartment all this time," Frank said.

"Not all the time, just during the ceremonies at each port," Tombs said. "It's in between that you go to work."

"Here come the shiv," Beau said under his breath.

"After sunset, the four of you will board the ship's launch and be taken several miles south of Elat. You will deploy a rubber raft and use that to approach Aqaba under cover of darkness. Right off the bat, let me tell you that this operation is totally black—you will not wear or carry anything that can be identified as having been made in the United States. And this time, no exceptions—not a damned one. That means you can't use one of your usual RPBs. A substitute has been obtained and is already aboard the launch. Your weapons must all be of foreign manufacture, as well as the ammunition. That part's no trouble. No rifles or other long guns, strictly pistols and knives. Untraceable clothing, right down to skivvies and

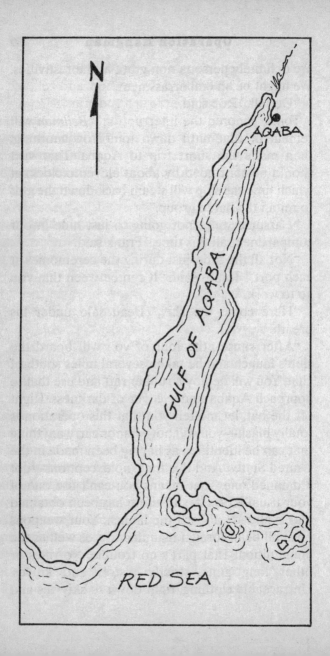

socks, has been brought in especially for this. You are to get in, accomplish the mission, and get out. No one is to be taken prisoner under any circumstances." He paused.

"You gonna give us suicide pills?" Rob asked.

"That shouldn't be necessary. I assume you can handle that job without pills," Tombs said. "You're going into Jordan on this one, therefore we don't make waves that say 'Made in the USA.' The new king has more than enough problems."

"Okay, we get the picture. So what's the job?" Frank asked.

Tombs paused before he answered. "Blow up the headquarters of one of the splinter groups that broke away from the PLO over the peace for land deals with Israel. The explosive devices will be of regional construction, ones we, ah, liberated from another of the groups that refused to go along with Arafat making nice with the Israelis. The manufacture is quite distinctive and very effective, exceptionally well suited to this job. More elegant, shall we say, than a truckload of fertilizer and fuel oil. No one will have any difficulty identifying the origin of the devices. The timing mechanism was constructed of parts available in the Middle East. Give yourselves enough time to get back to your boat before it goes off." He finally slid the target folder across the table to Frank . . . who did not open it immediately.

"You do realize that the northern end of the Gulf of Aqaba is one of the most heavily patrolled stretches of water in the world, from the air and on the surface as well as from shore," Frank said. "On the west you've got Egyptians. In the north, Israelis. On the east, both Jordanians and Saudis. It would be damned hard for a used condom to float ashore along there without being spotted."

"The Egyptians stay close to the coast of Sinai," Tombs said after his usual pause. "They go to extremes to avoid raising Israeli hackles. The Saudis respect the territorial interests of Jordan. Their patrol craft don't come as far north as where you'll be operating, and the Israelis will not be a problem. That just leaves the Jordanians. While they have competent people, they have political worries to distract them. They can't even raise the price of bread without risking riots that might overthrow the monarchy. Hussein couldn't manage that, and his son doesn't have the juice of his old man yet. The sizable Palestinian minority creates constant problems for the government. There is a certain amount of routine contraband brought in through Aqaba, and the authorities turn a blind eye to it. In addition, they're far more concerned with safeguarding the commercial traffic that uses the port. There is some risk of discovery, but no more than you have faced before. As long as you steer clear of the commercial facilities, the risk is minimal."

Frank finally opened the target folder. He just scanned the operational order on top—those never really said much about a mission; they were merely the covering document. The details came in the other papers. At this point, Frank was most interested in the maps and satellite photographs.

"Aqaba is on top of a cliff," he said. "Do we scale it or use this street going up to where most of the buildings are?"

"There isn't time for climbing," Tombs said. "That stretch is where your greatest risk of discovery comes, and going in after midnight there shouldn't be much activity. Remember, the population of Aqaba is under seventy thousand, and a large part of that consists of refugees who don't have much beyond the necessities of life. Night life is minimal."

"Be nice if there was something going on at the far end to distract the cops," Frank said, sliding the map and photos to Rob. "But I don't suppose we can get anything like that."

"Not this time," Tombs said.

"This is crazy," Beau said. "Like trying to sneak this ship into a wadin' pool."

"You doubt your ability to handle the mission?" Tombs's voice changed tone, raising warning flags in Frank's head.

"There's no call for that," Frank said, before Beau could reply. "If it can be done, we're the ones can do it. We've gone balls to the wall before, but this one ... well, this might be stretching things, especially since none of us speak Arabic."

"What does that have to do with it?" Tombs asked.

"If we had someone who could speak Arabic, we might be able to bullshit our way past anyone.

I can understand a little, but not much, and no one ever seems to understand me when I speak it."

This time, Tombs hesitated for nearly half a minute before he said, "I speak Arabic."

"I know," Frank said, meeting his stare. "You got the balls for this one?"

THE PREPARATION

"Are you crazy?" Rob asked, loudly, once the SEALs were alone together. "Inviting the spook along? Wasn't once enough?"

"Most times, I'd say you were right," Frank said. "But this time is different. Unless you think you can learn Arabic in the next few hours, he might actually contribute something more than four bullets. This op stinks, and having Tombs along might just mean we get to bitch about it tomorrow, back here. I'm not crazy about having his company again, but there it is. You got a better idea?"

"Yeah, tell our fearless leader to handle it by himself."

"You that eager to go back to Kansas and ride a tractor and slop the hogs?" Frank asked. "Besides, just supposing for a minute that we could get away with telling him to do this one himself, how would we look if he pulled it off without us?"

"Better than we'd look with that 'fall-on-your-swords' shit. I got better ideas for when I check out, and they don't include that."

Frank stared at Rob for a moment, trying to decide whether this was just normal grousing or something more serious. "You want out, you know how to do it," Frank said at last, softly, so Rob would know it was not banter. He had to *know*. "You volunteered for the Teams. You volunteered for Team Six. You can unvolunteer yourself all the way back to the fleet."

It was Rob's turn to stare before talking. "We started as a foursome and that's how we'll finish," he said.

THE MISSION

During the last part of *Bellman*'s journey north in the Gulf of Aqaba, it had seemed more like sailing up a river than being at sea. Land was visible on both sides, and—finally—ahead as well. The SEALs had done more than their share of looking, especially as *Bellman* passed Jordanian Aqaba near the end of the trip. Layers of buildings seemed to adorn the side of cliffs. Ike had checked an encyclopedia and reported that the entire gulf was a northern continuation of Africa's Great Rift Valley. "At one time, the land on the east and on the west touched," he told the others before they adjourned to their compartment below—just before the ship docked at Elat.

They were not totally cut off from the festivities on deck, the ship's loudspeakers and closed-circuit television system relayed everything that happened. Frank and his companions tried not to pay too much attention to the speeches and the music played by a local band. The ceremony was over before sunset though, and the SEALs went to supper.

Before midnight, they were rested, dressed, and equipped for the night's mission. The clothing was all civilian, and might have passed muster in any town or village in the Middle East.

Harry Tombs had come to their compartment and they had gone over each step in the plan. He even added a couple of extra photographs to the target folder. That afternoon, he had taken several photographs of Aqaba with a telephoto lens. They gave the team a better view of what they faced.

At 2355 hours, all five of them were on deck, near the fantail, on the side of *Bellman* away from the dock. The ship's launch was in the water. The two explosive devices, each weighing slightly less than fifty pounds, had already been lowered to the launch—with extreme care.

"We don't leave anyone behind," Tombs said softly before they started climbing down the Jacobs ladder to the launch.

Bellman's skipper had provided an excuse for having the boat out—fishing. During the meeting with Elat's politicians, the captain had mentioned hearing that there was good fishing in the area, that a couple of his officers were interested in giving it a try. The story was bizarre but had apparently drawn no suspicion. The launch had a perfect cover story both for going out and for remaining away most of the night.

"If it works, it works," Frank had commented when Tombs told him the tale.

"As long as they remember to actually *do* some fishing," was Tombs's reply.

In the launch, Tombs spoke with the lieutenant (j.g.) in charge, then sat with the SEALs as the boat started away from *Bellman*. The launch did not race out of port. Beau guessed that the boat never got above six knots. That was more than enough. They didn't have far to go.

Tombs and the SEALs did no talking among themselves during the fifty minutes the launch took to get them to the point where they would transfer to a rubber boat. The launch's crew took care of inflating the boat, trailing it over the side, and installing the electric motor and batteries.

After the team was in the raft, they finished preparing it for their purposes, spreading a black waterproof tarp over the top and securing it to the rope on top of the inflated sides. The fit was loose enough to allow air to circulate, but the SEALs knew that it was going to be a hot ride.

"Frank, you navigate from the bow. Give Beau his directions," Tombs instructed. "This gives us a little better chance to get in unobserved."

The trip in, nearly four miles, was uneventful, though tense. There would be no talking their way out of it if a Jordanian patrol boat came across five men trying to sneak into Aqaba, especially if the raft was inspected. Two bombs would be impossible to explain. Frank decided, for himself, that if they were spotted before they got more than halfway in, he would try to slip over the side and swim back to the launch. It might not work, but it would give him a chance.

They aimed for the edge of the port area, away from any activity that might be going on, or anyone standing watch on the single ship tied up at the dock. There were a couple of fishing boats tied up, and Frank directed Beau to bring the rubber raft in next to the last of them.

There were no lights on within fifty yards.

Frank was the first man out of the boat. He climbed into the open fishing boat and looked around to make sure no one was sleeping aboard it. Then he went ashore. He could see no one anywhere along the waterfront.

A gesture from Frank brought the others out of their boat, beginning with Harry Tombs. "Looks good, so far," Tombs whispered when he joined Frank. "Down there, up the street to the left, a block past the old fortress."

"I studied the folder," Frank replied. "You take point. We'll stay close, two by two. Rob and Beau will bring up the rear." The division of labor had been settled before leaving *Bellman*, but Frank repeated it to reassert his tactical command over Tombs after letting the spook's directions in the boat pass without comment. Ike and Beau would carry the explosives. Each fit into a large olive-colored satchel with a shoulder strap. Frank and

Rob would handle the detonators until they reached the target and did the final assembly of the bombs and set the timing devices.

Everything seemed to be made of stone, buildings and streets. The route up to the top of the cliff had been carved from the hillside, and the angle was steep enough to put a strain on calf and thigh muscles. There were few streetlights, and they were well separated, leaving considerable pockets of darkness.

The five men did not try to *sneak* up the hill. That would have been too suspicious. They walked along the street, staying close to one side but making no effort to dart in and out of shadows. The image they hoped to project—if they *were* observed—was that they might be crewmen from the freighter, taking a peaceful walk into town. For whatever reason.

Frank and Ike stayed only a couple of yards behind Tombs. Beau and Rob were somewhat farther behind them. Not all together, but close enough that they could be presumed to come from the same place. And close enough that Harry could do the talking no matter what side they might be hailed from.

Better he not have to talk, Frank reminded himself as they reached the top of the incline and turned toward the old fortress—that the British and French had shelled during World War One, before Lawrence of Arabia took the town from the other side. Better still if no one sees us. Ike and Beau both list badly; anyone will know those bags are heavy, heavy enough to be suspicious anywhere.

On the seaward side, the street and buildings had all appeared clean, scoured by wind and squalls blowing off of the gulf. Once on level ground, behind the first barriers to weather, the street and buildings had the dusty look common to desert towns.

They went past the old fortress—with signs in several languages announcing what hours the site was open for tourists. Frank could match their location with the map and photos he had studied. He could pick out the building they were to target as soon as he saw it.

Tombs led the way into an alley across the street and half a block from the target. This was where detonators and explosives would be assembled. The SEALs all had gone through considerable training in explosives, and they knew the steps necessary to arm this particular combination. The men who had carried the detonators did the assembly in near darkness, with only a faint glow from a streetlight near the entrance to the old fortress providing illumination. Frank and Rob worked slowly, knowing that this job could not be rushed. Tombs stood watch at the mouth of the alley, in the shadows, looking for any hint of approaching danger. He did not try to rush the SEALs.

When the assembly work was finished, Frank went along the alley wall, stopping just behind the CIA man. "They're ready. We get to the target, just need to set the time and arm the detonator. Ten seconds' work."

Tombs nodded without turning. "No sign of anyone moving anywhere around. What say we put the bombs in the middle? I'll stay up front. You and Rhodes bring up the rear."

"Best way," Frank said. Put you up front, he thought. That way, if you're wrong about there not being a bunch of armed men in that building you'll be the first to know. After all the strikes the team had made, he thought it extremely likely that any groups that might be targets would take extra measures to protect their assets.

Harry Tombs stepped casually out of the alley and stood in the open, a couple of feet from the nearest building. He stuck his hands in his trouser pockets and looked around—overplaying the part, Frank thought; he's doing everything but whistling "Over the Rainbow." After a moment, Tombs gave a minuscule nod of his head and started walking, sauntering, toward their target.

Frank stood at the end of the alley, where Tombs had been before, and gestured Beau and Ike forward. They walked together, still leaning to the side to balance the weight of the bombs they carried. Frank gave them only a few yards before moving out with Rob. This was not the time to get too strung out.

It's all going too easy, Frank worried, glancing over his shoulder to assure himself that no one was sneaking up behind him. No place can be as deserted as this burg looks. There weren't even many lights visible inside buildings. And they had not seen a single vehicle moving. There ought be police patrols, if nothing else, Frank thought. Almost involuntarily, his right hand moved to touch the butt of the pistol stuck in his belt, under his shirt. *Something.*

They were crossing the lone intersection remaining between them and the target when Frank saw something off to the left. A block away, a car had sped across the next intersection. He was startled, almost to the point of physical response. Damn, Frank thought. Next thing, I'll be jumping out of my skin. Good thing that car didn't come this way. He shook his head.

Ahead of Frank, Beau and Ike had both seen the headlights and heard the engine. I don't know 'bout using the spook to bullshit anyone, Beau thought. We get spotted, out best bet be cut and run, fire off a few shots then get away fast. It was a little late to wish he had thought about bringing along a hand grenade or two as escape insurance.

The car lights had startled Ike so badly his sphincter contracted and he was afraid he would brown out. He needed a few seconds to get control of his reactions, and longer to let his heart quit beating so rapidly. Then he found himself thinking that it was a good thing that the bomb he was carrying was hung from his shoulder. Otherwise, he thought, he might have dropped it. According to everything he had been taught, the mere shock of a drop would not have caused the bomb to detonate, but he wasn't absolutely certain—not *dead* certain.

When he reached the target building, Harry Tombs stopped at the near corner. He turned facing the street, looking both ways, and scanning the windows of the building across from the target.

The building that housed the headquarters of the terrorist faction had been built just after World War One. Its predecessor had been destroyed in the naval bombardment of Aqaba. Tombs had studied roughly drawn plans of the building, not blueprints or anything approaching that level of detail. The building was unusual for the area in that it had a cellar—intended, Tombs supposed, as a haven in case Aqaba again underwent the kind of shelling that had destroyed the previous building on the site. There was an exterior stairway in the narrow passageway between that building and its neighbor, and a door leading directly into the cellar. That was where Tombs hoped to gain entry—to place the bombs against interior load-bearing members. It was the optimal way to use the two bombs.

Tombs remained at the street while the four Navy men went back into the passageway. Rob had a long pry bar stuck under his belt. He went down the stairs and examined the cellar door. The door was constructed of what appeared to be two-by-fours banded together with wrought iron. The wood showed the effects of long exposure to the weather, and the door and jamb did not meet as securely as they might.

"If there's no alarm system, this should be a snap," Rob whispered to Frank, who was behind him in the stairwell.

Frank had drawn his pistol as soon as he was between the buildings, out of casual view. He glanced back toward the street. Beau and Ike were leaning against the wall, as deep in the shadows as they could get. Tombs remained out by the street. Frank shook his head when he saw the CIA man take out a cigarette and light it. He's seen too many James Bond movies, Frank thought. He turned his attention back to the door.

Rob had edged the pry bar between door and jamb and was wiggling it closer to the latch, working the bar back and forth. The wood was complaining, but not loudly. Not yet.

"We don't want it to snap loud enough to draw attention," Frank whispered.

"I know," Rob replied, "but it's gonna be hard. This wood is so dry it could make enough noise to wake the dead. I'm trying to work it to pop the bolt without splitting the wood."

"Maybe with you prying and me pushing?" Frank suggested.

"Maybe. Let's try."

Frank stuck his pistol back in his belt, then leaned into the door, as close to the latch side as he could get his weight. He could feel some give in the wood, but the door resisted.

"Hang on. Let me get a new entry under the latch," Rob said. He pulled the pry bar out and worked it in again lower, wiggling it into position again. "Okay. Here we go again," he said, when he was ready. He pulled on the bar. Frank leaned into the door.

The wood strained. Frank could feel, more than hear, the protest of door and jamb. He got one foot up behind him, against the rock on the other side of the stairwell, and fought for every ounce of leverage he could get. When the door finally popped free of the jamb, Frank nearly went head-first into the cellar. He grabbed the edge of the door, keeping it from flying all the way open and arresting his own momentum, but it did expose him for an instant. If there had been anyone waiting inside the cellar, Frank would have been silhouetted clearly against the doorway, an unmissable target. Rob got his pistol out, but if there had been an armed watchman in the cellar, Rob would have been too late to save the chief.

There was no one waiting, though.

The other SEALs did not wait for an invitation. They were down the steps and in the cellar with Frank and Rob in less than ten seconds. Harry Tombs was only a step behind them. He pushed the door almost closed. Then he pulled out a small flashlight and started scanning the cellar, particularly the ceiling, looking for places to set the explosives.

"Be careful with that light," Frank said in a forced whisper. "Rob, you watch outside. Stay in the stairwell, but make sure we know if anyone comes this way."

Rob slid through the doorway, opening the

door just enough to let himself through—after looking to make sure that Tombs had turned off his flashlight. As soon as the door was pushed to again, Tombs clicked the light on again.

"We can't do this in the dark," Tombs whispered to Frank. "We have to know where to put the charges."

"Leave this part of it to us," Frank said. "Give me the light. You go over there by the stairs leading up into the house, just in case they've got a nosy watchman."

Tombs complied without saying anything. Frank used the light to look around the room. There were stacks of crates along one wall. They weren't standard munitions crates, and Frank doubted that weapons and ammunition would be stored in what was supposed to be a *political* headquarters. It didn't matter.

The cellar was simply one large room, with two metal columns—little more than glorified jacks— along the center line, about ten feet apart, supporting much of the weight of the building. Rafter and joist construction above. Crates along one wall. Electrical service and plumbing against another. No sign of a furnace or water heater. Waste pipe.

"Ike, Beau. We'll set the charges where the columns meet the joists. Wedge 'em and tie 'em in place." Frank pulled two coils of copper wire from his pockets. "It won't be the best solution, but it's the best we can come up with in a hurry. The blast should knock out the supporting columns below and raise hell with the structure above. If the wood in the rest of this place is in the same shape the door is, we ought to bring the whole thing down."

Even though the ceiling height was only eight feet, Ike and Beau each moved a box over from the wall and climbed up on them to work. Frank watched as they got started, then went to the outside door and looked through to check on Rhodes.

"Not a breath of anything, Chief," Rob whispered when he saw Frank peering out at him.

"It won't be long," Frank replied. "We're putting the packages in place now."

Rob nodded and turned his attention to the street again. He was lying on the steps, only the top half of his head exposed—enough to get his eyes above street level. He had his pistol out, lying on the first step down from the top.

When Frank moved back inside, he saw Tombs coming down the other flight of stairs—more quietly than he had gone up them. He hurried across the cellar to where Frank was.

"There is someone upstairs," Tombs said, whispering directly into the chief's ear. "The telephone rang. Someone answered it."

Frank nodded, then looked at the men working on the explosives. "Just about done," he whispered. "Just need to set the timers and activate them."

"Ninety minutes," Tombs said. Frank went to each of the men setting the bombs and repeated the message. He waited until the last wires were tied around the bombs and the timers set, then made a gesture with his right hand to tell the men to activate the bombs. They ought to go off within a fraction of a second of each other—if the timers were both accurate, and he was far from confident of that.

"Let's get out of here," Frank said, pushing Tombs toward the door. "I'll be last man out."

Tombs went first, then Ike, followed by Beau. Frank shoved the flashlight in his pocket and started to the door. Just then, the other door, at the top of the interior stairs, opened, and the single light in the middle of the cellar ceiling came on.

Damn! Frank thought. We can't take a chance on someone seeing what we've done. The crates Ike and Beau had climbed on were still sitting directly under the bombs. Frank's reaction was reasoned, even if the thought processes went too quickly for him to be consciously aware of every step. By the time a pair of boots and the lower half of a pair of khaki trousers appeared on the stair, he had moved along the wall and around toward the front of the building, until he was directly under the open wooden stairway.

Frank drew his knife and held it in a fighting stance, thumb resting on the guard, along the flat of the blade. For perhaps ten seconds, the man above just stood where he was, looking down into the cellar without moving. Then both feet shuffled and one came down to the next step.

He saw the crates! Frank thought. He moved

half a step to his left, near the edge of the stairs. For just an instant, Frank had to take his eyes off of the man above him. He thought about the others, waiting for him to emerge. God! Don't let any of them open that door again, Frank thought.

The watchman, or whoever he was, came down one more step. His boots were level with Frank's face.

I can't wait any longer. Frank reached up as he moved out from under the stairs, grabbing the man as high as he could and pulling him sideways. The man made a grunt of surprise but had time for nothing more before his body slammed into the cellar floor. His head bounced off the end of a tread. Before he could get his wits and his wind back, Frank was on top of him, one hand over the man's mouth, the other drawing his knife across the exposed throat. His victim had no chance to struggle, no opportunity to defend himself. Blood poured out of a six-inch-long cut, along with a strangled gurgle as the last of his breath bubbled through the gushing blood. Frank took no chances. He shifted his position and stabbed between the ribs of the man beneath him, directly into the heart. The body trembled violently for a few seconds, then was still.

Frank pushed himself to his feet, looking toward the top of the stairway. If there was anyone else there, he might be finished. But there was no shout, no sign of anyone. Frank hurried around the perimeter of the room, heading toward the door. Halfway there, Frank stopped.

After another glance at the top of the interior stairs, he crossed to the middle of the room and moved the two crates back to where they had been originally, along the far wall. And he unscrewed the single light bulb in the cellar. When he finally got to the exit, Beau and Rob were both at the bottom of the exterior stairwell, pistols in hand.

"You okay, Chief?" Rob asked, an urgent whisper. "We saw the light come on."

"I'm okay. Let's get moving. I left a body in there."

"You better wipe that blood off," Beau said as they started up the stairs. "That stand out a mile." He handed a red bandana to the chief, who mopped as much of the blood off his arm and hand as he could. There was nothing he could do about the stains on his shirt.

It was difficult to walk casually back toward the dock. Frank had to consciously will himself to walk slowly, to give the appearance of a man simply out for a late-night stroll. He could see the startled look in the eyes of the man whose throat he had slit, smell his sour breath. The man had been past middle aged, gray haired and grizzled, not some young hothead out to change the world at any price. It was only after Team Wolf was halfway back to their rubber boat that Frank realized that the pistol in the man's belt had been an antique, a Mauser that must have dated back to at least the First World War. The man had never drawn the weapon, had made no attempt. He had only had time to realize that he was going to die.

The blood that had soaked through Frank's shirt felt cold against his chest. He moved from side to side, staying in the deepest shadows, where the wet stain would not be so immediately obvious if they were stopped.

The five men started back down the slope to the water. The sound of a car or light truck rose and faded above and behind the five men. Beau, at the back of the team, glanced over his shoulder and watched for a few seconds, but no lights came into view. The vehicle was not coming after them. I hope nobody finds that body 'fore the bombs go, Beau thought. Might waste all this effort. They had not booby-trapped the bombs so they would go off if anyone attempted to remove or disarm them.

Ike, walking next to the chief, was the first to see the man on the deck of the lone freighter in port. He was leaning on the railing, smoking a cigarette. There was no place to go to escape notice. Ike nudged Frank and gestured with his head.

"Just keep going like we belong," Frank whispered, so softly that Ike barely heard him. Frank could tell when Tombs spotted the sailor, but Tombs kept going as well, just—gradually—sliding a step closer to the wall at his side, deeper into the shadows. The other SEALs eventually saw what was going on and were just as subtle in their own movements.

The merchant seaman spotted the five men. His head moved as he watched them come the rest of the way down the slope and turn toward the fishing boats. The man waved, but did not call out a greeting. Tombs waved back. So did Frank. Ike was too nervous, afraid of making a wrong move, so he pretended that he did not see the seaman. Rob nodded. Beau hunched his shoulders up a little—giving the impression he did not want to be bothered.

I hope that ship's leaving in the morning, Frank thought. Maybe it'll be gone before anyone thinks to ask questions down here.

The lit end of the cigarette traced an arc as the seaman tossed it into the harbor. He turned and moved out of sight of the five men on shore.

Once they got to the rubber boat, Frank and his men worked quickly to get away from the shore. "Twist that throttle off," Frank told Beau. They kept the tarp over their heads, but everyone but Beau spent nervous minutes looking out from under it, worried that there might yet be some pursuit before they got to safety. The seaman might say something to one of his crewmates— someone more suspicious by nature. Someone might find the body in the cellar. Anything.

As soon as they were five hundred yards out, Frank ripped his shirt off and balled it up, with the bloody section in the middle. He mopped at his chest and stomach, trying to get rid of the sticky reminder. Then he tied the shirt around the knife and sheath. By that time, the boat was nearly to its rendezvous. Frank slipped the package over the side and into the water, and pushed it under, and he watched to make certain that it did not bob back up. The knife would, he thought, be heavy enough to take itself and the shirt to the bottom of the gulf.

The launch was within twenty yards of *Bellman*, slowing down, when the bombs detonated. None of the SEALs noticed the initial flare. It was the sound of the blasts, rolling across the gulf, that caught their attention. Even at a distance of four miles, it was impossible to miss what the sound was. They looked across the water toward Aqaba. There was more smoke than fire visible, but the mostly unseen flames cast an orange hue to the billowing cloud above the port. From this angle, the smoke seemed to rise directly over the old fortifications.

The officer in charge of the launch whistled under his breath. Ike, who was the nearest SEAL, heard him whisper, "I don't want to know," very softly as he shook his head. The lieutenant (j.g.) wanted nothing more at that moment than to get aboard ship and forget all about this fishing expedition.

POST-MISSION

"Our ambassador to Jordan is in Aqaba tonight," Tombs said, when the team gathered for the debriefing. "He came to be present for *Bell-*

man's visit in the morning. Several high-ranking officials of the Jordanian government are also on hand."

"You know all this before we went out?" Frank asked.

Tombs shook his head. "It was to be expected, but, no, I didn't *know*, not for sure. Actually, I never even considered that possibility. We had our orders."

We really *were* on the hot seat, Ike thought, swallowing hard. They'd caught us, we would have just disappeared.

"According to early reports from inside Jordan, nobody knows what to make of it yet," Tombs continued. "The last I heard, the fire wasn't out." He paused, and focused on Frank. "That means they haven't been into the cellar, haven't found the sentry who stumbled in on us."

"They will," Frank said. "And they'll probably be able to tell how he died."

Tombs shrugged. "They'll be able to determine that the place was blown up by explosives, and might be able to pinpoint where they were planted. Depends how much effort they put into the investigation. That's not certain here. The one thing that does seem certain, at least from the reports I've been able to gather since we got back to the ship, is that there were no casualties outside that one building. No collateral damage."

"That's good to know," Rob said.

"Get your written reports to me in the morning," Tombs said. "After *Bellman* leaves Aqaba."

"You don't think Jordan will cancel the visit?" Ike asked.

"I doubt it, but it's possible," Tombs said. "When diplomats and politicians get involved, it's not always easy to predict what will happen."

THE REPORT

Harry Tombs drafted his own report before he had those of the SEALs. Their takes on the mission did not force him to change anything in the master document though, not even his summary.

```
I decided that it was essential that I
accompany the SEAL team on this mission
since I was the only member of the group
whose   command   of   Arabic   was   fluent
enough to offer a chance to talk our way
out of any potential trouble. Since we
needed to rely more on stealth than the
combat  abilities  of  the  SEALs,  there
seemed no reasonable alternative.
  We were spotted by a sailor in the
harbor,  and  that  command  of  Arabic
might  have  proven  necessary.  Fortu-
nately, we were able to depart without
delay.
```

Serenity came more easily than it normally did for Faud ibn Landin, despite the spate of bad news. He had just come from prayers. Now he sat with his eyes closed, savoring the moment of contentment. Rashish Suleiman stood across the desk from his boss, waiting, feeling a certain amount of surprise at the expression of—almost—happiness on ibn Landin's face.

"The infidel fools are playing right into our hands, Rashish," ibn Landin said without opening our eyes. "They think they are hurting us with their puny mosquito bites but all they are doing is strengthening us, God be praised."

"I'm not certain I see what you are leading to," Rashish said. "We have lost good people, and good friends. The people we hope to unite are in fear, looking to their own safety rather than taking jihad to the infidels."

Faud shook his head, very slowly, then opened his eyes. "The fools carry things too far, Rashish. At first, yes, their actions seemed likely to drive a wedge into our plans. Some of the groups might not have come to our conference, or might not have agreed to union. They worried that brothers were attacking brothers, but not now. Now, it is clear to all that we are being attacked from outside, and that drives us together, makes union almost a certainty, God willing. We will be unstoppable!"

"God willing," Rashish echoed.

"Everyone will come. Everyone will join, Rashish. Mark my words. The infidels do our work for us!"

8: DÉJÀ VU

PRE-MISSION

Bellman had made its visit to Aqaba, then proceeded back along the gulf, taking nearly two full days to rejoin the battle group, once again steaming south down the middle of the Red Sea. The SEAL team had taken a night off. Except for Frank, none of the SEALs had even seen Harry Tombs in fifty-four hours. Frank had delivered the written reports, his own and those of his men, to Tombs just after *Bellman* left Aqaba. That evening, Tombs had called Frank to his cabin to tell him that the latest reports confirmed that there had only been one fatality in the blast in Aqaba, and that the local authorities still professed to have no idea who had planted the bombs or why.

"The official line is that the police suspect that it was the work of some group protesting the visit of *Bellman* to the port," Tombs said. His grin came and went so quickly it might have been subliminal. "They're looking for rivalries among the terrorist groups."

"You have any idea how much longer we're going to be out here?" Frank asked, ignoring Tombs's glee at the misdirection.

"Not exactly. It depends on when—or if—ibn Landin gets his big meeting going. Once that ends, our job is done."

The following day, Tombs saw Frank just long enough to tell him that the tcam would not be in action again that night. The next morning, word was passed to the SEALs to report to the conference room at 1100 hours.

THE BRIEFING

"I have some positive news for you," Harry Tombs said, as soon as the door was closed behind the last man and everyone had taken seats at the table. "We have hard intel that the terrorist summit is definitely on again, scheduled to start in three days, and it will be at one of the sites we know about in Sudan. The precise location won't be decided until within twenty-four hours of the start. But we may be able to influence that choice. That is the mission for tonight."

Tombs raised the target folder and dropped it on the table. He put his hand on top of the folder then before Frank could reach across the table for it.

"One of the Libyan-sponsored groups has already moved its advance unit into Port Sudan,

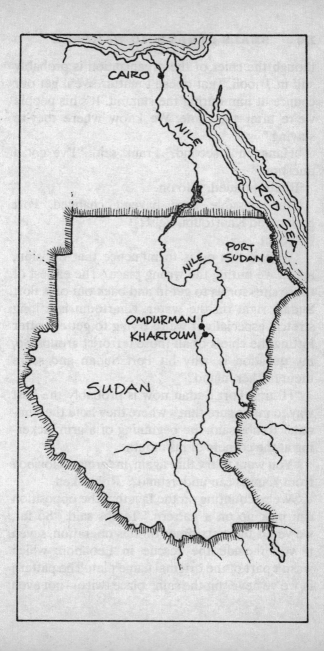

CAIRO

NILE

RED SEA

PORT SUDAN

NILE

OMDURMAN
KHARTOUM

SUDAN

though the chief of the organization is probably still in Tripoli. That doesn't matter. We'll get our chance at him during the summit. It's his people we're after this time. We know where they're staying."

"Hang on a second," Frank said. "I've got a question."

Tombs nodded. "Go on."

"The possible sites haven't changed, Port Sudan and Khartoum, right?"

"Right."

"Well, if this op is to influence that decision, aren't we hitting the wrong place? The easiest of those sites for us to get in and back out of is Port Sudan, right on the water. Khartoum is a long stretch, especially if we're trying to get out after hitting the chiefs of all those terrorist groups. So, my question is, why hit Port Sudan and scare them farther inland?"

"Hitting Port Sudan now is probably the best way to make sure that's where they hold the summit," Tombs said, the beginning of a grin flickering at the corners of his mouth.

"You want to try that again, in terms a plowboy from Kansas can understand?" Rob asked.

"We're counting on the fact that the opposition can pick up on a pattern," Tombs said. "So far, we've hit them six times on this operation, seven if you include the rescue in Lebanon, which wasn't part of the original game plan. The pattern is, we've never hit the same place twice—not even close. If we hit Port Sudan now, it's apt to look like the safest location in the region to the people we're after."

"Okay, I see where you're going," Rob said. "Maybe you've got something, but I hope you're not betting the farm on this being enough to make them choose Port Sudan over Khartoum. You didn't go far enough with your pattern. We haven't even hit the same *country* twice, so that might just make them think that anywhere in Sudan will be safe."

"There are no guarantees," Tombs said. "In the end, ibn Landin might flip a coin to decide where to hold the meeting. But, among other considerations, these terrorists leaders have got to remember that the U.S. hit Khartoum with cruise missiles after the embassy bombings in east Africa. And more than one of the men we're after is paranoid enough to believe he is worth the million-plus dollars a cruise missile costs."

"We'll handle the final target when the time comes," Frank said, glancing at Rob. "Wherever it is. What about tonight? That's what we need to concentrate on now."

Tombs slid the target folder across to Frank. "Tonight, we hit a small hotel near the Port Sudan airport, on the southern edge of the city. It's right on the highway leading south out of Port Sudan and on to Khartoum. A side note: that highway accounts for about half of the paved road in the entire country. Back to the mission.

"The hotel dates back to the decade before World War One, when Great Britain and Egypt jointly ruled the Sudan. The rooms are large and airy, intended to serve the imperial elite. A veranda extends completely around the first floor, a balcony completely around the second floor, with doors to each guest room. Also interior corridors and doors. In its early days, the hotel served mostly colonial officials and travelers doing business with them, and the occasional member of nobility off to see the empire. Currently, the guests are usually tourists or business travelers. But there are no regular guests at the hotel just now. We have that for a fact. The entire establishment—some two dozen guest rooms, dining room, and a bar to serve non-Muslims—has been taken over by the African World Liberation Front, the latest in a series of names this group has gone by. Karim Nazir is, we believe, originally Syrian, but he's worked out of Libya at least since the Iraqi quarantine began. Right now, there are perhaps fifteen members of his organization at the hotel, making preparations for the arrival of their leaders, who are expected the day before the summit conference starts."

"Is the target the building or the people?" Rob asked.

"The people. We hit late at night, when hotel staff is at a minimum," Tombs said. "We have a chance to cripple Nazir's organization, at least temporarily, take out some of his top people, men responsible for at least a half dozen terrorist attacks in Africa and Europe. There are photographs of several of the men we believe are at the hotel in the packet." He gestured at the target folder Frank was leafing through.

In addition to the usual maps and satellite photographs, there were a dozen photographs that had been taken on the ground, showing the hotel and the approaches from the shore of the Red Sea. Detailed sketches were also included, as well as floor plans for the hotel's interior. None of the photographs of individuals were particularly good. They were all grainy, enlarged portions of long-range snapshots, with the rest of the originals cropped out. Recognition based solely on those photographs would be difficult.

"According to the information we have, Nazir's men are handling security within the hotel. At night, that probably means one man in the lobby, another perhaps roaming the halls. Local police are responsible for outside security, but until the principals arrive that probably means no more than their usual patrols taking a look now and then," Tombs said. "Our operating protocol calls for evading any police going in, and engaging them on the way out only if there is no practical alternative. But if it's necessary, you are authorized to take all necessary action. The Sudanese are definitely not on our most-favored-nation list. They're still listed as a state supporting terrorism. But the plan is to get in and out before there is time for the local authorities to mount a significant response to the attack."

"Twenty-four guest rooms, public rooms. Fifteen targets, perhaps a handful of hotel employees who are not targets. Four of us," Frank said, as he passed the last sheets of paper from the target folder to Rob. "I didn't see anything here to show where the telephone lines enter the hotel. The best way to give ourselves a couple of extra minutes before the cops show up is to cut the telephone line before we start. With all the cell phones around these days, that's no guarantee, but it's still a necessary bit of insurance."

"Good point," Tombs said. "Let's get to the tactical planning."

The four SEALs spent nearly two hours going over the photographs, charts, sketches, and other material in the target folder, talking out plans for the operation, and deciding on details of the weapons and methods they would use—subject, always, to what they found when they reached the target.

"This worries me," Frank said, tapping one of the satellite photographs. "There's a police station less than a mile from the hotel. That means we don't have a lot of time. We're not going to be able to go through that hotel room by room. Not with just four of us. The first noise loud enough to be heard outside the hotel, the first chance anyone inside has to call for help, and we could be counting seconds instead of minutes before the local cops show up."

"Silencers, knives," Beau said, shrugging. "Be better we knew what rooms were empty."

"Nowhere in the orders does it say we have to take out all the bogeys," Rob said. "We go in the back way, take out as many as we can without making it a one-way job, then head back for the shore and leave a final noisy farewell."

"Our problems might not end at the water's edge," Frank said. "After being hit with cruise missiles, the Sudanese government has to be viewed as definitely hostile to Americans. We sure as hell won't get the benefit of the doubt. The police have a couple of launches to patrol with, and Sudan does have something of a navy, probably at least a couple of glorified gunboats available at Port Sudan. We don't want their navy chasing us back here. Embarrassing to say the least. The skipper would probably be annoyed as hell."

"We got hot pursuit on us, we might not get picked up at all," Rob said. "*Bellman* might have orders to leave us behind, feed us to the wolves if necessary."

"I'd ask Tombs," Frank said, "but that wouldn't prove anything. If he thought it necessary, he'd lie up one side and down the other. We'll just take a few extra precautions, be ready for whatever happens. We're the only ones we can trust not to fuck with us."

THE PREPARATION

The men did not spend a lot of time deciding on armament. That was fairly well dictated by the mission. M-16s with the KAC suppressors.

Frank decided on the RPD, a Soviet belt-fed light machine gun easily carried and operated by one man Instead of the non-disintegrating metal link belt often associated with the weapon, he chose a drum with a 100-hundred round belt that could be attached underneath the receiver of the weapon. Unlike the belt, the drum is easy to remove and replace with a loaded one, which would probably come in handy.

Ike would carry a rifle with the M203 grenade launcher attached, and the bandoleer of grenades he packed for it was a mix of high explosive and smoke rounds. Automatic pistols with silencers. Knives. A pair of hand grenades each. Two ropes

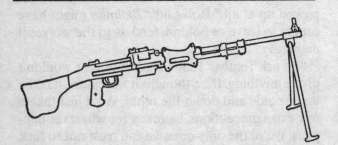

RPD

with padded grappling hooks. Ammunition for the rifles and pistols.

The extra precautions included diving gear, and a set of radio code words. Plan B.

THE MISSION

The SEALs boarded their rapid penetration boat on *Bellman*'s port side, the east, out of sight of anyone who might be observing from the Sudanese shore. Harry Tombs gave them a final wave from the deck above before the small craft started moving east and north, away from the ship and farther from shore.

"This goes on much longer," Rob whispered to Frank, "folks are going to put two and two together and figure out that *Bellman* must have something to do with our jobs. They'll start watching whenever she's around."

"Not much longer for us," Frank said. "After that . . . well, I don't think anyone's foolish enough to try to attack *Bellman*. Folks know just what sort of hell an American battle group can drop on their heads. Anyway, another month and the battle group is due to rotate home."

"And we should be home long before that," Rob said. "I'm ready for it."

"Just don't start salivating yet, Farmer. We got work to do first. Keep your eyes open. We're turning for the run into shore."

There were lights in Port Sudan and on the hillsides behind the city—an easy beacon. Fingers of light, reflections, reached out across the gentle swell of the water, appearing to be aimed directly at the men in the RPB. It might be an optical illusion, but it was enough to make all four men stay as low in the boat as they could, presenting the smallest target possible for any watching eyes.

Beau angled left, away from the greatest concentration of lights. A rotating beacon marked the position of the airport, and he kept the nose of the RPB pointed just left of that, south. There were no scheduled flights into the airport during the next several hours, no reason to expect any air traffic.

It was nearly twenty minutes before Frank, at the prow of the RPB, was certain that he could pick out the lights of the hotel from the clutter on shore. Not much light was showing on the seaward side of the building, just at the corners of the veranda and balcony, small yellow bulbs. As the boat moved farther southwest, he could see lights in one room on the first floor, at the far corner. That was, according to the plans Frank and the others had studied, the manager's office.

The boat was halfway to shore when Ike suddenly realized that he had not been at all nervous this time. I guess I've finally got used to it, he thought. Later, he might worry that it was becoming *too* routine, that he should have some feeling more than "going to the office" on the way in.

Later, not now. Ike just continued to scan his side of the boat, against the chance that a local patrol might happen upon them.

Two hundred yards out, Beau put the tiller over to run almost parallel to shore, south. The plan was to land a couple of hundred yards away from the direct line between sea and hotel. The SEALs had debated their landing point at some length during the planning session, the advantages of having the boat as close as possible when they were ready to exfiltrate against the possible benefits of that extra distance. The likelihood that there would be hostiles left alive in the hotel had settled the matter. "We don't want to let them stand on the balcony and pot away at us," Frank had said. "Give them a longer shot this way."

Finally, they were directly off the spot they had chosen for their landing. Beau turned the RPB again and headed toward shore, throttling back a little, more concerned about minimizing the boat's wake and noise than in speed.

The shore was rocky, and there was little room for the boat below the first rise. The four men dragged the RPB clear of the water and into what little cover they found available for it.

Once the boat was secure, Frank led his team toward the hotel. At first, they stayed right at the shore, taking advantage of the several feet of cover the rising bank provided them. Then they moved up and toward the road. A line of shops helped to shield them from direct observation from the road. In any case, there was little traffic. Two cars headed south, away from the city, while the SEALs were moving into position.

Eighty yards from the nearest corner of the hotel, Frank and his men went down, spread across about twenty yards, to observe. There was no hurry now, not before they struck; the hurry would come once they made their presence known. Frank used compact binoculars to survey each window he could see on the hotel, working across the first floor and coming back along the second. The only visible light was still in the manager's office on the first floor. Frank assumed that there would also be lights on in the lobby, but that faced the road, and he could not see that side of the building.

Frank put the binoculars away, then waited for another car to pass on the road, also heading away from the city. Then he got to his feet and started moving. The others got up and moved into position behind him. It wasn't necessary for Frank to give any commands now. Ike took the right flank, Rob the left. Beau held back a few yards as rear guard.

Parking for the hotel was on the south side. A half dozen cars were in the lot. Checking those was the next order of business for the SEALs. They went from vehicle to vehicle, glancing in, making certain none were occupied.

Then they moved around to the seaward side of the building. Beau uncoiled one of the ropes with the padded grapples. Standing back from the

edge of the first-floor veranda, he started twirling
the grapple, then, when he had enough speed to
the plastic-covered steel hooks, tossed it. The
grapple caught on the railing of the balcony on
the first try. Beau gave the line a couple of exper-
imental tugs, then moved in closer to the building
and scaled the rope hand over hand. He ran
silently along the balcony, toward the road, heading for the point where the telephone line came
in from the road. Beau had to climb up onto the
railing and stretch to reach the line. He sliced it
with his knife. The severed line fell away.

Frank followed Beau up the rope, then Ike and
Rob came up. It took less than a minute for all
four men to get to the second floor balcony and
spread out along the seaward side of the building.

Here's where it starts to get tricky, Frank
thought. We don't know how many rooms are
occupied, or which ones. Each man was between
the door and window of a different room. Frank
counted to thirty, silently, his left hand near the
door handle. His men were watching him for their
signal to move. If any of the doors were unlocked,
that would give the team a silent point of entry.
They would try doors, then windows. Any rooms
they could confirm as being unoccupied would
give them that much more of an advantage. They
would work silently for as long as possible.

. . . *Twenty-nine, thirty.* Frank took in a deep
breath and held it while he slowly tried to move
the door's handle down. There was no give; it was
locked. Frank looked to either side. None of the

others had found an open door, either. All four men moved to the windows. They were all casement affairs, made to open out onto the balcony. All were secured.

Shift right and try again, Frank thought. That spread his men around the far corner. Ike and Rob were out of his direct view. There was no need to wait this time. Frank tried the door's handle and, when it didn't give, moved to the window. It had been pulled closed, but there was a tiny gap in the center. The windows had not been secured.

Frank pulled the window pane slowly, anxious that he not make any noise. Beau, to his left, saw the window come open. Frank moved to the corner of the building and gestured to the other two men. They had a quiet way into the hotel.

Beau was the first man through the window, with Frank standing by, in case Beau needed help—in case there was someone sleeping too lightly in the room.

"No one here," Beau whispered, after just a few seconds. The other three came in. Ike, the last man through the window, pulled it shut, an instinctive precaution. Leaving the window open would be a clear signpost if anyone saw it.

Sixteen of the hotel's twenty-four guest rooms were on the upper floor. The rest were on the seaward side of the first floor. Public rooms were in front of them. The lobby was open to the second floor, with a large skylight above the atrium. Once the SEALs left the room they were in, they would be visible to anyone looking up from the first floor.

There was a gentle hum from an air conditioner. The room the SEALs in was cool—cooler, at least, than the outside.

After a few seconds, Frank thought that he could almost feel the vibrations of machinery through his feet, a gentle throbbing, almost like the feel of a ship under way.

Maybe we should have worn night-vision gear and knocked out the electricity, Frank thought. Too late now. My brain must be rusting up. It was an unusual time—for Frank—to have misgivings surface. He gave himself an extra couple of seconds to go over the next steps in his head. Once the action started, there would be too little time. Then it might all reach the point of act and react. Mistakes then could quickly be fatal.

Frank checked the selector switch on his rifle by touch. To start, he wanted it on single shot—until the opposition was roused and started to respond. A single silenced shot might not be recognized for what it was at first. It could give the SEALs a few extra seconds to operate unmolested.

"Get ready," Frank whispered, a warning to his men. Rob was across the room, at the door leading out to the balcony. Ike and Beau were closer to Frank, ready to follow him into the corridor ringing the atrium, ready to back up their leader if the action started too soon. Frank was at the side of the door leading to the interior corridor, pressed against the wall—one hand on his rifle, the other on the door handle. A deep breath: Frank took it in slowly and let it out in a long whisper.

Now.

Frank pressed down on the handle and drew the door open, slowly, and just far enough to let him look down the corridor to the left. He had no idea where any sentry might be. There was no one in sight in the narrow angle Frank permitted himself at first. He opened the door a little more, giving himself a slightly broader view of the second story corridor and a partial view of the front of the lobby, downstairs.

Nothing.

The open central area of the hotel was poorly lit, but it seemed bright to Frank, coming out of near total darkness. On the second floor, there were single light bulbs in each corner of the open corridor—no more than twenty-five-watt bulbs. In the lobby below, there was the glow of a light coming from the right, but the light itself was not visible.

Frank pushed the door open the rest of the way. Beau had been waiting for that. He went down on his stomach, across from Frank, and crawled forward just enough to be able to see the other half of the second floor corridor—his rifle ready in case someone was there.

Empty.

The reception desk in the lobby was to the

right, under the overhang of the upstairs corridor. From the doorway where the SEALs were, only the front of the desk was visible.

Ike stepped over Beau and moved to the right, into the open corridor, staying as near the wall as he could, and taking care to make no sound at all. His job was to cover the doorway to the manager's office, to the left, at the front of the hotel, and he had to move several steps along the corridor to get an open view of that door under the overhang. That movement also made him the closest person to the stairway at the right front of the hotel.

If all of them are in the rooms downstairs, we could turn this into target practice, Ike thought. Space ourselves to cover all the doors down there. He knew it wasn't likely. At least some of the terrorists would be in rooms on this floor, a more immediate threat.

Frank also stepped across Beau, moving left. Frank figured to be the one who would have to take out the sentry below, especially if he was behind the reception desk—which seemed likely. He moved his rifle, holding it in both hands now, slowly bringing the butt up to his shoulder.

All four SEALs were ready for action. Rob was at the side of the interior door now, his rifle out and covering the front of the second story. Too much light, he thought, blinking until his eyes adjusted. Be better in the dark.

Ike had the same thought. Although it had not been covered in the planning, he moved to the corner nearest him, then reached up and unscrewed the light bulb, just until the light went out. Beau and Frank both glanced at him, quickly, then looked back the way they had been looking. In the open doorway, Rob gave a little nod, just to himself. A good idea, he thought. We get a chance, we should douse the others up here.

All four men heard the scraping of a chair below, and an unintelligible mumbling. Heavy steps were the next sound from the first floor.

Frank eased his finger onto the trigger of his rifle. Whoever was manning the front desk was on the move. He noticed that a light went out, Frank thought. He waited. It was no more than a few seconds, but seemed longer. A man—carrying a light bulb in one hand and an AK-47 in the other—came out from behind the reception desk and turned toward the stairs.

He did not reach them. Frank sighted and squeezed off a single shot. Despite the KAC suppressor, the shot sounded incredibly loud to Frank, though it was nowhere near as loud as the sounds made when the bullet struck its target—a final grunt from the man below, the clatter of his rifle dropping to the floor, the light bulb popping on contact, and even the softer sounds of the body as it collapsed, dead before it came to rest.

Frank let out his breath as he looked for any reaction from the other terrorists in the hotel. It was time for the SEALs to start moving quickly, checking the other rooms on the second floor, looking for the rest of the men alleged to be in the establishment.

The others had already started. Rob and Ike each moved to the nearest room doors and tried the handles. Rob was the only one to get an unlocked door. He swung it open and entered quickly, moving off to the side, his rifle tracking toward the double bed in the room—an empty bed. He came back to the doorway, careful about exposing himself again, moving left, to the next room.

Ike kept his eyes on the manager's office as he moved toward the next door on his side of the corridor. He thought he heard a voice below, muffled, perhaps questioning. He'll come out to look soon, Ike told himself. Either the night manager or another of the terrorists. No matter which, Ike's job remained the same ... to put the target down. Harboring a terrorist was as much a crime as being a terrorist.

The first warning that the office door was open was light coming out of it, followed by a voice speaking in Arabic. Ike could understand nothing of what was said, but could make a good guess of the gist: *What happened out there?* It wouldn't take long for whoever had asked the question to spot the body. Ike brought his rifle up, ready to shoot as soon as he had a clear target—and he hoped that it would be soon enough to forestall a shouted warning.

It was close. Ike thought that he heard something from the man below just as he pulled the trigger on his M-16. Whatever the man who had come out of the manager's office had to say was cut off after no more than a word though. At least he didn't shout, Ike thought as he tracked the man dropping to the floor. Maybe we've got a little longer.

A second man came out of the manager's office. This one did have time to shout before Ike shot him.

"Move!" Frank ordered. Ike turned and kicked open the locked door he had tried less than a minute before. As he did, he was aware of another corridor light going out, but did not see Rob reach up and smash it with the suppressor on his rifle.

A figure moved on the bed in the room Ike had broken into, roused from sleep by the sound of the door being forced. He had no time to do anything more than blink twice before the muzzle of Ike's rifle flashed. The man died without a sound, flopping over onto the rifle that lay next to him in bed.

Frank and Rob each broke into occupied rooms and took care of the occupants as efficiently as Ike had. Only Beau did not join in the smash and shoot. He slid forward a little, and remained prone in the corridor, his rifle covering the bottom of the stairwell and the front of the lobby.

During the next forty-five seconds, so much happened that none of the SEALs was ever completely certain of the order in which the events took place. Two more doors were smashed in, two more terrorists—sleeping or just coming awake—were killed. Men came out of one of the rooms on the first floor, ready for trouble. They started spraying bullets—unsilenced—toward the second floor before they could consciously look for targets. At the same time, someone in one of the front rooms on the second floor started shooting, the bullets tracing a pattern in the door before the man inside pulled it open.

Ike had swiveled toward the sound of the latest shooting. As soon as the door on the second floor opened, he moved his right hand and fired the HE grenade in his M203 launcher into the opening. The man coming out of the room, still firing his AK-47, was caught high in the chest by the grenade. When it exploded, the man's torso virtually disintegrated with blood, bone, and bits of flesh being blasted for yards in every direction.

Frank took one of his hand grenades and tossed it over the railing, angling his throw so that it would bounce under the overhang. When it went off there was a temporary halt in the fire coming toward the SEALs.

"Go!" Frank called, loud enough for his men to hear. He gestured with his left hand to make certain that everyone got the message. It was time to get out.

Ike and Rob backed through the nearest rooms, heading for the veranda. Frank moved back to the room the SEALs had originally broken into, then waited in the doorway—spraying bullets at still unopened doors and down into the lobby—while Beau withdrew and crossed to the veranda door.

Beau covered Frank as he followed.

Outside, Rob had uncoiled the second grappling line, secured the hook, and dropped the rope over the side. Ike and Rob went down the ropes together. Rob controlled his descent with his legs and one hand. He had his rifle in the other hand, searching for anyone who might be waiting for them below. The rope burned Rob's left hand, and he dropped the last several feet to the ground, falling backward but landing sitting up, his rifle still pointed toward the building.

Ike and Rob backed away from the building together, giving themselves better angles to cover the corners. Beau and Frank came down the ropes, scarcely checking their speed at all—just enough to minimize the odds of breaking or spraining something that might slow them down on the ground.

Once all four of them were out of the building, they moved by twos—two scurrying toward the sea, the other two spraying additional bullets into the hotel to discourage pursuit. After they were fifty yards from the building, Ike launched another grenade, aiming for the open door on the second floor, hoping that the round might catch one or two more terrorists.

After that, there was some return fire from

inside the hotel, but it did not seem to be aimed very carefully—automatic fire sprayed in the general direction of the shore.

When the SEALs heard the not-distant-enough tones of a police siren, Frank called for the others to quit firing. "We're just showing them where we are," he added. "Down to the water, then turn for the boat."

They ran.

At the water's edge, behind the short embankment, Frank paused and looked back. Trouble was gathering at the hotel. A police car, flashing lights identifying it clearly, had pulled up near the corner. A small searchlight started to probe the darkness between hotel and shore. Men were shouting. Two men with rifles were visible on the southern side of the veranda.

Farther off, more sirens were walling.

We don't want to wait for the party, Frank thought. They got to the hotel faster than I expected. He trotted toward the boat, shaking his head while he ran. Unless luck started running with them, the night wasn't over yet.

By the time Frank caught up with his men, they had the boat in the water and the engine running. Frank climbed in and Beau opened the throttle. He wasn't worried about stealth, just putting as much distance between boat and shore as possible.

"Rob, get on the radio and send the code that

we're on the way," Frank said after catching his breath. "Everybody, watch for any move to intercept us."

Frank put a fresh double-drum magazine in his rifle, then took off his web belt with the rest of his ammunition. One by one, the others did the same. If they had to abandon the RPB, the seconds they saved themselves now might make all the difference in the world.

"Look to port, Chief," Beau said. "Racing right along shore."

Frank looked, then picked up his binoculars to confirm what he had already guessed. A large launch, probably police, was hurrying from the port toward the hotel. Its searchlight was scanning the water ahead of it, though the beam was still not within a thousand yards of the SEALs.

"I see it," Frank said. "Several men on the foredeck, armed. Get into your diving gear. There's still a chance they won't spot us, but let's be ready to swim if they do."

Ike was the first man to get his boots off and his air tank on. Carrying his flippers and mask with him, he went to the stern and took over the tiller to give Beau a chance to get into his equipment. Ike divided his attention between the beam of light moving across the water and the more distant running lights that marked the position of *Bellman*. The ship was still more than three miles away. That's gonna be a long swim, Ike thought, turning to look at the launch again. He eased the throttle open a little farther.

"Okay, kid, I'll take it," Beau whispered after less than a minute. His face mask was resting on top of his head. He had his flippers in one hand.

Ike moved out of the way and let Beau get back in position. "Let's get as close to home as we can before we have to swim," Ike said.

Beau grinned. "I got no argument with that. Better we don't swim at all." He glanced toward the launch. "Still a chance."

That chance faded seconds later. "Another boat putting out from the port," Rob said. "Looks like it's moving fast."

All four men looked for the new set of lights, the distant shape on the water. The second boat was larger, its searchlight clearly more powerful. "Some sort of cutter, I think," Frank said. "Looks like we've got their navy after us now too."

"How good's their fire control?" Rob asked.

Frank shook his head. "I don't want to test it." He trained the binoculars on the bow of the boat. It was clearly larger than the launch that had put out first, perhaps over a hundred feet long, and there was a gun turret on the foredeck. "About a five-incher, I think," Frank said. The cutter was not aimed directly at the RPB, but it was not simply following the shoreline the way the police launch was.

"Time for Plan B. Let's get out of here before they start shooting," Frank said, dropping the binoculars and reaching for his fins. "Scuttle the boat and into the water. Ike, send *Bellman* the code that we'll be swimming."

Ike had already started bringing the hand radio up. He checked the frequency, keyed the transmitter, then spoke a single word: *Barfly*. As soon as he released the transmitter key, there were three short clicks, *Bellman*'s acknowledgment.

Fins and masks on. Air regulators in mouths. A quick test to make certain systems were functioning. Rifles and pistols would be left in the RPB, extra weight to help it sink once the four men had slashed at the sides and bottom with their knives. They rode the boat until it was awash, then each man rolled clear after taking a compass reading— a heading for the swim to *Bellman*. The ship was still nearly three miles away.

Do they have depth charges? Ike wondered as he took up station to Frank's right. It might take the cutter three or four minutes to reach the divers, if the ship had a fix on where they went into the water. A depth charge did not have to be particularly accurate to disable a diver in the water. The concussion of an explosion could be devastating fifty yards or more from the detonation.

There was no need for the divers to go deep. Depth would give no advantage, and the need to come up slowly for decompression at the far end of the swim would simply extend the time they were vulnerable. Frank had decided earlier that, unless the Sudanese got directly overhead, they wouldn't go deeper than fifteen feet. *Bellman* would be looking for them to be shallow. The ship would be able to track the swimmers.

It would slow down to pick them up, and stop the propellers completely at the critical time to avoid any danger of a diver getting caught by a blade or the turbulence they kicked up in the water around them. The only tricky part might be if the Sudanese cutter decided to get close enough to see the divers come out of the water, and that would be dangerous for the Sudanese. Even without a clandestine operation under way, *Bellman*'s normal security protocols would require that it warn the cutter away. Sudan would not dare challenge. The U.S. battle group packed more firepower than the entire nation of Sudan could assemble.

Even shallow, the water was dark. The only illumination they had came from the luminous dials of their instruments—compasses, watches, and depth and air gauges. The four divers stayed bunched up, shoulders almost touching. Frank set the pace, not just because he was the team leader, but because he was also the slowest swimmer in the group. He made frequent checks of his compass and gauges. Without attention, it would be too easy to drift off heading or depth.

Easy, even leg kicks. A glance to either side now and then to make sure that the others were still with him. Check instruments. Keep the breathing regular, steady. That was one of the first lessons a diver learned, but even after many years, it could sometimes be hard to remember.

Rob was on the right flank, outside Ike, staying a head back. *Bellman* will stay at least three miles offshore, he reminded himself. They might come close to that limit for the pickup, but they would not come closer. At least a two-mile swim for us, maybe two-and-a-half. Time for a lot to happen if the locals decide to play rough. I'd like to know what's going on, if that cutter is coming after us.

The only way to know that would be to surface long enough to scan the horizon. That would slow the swimmers, and might do nothing more than give the locals a good fix on their position. Frank would have to be the one to make the decision to surface. Rob did not expect him to.

Beau was on the left of the formation. Closest to the enemy, was the way he thought of it. Not that he expected the enemy to do anything. They be fools to, he thought. Uncle Sugar not gonna take no crap from these bastards. Beau tried to focus on what he could hear, beyond the sound of his own breathing and his regulator supplying air. If one of the Sudanese craft did come close, they would hear it before it was directly over them, the pulsing of propellers beating water, perhaps the throbbing of an engine. It might not provide very much warning, but a little, enough to let the divers take evasive action. The approach of an enemy vessel would mean that the swimmers would have to go deeper, to avoid getting sucked into a propeller and to make it harder for the enemy to get at them.

The SEALs had been in the water forty minutes when the divers first started to become aware of a faint throbbing sound in the water. It was coming from in front of them, rather than behind. Then a sharp pinging—three close together, followed by two spaced farther apart. *Bellman*.

The throbbing noise stopped. *Bellman* had shut down its propellers.

Frank took his men deeper, to give the ship's hull plenty of clearance. The plan was for them to come up east of the vessel, to keep *Bellman* between them and the Sudanese coast. Home free, Frank thought. If there had been potentially hostile craft close, where they could see the pickup, the signal would have been different.

POST-MISSION

Ten minutes after he had drunk it, Ike could still feel the warmth of the long shot of whisky. Harry Tombs had pulled out a bottle as soon as he was alone with the SEALs, before they had a chance to go to their compartment and change out of their wet clothing. And he went with them.

"We're picking up all kinds of good stuff from shore," he said while the men dried off and put on dry uniforms. "Police and navy traffic, a scream of protest from the government. All kinds of good stuff," he repeated.

"We gave them something to think about," Frank said. "But that was one hairy mother."

"In one ten-minute broadcast, they managed to suggest that the attack was staged by Ethiopian terrorists, Israeli agents, and American-backed mercenaries. They don't know who to blame."

"They say anything about casualties?" Ike asked.

"According to the last report, local authorities killed at least five members of the attacking force," Tombs said, grinning so widely it looked as if his face might split open. "By that time, we already knew all four of you were safely in the water."

"What about their casualties?" Frank asked. "I'm sure we greased at least six of them, maybe as many as ten or more."

"The news report said that six civilian tourists were murdered in the hotel, along with two employees."

"Bullshit," Rob said. "Civilian tourists and hotel employees don't run around with Kalishnikovs."

Tombs shrugged. "Doesn't matter what they say. People will believe what they want to. We should know for certain how well you scored within twenty-four hours. It looks good though."

THE REPORT

A few hours later, as he completed his after-action report, Harry Tombs was less certain. He was puzzled, and did not try to hide that in his summary.

After three hours of almost hysterical screaming about the "outrage" of the attack, Sudanese media went completely silent on the subject, and Sudanese government spokesmen retreated to a firm "No Comment" in reply to every question by the few representatives of the international press in Sudan. They have not gone so far as to deny that any attack took place, but they do not confirm it either. The reasons for this abrupt change of approach are not at all clear, and must be seen as troubling for that reason.

"Either they know something, or they think they do," Tombs whispered, staring at the screen of his portable computer. The worry was enough to trouble his sleep.

9: PEPPERMINT

PRE-MISSION

"I thought we weren't doing anything else until the big op," Rob said, after the call came for the SEALs to report to the conference room aboard *Bellman*.

"That was the last word I had from Tombs," Frank confirmed. "Who knows what the spook has come up with? Maybe the summit meeting has been cancelled, or postponed again. Just keep your shirt on. We'll find out soon enough."

"Maybe Tombs guessed wrong about the effect hitting Port Sudan would have," Ike said. "Maybe they've moved the summit to Afghanistan or Timbuktu."

"It won't be Afghanistan," Frank said. "Some of the terrorists scheduled to attend wouldn't put themselves that completely in ibn Landin's power. That's why he had to set it up in Sudan in the first place. Those buggers don't trust each other." One of the early briefings Frank had attended that the others had not had laid out a

list of conditions that had apparently ruled the
choice of a site for the meeting. There had to be
an amenable government in the country. There
had to be a variety of easy transportation options
in and out. The location had to be acceptable to
all of the groups invited. Libya was objected to by
several leaders; they feared Khadafi might try to
take control. Lebanon wasn't secure; there was
too much chance of Israeli intervention, and the
Lebanese government wasn't completely reliable
as far as several of the groups were concerned.
And ibn Landin had ruled out anything on the
Arabian peninsula. The Saudis had a million-dollar price on his head, in addition to the five million dollars being offered by the Americans. The
Gulf states were all too beholden to the Saudis to
be trustworthy; and most of them were too ready
to deal with Americans. Yemen was almost an
alternative, but it was too close to the Saudis, and
not entirely reliable.

"I don't think it'll be moved," Frank said. "Postponed or cancelled, maybe, but if they hold it, figure it's going to be in Sudan. Now, let's go find out
what Tombs has to say."

THE BRIEFING

The trek to the conference room was routine
by now. The SEALs went in and took accustomed
seats at the table. Harry Tombs came in less than

a minute later. The first thing the SEALs noticed was that Tombs was carrying a target folder.

"Okay, I know I said that we were done until the big dance," Tombs said as he moved to his usual position at the table. "I thought we were, but we've got maybe a big bonus dropped in our laps, something just too sweet to pass up."

"Don't bury us in soft soap," Frank said.

"Uh, right. First off, we've replaced everything you were forced to abandon last night. And then some. I had some special extras flown in for the final strike. They'll think they're being attacked by a whole damned battalion."

Rob snorted at the last word. "Tombs, we've got teams, platoons, detachments, special operations groups. We don't have battalions. At least get your lingo right."

"You know it, and I know it, but the terrorists we hit won't know who's clobbering the hell out of them." Tombs grinned.

"Hey, we're getting off the track again," Frank said before Rob could get in another comment. "Let's get this op out of the way before we start thinking about the next one."

Tombs nodded. "You're right, Chief," he said. "My enthusiasm is running over. Tonight's op." He paused while he looked around at the four SEALs.

"We've learned that there's an extra delegation coming to the terrorist summit, an unexpected addition. The Iraqi government has decided to send two members of its Revolutionary Council,

and one of the leaders of the Bath party, to urge
the terrorists to step up their activities against
American and British interests. Because of the
continuing sanctions, and what they see as their
own security concerns, the Iraqis traveled by land
from Baghdad to Amman, Jordan. They planned
to fly out of Amman, but were forced to make
other plans because of diplomatic pressure and,
ah, suggestions that air travel would not be safe
for them. That took them to Aqaba. They arrived
there less than twelve hours after your visit."
Tombs chuckled.

"Conditions being what they are, they decided
to travel by sea from Aqaba to Port Sudan. The
boat, *Georges*, is registered as Jordanian, but is, as
far as we can determine, owned by the Iraqis, and
the crew is Iraqi, probably all members of the
Republican Guard."

"In other words, fair game," Rob said under his
breath.

"Fair game," Tombs agreed. "And the members
of the Revolutionary Council and the Bath party
bigwig are wanted for crimes against humanity,
for the attacks made against the Kurds in northern Iraq and against the Shiites in the Basra area.
You will intercept and board their boat tonight. If
practical, the principals will be taken into custody
and brought back for trial. If that is not practical,
and I doubt it will be, our mission is to leave
vacancies for Saddam to fill."

"We know the name of *that* game," Beau muttered, but no one took any notice.

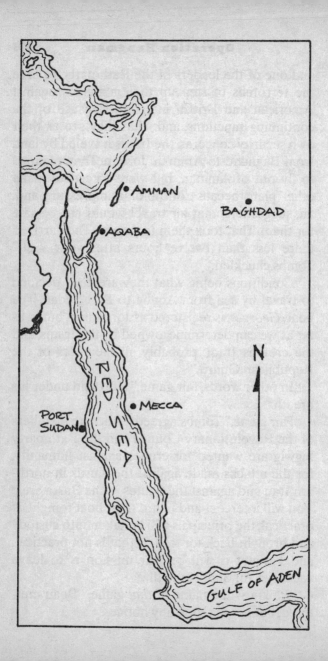

"We are tracking the progress of the Iraqis' boat," Tombs continued. "After sunset tonight, you will be dropped, along with an RPB, into position to intercept the vessel while it is still well away from either shore. We expect them to make for the nearest point of Sudanese territorial waters, then follow the coastline to Port Sudan, as close in as practical. Your job is to make sure they don't get there. If the Iraqis don't know who to blame afterward, all the better, so plan to deep six the boat and any remains."

THE PREPARATION

"Let's keep this simple," Frank said, when the team gathered to select weapons and other gear for the mission. They were already dressed, all in black, with dark camouflage paint on their hands and faces. Each carried the classic Ka-bar knife strapped to their sides. A variation on the famous Marine Corps fighting knife, the SEAL version featured a waterproof gray plastic sheath and a canvas web hanger strap. Cheap, rugged, and reli-

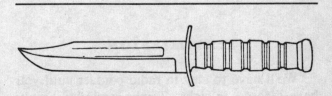

Ka-bar

able, the bowie-style knife had been standard gear for the Teams for as long as any of the current members could remember.

"If we can, we'll board and do this in and dirty. There might not be a lot of room belowdecks on *Georges*. Farmer, you stick with a rifle. The rest of us, submachine guns. Pistols. Hand grenades. Half concussion, half incendiary."

"Be better if you can sink that boat without a fire," Tombs said. "Make it disappear cleanly." He held up a hand. "We want it gone, one way or the other. Whatever you can do."

"A couple of shaped charges, then," Frank said. "No guarantees, Tombs. You want us to disappear it, blowing it out of the water is surer and faster, but we'll try it your way, if we can. Good enough?"

"I can't ask more," Tombs said.

"There's one more possibility we need to prepare for," Frank said. "There's a chance we might not be able to get close enough to board the boat. In that case, we could use a couple of LAWs rockets. If we don't destroy the boat, we should at least be able to do enough damage to let us catch her and finish the job."

THE MISSION

"We'll have to stay in radio contact until you have *Georges* in sight," Tombs reminded Frank, as the SEALs got ready to board the helicopter.

"I've got the scrambler set on both radios," Frank said.

"I'll be in CIC. They've got the boat on the plotting board and a radio hookup for me."

"Just make sure you get pickup out for us if that boat changes course so we can't get to it after we're in the water," Frank said. "I don't want to spend all night waiting for a date that isn't coming. If they push it, *Georges* can do twice the speed an RPB can. We can't chase it down, can't head it off if it turns much before we can see it."

"As of five minutes ago, *Georges* was still making only seven knots. If it changes course early enough, we might be able to pick you up and set you back down," Tombs said. "We're keeping our options open, and you've got those disposable rocket launchers if all else fails."

"An operation like this needs two, even three, teams waiting," Rob said, after the helicopter had deposited the SEALs and their boat in the water. "Spread out across the course so that one of the boats has a good chance of intercepting the target." He spoke softly, almost without inflection, but the others could all hear. "Like this, if the crew has their eyes open, they could change course the minute they spot this boat, crank up the revs, and leave us behind. We might not even get close enough to hit them with those throwaway bazookas."

"Always that chance," Frank said. "*If* they've got enough eyes looking. *If* they spot a low-riding dark lump on dark water. *If* they suspect we're more than flotsam. *If* they think we might be a threat."

"A bunch of paranoids sneaking to a supposedly clandestine meeting of terrorist leaders." Rob snorted. "A damned seagull might spook them."

"Saddam told them to go to this meeting," Ike said. "Iraqis don't last very long if they don't do what the boss tells them to, no matter how scared they might get."

"You're turning into a cynic, kid," Rob said.

"I watch the news," Ike replied. "Chief, how far off are they now?"

"Three miles, almost due north."

"We should be able to see their running lights," Ike said, scanning the northern horizon.

"Pretty quick, if they've got lights on," Frank said. He was also scanning the horizon, using binoculars. "We're at water level, and *Georges*'s masthead is thirty feet above the waterline. Even without lights we should be able to spot the silhouette in the next few minutes."

It was only thirty seconds before Frank spotted *Georges*. "No masthead light, but they've got port and starboard lights at deck level."

"You sure that's *Georges*?" Rob asked.

"The position is right and Tombs said there wasn't anything else in the neighborhood," Frank said. "It's heading straight for us on the right course. Pretty safe bet."

"Hey, we're going to board it. If we've got the wrong address, we'll know," Ike whispered.

"Right," Frank said. "Beau, start moving us toward her. We'll tie on as close to the bow as we can get."

With the throttle kept low, the RPB's engine was almost totally silent, the minimal noises it made covered by the sounds of the water. The Red Sea was not as glassy calm as usual. The water had a bit of a chop, the ragged edge of a squall running along it two hundred miles away.

Georges looked as if she were a cross between a barge and a small freighter. The boat was broad and low, with no more than four feet of freeboard—the space between the waterline and the deck. The superstructure was a rectangular cabin near the stern. The radio mast and crane were ten feet forward of the cabin, with the hatch leading into the boat's single hold a dozen feet ahead of them. The boat had clearly been designed for coastal trade and sheltered waters. It did not look as if it had been designed to provide a comfortable voyage for passengers on the open sea.

Beau maneuvered the RPB's tiller and throttle to let *Georges* come up on it as gently as possible, almost like a docking maneuver in space. Frank stood in the bow and hooked the RPB's painter over a bitt near the bow on the starboard side of *Georges*, and secured the line. Rob kept the RPB from smacking the side of the other boat too severely, and Ike was the first man to clamber up onto the deck of *Georges*, rolling into position, careful not to get any higher than absolutely necessary. Frank and Rob followed within seconds, and Beau joined the others as soon as he had shut off the rapid penetration boat's engine.

At first, the SEALs all went prone, Rob's rifle and the Uzi submachine guns of the others pointed in the direction of the cabin at the boat's stern, ready for action, in case they had been seen coming aboard. The deck of *Georges* stank, a combination of odors that included both diesel and olive oils, and other things that the SEALs could hardly guess at.

I can't believe they didn't see us, Ike thought. Aren't they even watching where they're going? There were two glass panels on the front of the cabin, stretching nearly the entire width of the superstructure, and Ike could also see a long rectangular window—definitely not a porthole—on the near side of the cabin. The glass appeared to be backlit in green and red, undoubtedly the glow from various instruments inside.

Then he saw movement in the cabin, the vague silhouette of a face turning, illuminated by the glowing end of a cigarette in a mouth. The helmsman had obviously been looking aft. Now he was looking toward the bow of *Georges*, at or over the four men lying on its deck.

Frank tapped Ike's leg, and when the youngest member of the team turned his head, the chief gestured toward the cabin. He "walked" his fingers along the deck. Ike nodded, understanding the order.

As much as possible, Ike used the minimal cover provided by the hold's hatch lid, which projected fifteen inches above the deck. He slid to his left, pulling with fingers and pushing with toes, trying not to lift off the deck by even an inch. Slithering on a wooden deck was slow and uncomfortable. Ike picked up a couple of splinters along the way. Patience was the key word. He scarcely dared to breathe, unwilling to do anything that might give the man in the cockpit any clue that the ship had been boarded.

Rob was the next SEAL to start moving toward the superstructure, sliding to his right—the port side of *Georges*—and moving as cautiously as Jensen was. Beau glanced at Frank, who gave him a "wait" signal with his hand.

Ike took nearly five minutes to reach the starboard side of the cabin. He allowed himself a little leverage then, getting up to hands and knees to scurry to the rear of the cabin. He glanced cautiously around the corner. The single door leading inside had been lashed open.

After laying his Uzi on the deck, with exaggerated care to make certain that he made no noise, Ike crawled toward the door and peeked into the cabin. There was only one man inside, standing at the helm, looking forward.

Just stay that way, Ike thought. He reached for the knife at his belt, slid it out of the sheath, and got slowly to his feet. Three steps, Ike told himself. He took a breath first, then held it as he moved into the cabin, stepping as lightly as he could.

The helmsman either heard or felt something. Ike had just taken his second step when the helmsman turned his head. The apparition of a dark figure coming at him appeared to leave the man in shock for a split second, and that was all the advantage Ike needed. He plunged his knife into the man's chest while his left hand reached for the man's mouth. The dying gurgle of the helmsman was only partially muffled by Ike's hand, but there was no scream of warning, and Ike caught the body before it could fall to the deck.

By the time Ike had lowered his victim softly, wedging the body into a corner to keep it from rolling, Rob was at his side, carrying Ike's Uzi as well as his own rifle. A nod, and a pat on the shoulder, provided Rob's appreciation for a job well done. Then he waved broadly, his hand near the window, to let the others know that they could come along.

A ladderway at the starboard side of the superstructure led below deck. The hatch was closed, but the louvered panel showed dim light beyond.

"Handle the wheel, kid," Rob whispered, his mouth right against Ike's ear. "Hold her on course."

Forward, Frank gestured for Beau to stay put and watch the hatch to the hold. Frank got up and went toward the stern of *Georges*, his feet almost sliding along the deck to keep from making noise that anyone below might wonder about.

Frank paused in the doorway, picking out the positions of his men, the body on the deck, and the hatch leading below. He nodded, then crossed to the hatch. He bent close to the slats, moving his head, trying to see what might be waiting in the companionway below. He heard no sounds of people, saw no indication of movement in the feeble light.

Can't stand around all night, Frank thought. He tapped Rob on the shoulder, then gestured for Ike to leave the helm and come along. Frank pulled open the louvered hatchway, and bent low, looking along the low passage at the bottom of the ladder. There was no one in it.

Going down the six steps, Frank kept his Uzi in front of him, ready to fire if anyone came out of one of the doors along the companionway. There were two on either side, and another at the end. In the bulkhead behind the ladder, another hatch led aft, into the engine room.

Six ways to trouble, Frank thought. He gestured for Rob to take care of anyone in the engine room, then waved Ike forward.

"Here we go," Frank whispered. He opened the first door on his left, just a few inches, then reached around the edge to search for a light switch. His hand closed over a knob. He twisted it and an overhead light came on in the room.

At the same time, he heard the quick stutter of

a three-shot burst from an M-16—Rob taking care of whatever he had found in the engine room. The two men sleeping in the berths in the cabin came awake instantly. The man in the upper berth reached for a rifle on the mattress next to him.

Frank pulled the trigger on his Uzi, spraying the man in the upper bunk, then he lowered his aim and shot the man below him—who had been slower to come alert.

"That tears it, kid," Frank said, turning toward Ike. "Kick 'em in and watch your ass."

Ike turned and kicked in the door on the opposite side of the companionway, moving to the side, his submachine gun tracking across the room. Ike did not wait to give anyone inside a chance to target him. He sprayed bullets liberally into the cabin, then tossed in one of his concussion grenades.

Frank and Ike both ducked to the side as the grenade went off.

"Grenade first, then bullets," Frank suggested. Rob joined them then.

Ike and Rob took the next pair of cabins simultaneously, kicking open doors, tossing in concussion grenades, then moving out of the way until after the stunners went off. They were just moving back to make certain that the inhabitants of the cabins were accounted for when the door at the end of the passageway came open and two rifles started firing.

Frank dropped to the deck at the first sound of

the door, so he was under the first bursts of hostile gunfire. Ike and Rob had both made it into the cabins on either side of the passage. From the deck, Frank fired back, and he continued shooting through the hatchway even after the hostile gunfire stopped—after two rifles clattered to the deck.

Ike did not want to leave the chief to face the guns alone, so he wasted no time with the three men he found in the cabin. They had apparently all been sleeping. Two were holding hands to their ears. Blood flowed through the fingers of both of them. The third man was unconscious or dead. There were burn marks on his face. Ike sprayed them with 9mm bullets.

Across the way, Rob was as summary in his handling of the passengers in the last cabin. Two men, only one of whom had been moving after the concussion grenade went off.

Rob and Ike both returned to the doors of the cabins they had gone into. Together, they added their weapons to the fray, shooting into the darkness beyond the door at the forward end of the passage. On the deck, Frank fitted a new magazine to his Uzi. He whistled sharply. Rob and Ike quit firing.

"Anybody recognize any faces?" Frank asked.

"Yeah, at least one of the buggers Tombs showed us," Rob said. "One of the men from the Revolutionary Council."

"I spotted one of them too," Ike said. "And I think the party guy."

"Any of them in any shape to stand trial?" Frank asked.

"I don't think so," Rob said.

"Then toss a match through that door and let's get out of here," Frank said.

"What about the shaped charges?" Rob asked.

"They're back in the RPB."

"I'll get them," Ike offered.

"Hell, don't bother," Frank said. "Let's do the job clean. Farmer?"

Rob took one of his incendiary grenades, pulled the pin, and tossed the weapon through the doorway at the end of the passage. He and Ike both ducked back into the rooms they were in. Frank flattened himself on the deck. The grenade exploded, sending tongues of flame in every direction.

It was time to leave. Frank got to his feet and ran aft and up the ladderway to the cockpit. Rob and Ike were almost on his heels. Ike, last man out, tossed another incendiary grenade—into the engine room. After that, the three men sprinted toward the bow of *Georges*. Beau moved to the bitt and had his hands on the rope holding their RPB to the burning ship before they reached him.

The grenade in the engine room exploded. Seconds later, there was another blast as the ship's fuel lines ruptured. The secondary explosion lifted the stern of *Georges*. The sudden motion tossed both Ike and Frank over the side. Ike landed in the SEALs' boat with the wind half knocked out of him. Frank landed in the water and lost his Uzi. Rob managed to catch the ship's railing and kept himself from going overboard. And Beau had been holding on to the painter. He lost his footing and slid toward the side, catching a stanchion between his legs—painfully. He grunted in pain and doubled over, but did not lose his grip on the rope.

Rob grabbed Beau's arm. "Let's move before this whole tub blows," he shouted.

Beau got to his feet gingerly, one hand going to ease the pain in his groin. He was seeing stars, and having difficulty getting his breath. "Go!" he grunted.

Rob hesitated only fractionally, then went over the side and lowered himself into the boat. Ike had recovered and was pulling Frank aboard. Beau was the last man into the RPB, moving half doubled over from the continuing pain. But he cast off and got into position at the stern.

"Steer due south," Frank ordered after coughing out sea water. "Rob, get on the horn and tell them to come get us."

Georges burned quickly. The engine room explosions had blown a hole in the hull. The ship settled by the stern. As the RPB pulled away from the hulk, *Georges* lit up the sky, a torch slowly being overtaken by the sea. Diesel fuel spilled and burned, a sheet of fire on the water.

"They'll be able to see that from twenty miles away," Ike said, looking back at the fire.

"Farther than that, kid," Rob said. He chuckled.

"By tomorrow, they'll be seeing it all the way to Baghdad."

POST-MISSION

Frank Lucan sat on the deck of *Bellman*, on the port side, in the lee of the superstructure, doing something he hadn't done in more than a decade—smoking. He had borrowed a pack of cigarettes from the duty chief in the engineering section after the mission debriefing, and after he had sent his men to bed. Frank had been sitting on deck for more than an hour, smoking one cigarette after another—uncertain why, other than an unusual uneasiness. The only time he had been disturbed was when the junior officer of the deck had spotted him and come to ask what he thought he was doing. Once Frank had identified himself, the Junior O. D. seemed to lose interest. He left with a mumbled, "Carry on."

Pickup after the burning of *Georges* had taken only twenty minutes. The helicopter had been waiting on the pad for word from Team Wolf. Frank had been chilled after his unexpected dunking, and possibly a little shaken; he had ridden back to *Bellman* with a blanket wrapped around him. Harry Tombs had produced a bottle of Jack Daniels; a couple of sips of that had taken Frank's chill away. Ike and Beau both seemed worse for wear than Frank. Ike kept flexing his left arm and shoulder, as if he were in pain . . .

though he denied it. And Beau was walking gingerly. He had been quite graphic about what had been hurt, and how, but refused to do anything about the injury. "I be okay," he said. "Been kicked there before."

Tombs had been so delighted with the results of the operation, and confirmation that all three primary targets had been eliminated, that he made only perfunctory complaints about the team's failure to try to sink *Georges* without burning her. He already had a satellite photograph that clearly showed the burning ship and—with the use of a magnifying glass and a little imagination—the smaller boat the SEALs had used, caught at the edge of the light of the fire.

Frank chainlit a new cigarette from the old one, then tossed the stub into the Red Sea. The battle group was headed south again, the official plan to sail all of the way to the Balal Mandeb, the strait at the southern end of the Red Sea, before turning north again—to head through the Suez Canal and the Mediterranean on its way back to the United States, its six-month deployment over. Unofficially, *Bellman* would be operating detached from the rest of the battle group for several days, not making the trek all of the way south. It would remain within reach of Port Sudan to support the final operation of the SEAL team.

The kid's gonna be all right, Frank thought. The changes in Ike Jensen over the past couple of weeks seemed remarkable. He had become a veteran, self-assured, confident. The nervousness that had been so obvious at the start had vanished completely. Beau Guisborne and Rob Rhodes remained as dependable as always.

Me...? Frank took a deep drag on his cigarette, then shook his head. That was the problem, and Frank was just realizing that, though he still didn't have any idea why he was suddenly so uneasy. *Maybe I just need some R and R,* he thought. *Or maybe I'm getting too damned old for this shit.*

He lit another cigarette and threw the old one overboard.

10: INCENSE

THE BRIEFING

"This is the big one," Harry Tombs said after he closed the conference room door behind him. "The blow-off." He moved to his usual place at the table. "Everyone fit?"

No one rushed to fill the silence. Ike's shoulder was still sore, and a little stiff, but he was certain it would not interfere with his ability to do his job. Beau had no real pain left from his injury, but the memory of pain, and a little tenderness in the region that might not have been completely imaginary, lingered. Frank felt as if he had slept four minutes instead of four hours. No one would admit, however, he was at less than one hundred percent. Only Rob had nothing slowing him down.

Tombs took silence for affirmation. He had worked with SEALs before. "Good. Most of the participants in the terrorist summit won't reach the site until tomorrow morning, but we have hard intel that the meeting is on, and that—as hoped—it will be at the Port Sudan location. From what we have been able to determine, at least nine of the ten heads of organizations will be there. We know that Faud ibn Landin has left his refuge in Afghanistan and is enroute, though we don't know his precise location. He will probably be the last to arrive. The opening session of the summit will be tomorrow afternoon.

"We'll put you ashore tonight. You'll have to find a place to go to ground in the hills behind the meeting site. The Sudanese government is providing heavy security for the terrorists, a full company of soldiers and perhaps as many as thirty members of the military security police, the force that provides bodyguards for the president of the Revolutionary Command Council. The convoy of troops is on the road now, perhaps an hour south of Port Sudan. A few members of the security police detachment are already in the city. Others will be accompanying delegates to the conference overnight and tomorrow morning. And we estimate that each of the ten principals will have two or three of his own people along for personal security."

"In other words, the total opposition right at the site could be over two hundred," Frank said.

Tombs nodded. "With perhaps another twenty or thirty local police available within minutes, and additional military forces within three quarters of an hour. We anticipate that the company of soldiers will be the best, and most reliable, the Sudanese government has available."

"You pack our blue tights and red capes?" Rob asked.

"You'll have what you'll need to get the job done," Tombs said.

"I'm not worried so much about getting the job done as getting out in one piece afterward," Frank said. "I know what you've got in those locked crates. But once we hit that conference, the Sudanese are going to put everything they've got into nailing us. If we leave an RPB on shore when we go in, the odds are way too heavy they'll find it. And they'll have troops, ships, and police crawling all along that shoreline."

"You're right about leaving an RPB," Tombs said. "You won't. I'll be riding in with you and bring the boat back to the ship tonight."

"That still leaves the question of extraction," Ike noted.

"Once you hit that conference, the need for secrecy ends. The United States will be ready to take credit for the strike. That means we can use any resources necessary to get you out. We're preparing for a number of contingencies." Tombs held up a hand to stave off an interruption. "That's not just a vague generalization. The primary extraction plan calls for helicopter pickup, with whatever air cover seems necessary, including helicopter gunships or fighters off *Roosevelt*. *Bellman* will be in range to use its five-inch gun as well. *Bellman* will keep any Sudanese coast guard or naval assets from interfering. The ship's launch and an RPB will be ready to make a surface pickup. And our friends from the Aden mission will be joining us within the next few hours. *Pompano* will have an SDV in the water with gear for the four of you. That's also a fallback in case anything goes wrong with any of the other options. They'll also have a backup team to put ashore if you need reinforcements."

"No battalion of Marines?" Rob asked.

"No battalion of Marines," Tombs said. "I was told you heroes wouldn't like it."

"We're not heroes," Frank said, very softly. "Just men doing a job that, maybe, has to be done. But, since you say that the government is ready to take credit, ready to use the entire *Roosevelt* battle group to get us out if necessary, why not just use them to take out the conference. Cruise missiles or bombs and rockets from the fighters?"

"You know the reasons as well as I do, Chief," Tombs said. "We want to be sure we get the people we're after, and bombs and missiles can't be counted on for that. You know what we've tried in Iraq and Serbia. We need people in on the ground."

"Just to get everything straight," Frank said.

Tombs slid the target folder for the mission across the table to Frank. It was considerably thicker than any of the others had been. "This is a job that has to be done," Tombs said. "If we can take out the leaders of the ten most militant terrorist groups in this part of the world, we'll sow

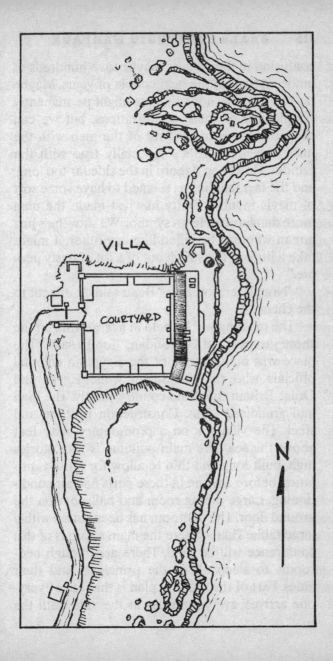

VILLA

COURTYARD

N

confusion in their ranks, maybe save hundreds of innocent lives in the next couple of years. Maybe it's too much to hope that we might permanently cripple any of these organizations, but we can chop the heads off, get rid of the men with the juice, the ideas. That's especially true with ibn Landin. He's been a thorn in the side far too long, and the fact that he has seemed to have some sort of magic invulnerability has just made the man more dangerous. He's a symbol. We show he's just a man who can be killed like any other, it might take a little of the starch out of a lot of nasty people."

" 'Nough sermonizing," Beau said. "Let's cut to the cheese."

"The meeting will be held in a large villa on the shore just north of Port Sudan," Tombs said. "The place was built by one of the Egyptian colonial officials who ran the Sudan while Egypt and Great Britain ruled the country jointly. The man had grandiose ideas. Construction is stone and steel. The villa sits on a promontory sixty feet above the sea. The main building is four stories high, built long and thin to allow for cross-ventilation before anyone in these parts had air conditioning. Large dining room and ballroom on the ground floor. The ballroom has been set up with a large table. That's where the main sessions of this conference will be held. There are enough bedrooms to sleep all of the principals and their aides. Part of the security plan is that once everyone arrives, everyone stays at the villa until the summit ends. Which makes it convenient for us. The domestic help, cooks, maids, and so forth, have all been brought in by the Sudanese government, the names circulated among the major groups coming to the conference for approval.

"On the inland side of the main building, there is a courtyard that's a hundred feet square. Ten-foot-high walls, four to six feet thick. Garages and other outbuildings have been incorporated in the wall structure. Gate house outside the wall. That will be staffed with security people, and the military will probably have a machine gun set up somewhere nearby, as well as patrols extending out for several hundred yards."

"Which means we'll probably have to deal with the army before we can get at the terrorists?" Frank gave it the inflection of a question though it was more a statement of what he saw as an unavoidable fact.

"Before or simultaneously," Tombs conceded. "Until you see the dispositions and movements firsthand, there's no way to be certain. But it's unlikely that these troops will be prepared for the sort of concentrated firepower the four of you will bring to bear."

"Blow the crap out of them before they know they're under attack," Rob contributed.

"Something like that. Which brings us to the assault on the conference itself. And the contents of those locked crates the chief mentioned earlier," Tombs said. He smiled. "I know that at least three of you have fired the XM18 for familiarization." He turned his attention to Ike. "All but you, Jensen."

"Okay, I'll bite," Ike said. "What the hell is an XM18?"

"The XM18 projectile launcher," Frank said. "Picture a Thompson submachine gun that fires 40mm grenades. Holds eighteen rounds and you can empty the magazine in five seconds. Same kind of range and accuracy you'd have with an M79 or M203." He turned to Tombs. "The kid can handle one. He's fired other grenade launchers enough."

"I made preparations based on that assumption," Tombs said. "There are four weapons and three hundred and sixty rounds of ammunition—high explosive, armor piercing, incendiary, fragmentation. Concentrated mayhem. The four of you lay down seventy-two projectiles in five or ten seconds, you'll have plenty of time to reload, move closer, or whatever else you need to do

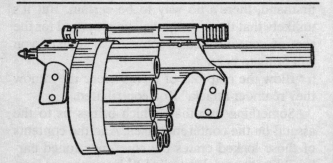

XM18 Projectile Launcher

before the opposition knows what the hell hit them. As Rob said, 'Blow the crap out of them before they know they're under attack.' "

"Takes a lot longer to reload than to empty it, kid," Rob said. "Figure a minute to eject empties and replace them."

"We'll give you a chance to practice loading and reloading in the armory, kid," Frank said. "We could all use a little practice before we go in. It's been . . . since the build up to Desert Storm, I guess, since I handled one of these crackers. I didn't know we had any in stock yet."

"There are a few around," Tombs said. "In brief, here's the plan. You go in tonight, find a secure place to hide, then hit the conference just after sundown tomorrow, and we pull you out. Then we all go home."

"One way or t'other," Beau said.

THE PREPARATION

Ike Jensen whistled softly as Frank Lucan took the first XM18 out of the crate and handed it to him. Ike moved the weapon around, looking at it from every angle.

"This looks almost like a toy, something to shoot Ping Pong balls with," Ike said.

"It's no damned toy," Frank said. "It's one serious piece of ordnance. A little too heavy for regular use. I guess that's why the Teams never formally adopted them. The first of these we used, some years back, were as shiny as the ends of a beer can. Glad to see they had the sense to give us a black finish on these."

"Big appetite," Rob said. "Eats ammo faster'n you can possibly reload."

"Four of these going at once, we might be mistaken for a cluster bomb," Ike said.

Beau chuckled, then pulled another of the weapons from the crate. "We make pretty music, I think," he said.

Frank took Ike's weapon back, and showed him how to open the drum magazine. "We'll all take some time practicing loading," Frank said. "Not too bad, once you get the hang of it."

THE MISSION

"We've got one little extra bonus going for us this morning," Tombs said when the team gathered in a red-lit companionway at 0130 hours. "All but one of our ops so far have started earlier. Even if the locals are concerned about something going on, they should be lulled a little by the time we get close. It's nothing to take to the bank, but every little bit helps. At the moment, there's a single boat patrolling the coast off Port Sudan. It's a police launch. We'll time insertion to put that launch at the far end of its beat, and the captain is going to provide a little distraction. The ship's launch will be sent off to the south, close to the three-mile limit. Give the locals something to look at while we sneak you in."

"What about patrols on shore?" Frank asked.

"The security police have set up a checkpoint between the villa and town, a half mile south of the villa. Closer in, the military has two outposts manned outside the walls, one off the northwest corner, the other a hundred yards up the road, toward town. Earlier, they were running two patrols, five or six men in each, but it appears that they've been pulled in. At least temporarily. We plan to make landfall two hundred yards north of the farthest limit they were patrolling before."

"We trip over a patrol going in, it's going to screw up the whole mission," Rob noted.

"So don't trip over them. That's supposed to be your forte, isn't it?" Tombs said.

"Yeah, but just for the sake of covering all the bases, what if we *do* hit trouble going in?" Frank asked.

Tombs hesitated for what seemed to be an extraordinarily long time before he replied. "Cover your asses and call for extraction. We'll do whatever we have to in order to get you out. But that would leave a lot of people very unhappy. You get spotted going in and the conference is sure to be moved or cancelled, and we might not have a second chance. We may never get another opportunity this good to bugger these terrorists—especially ibn Landin. Washington wants him badly."

"Not as badly as we want to keep our butts in one piece," Frank said.

Waiting to board the RPB that would carry them to shore, the four SEALs looked as if they might have been posing for an editorial cartoon lampooning the military. Each man was heavily weighted down with weapons and ammunition—far more than a normal combat load. Each man carried an XM18 with its drum magazine loaded, and bandoleers and pouches carrying another fifty-four projectiles each. Rob and Beau also carried M-16 rifles with two of the hundred-round double drum magazines, and the team's two radios. Frank and Ike carried Uzis with spare magazines. Everyone wore night-vision goggles, knife, and pistol as well, and, since they would be out for nearly a full day, the men had to carry canteens and rations. They wore desert camouflage BDUs and slouch hats, with visible skin painted in three colors.

Tombs looked at his watch. It was 0158 hours. "Time to go," he whispered. Tombs was wearing a pistol on a web belt and carried an Uzi slung over his shoulder. He was going only as far as shore, and would be bringing the boat back. His position during the following twenty hours or so would be in *Bellman*'s CIC, the team's liaison with the battle group.

The men filed out on deck single file and went to the Jacob's ladder leading down to the RPB that *Bellman*'s crew had already deployed. The ship's launch had been lowered and started out on its mission of deception fifteen minutes earlier. Climbing down to the RPB so heavily loaded took extra care on the part of the SEALs. This was not the time to fall. Shedding enough weight quickly to avoid drowning was an exercise none of them wanted to attempt.

Harry Tombs was the last man to step into the boat. He sat at the rear, near Beau Guisborne, who would handle the RPB on the way in. Above, on *Bellman*'s deck, the junior O.D. flipped a salute at the men as the boat pulled away.

Tombs wore a radio headset, to monitor traffic between *Bellman* and her launch for anything that might affect the insertion of Team Wolf. Low at his side, he kept clenching and unclenching his right fist, his only show of nerves . . . and he did all he could to keep any of the SEALs from noticing. He was not overly confident of the outcome of this mission. There was simply too great a chance of something going wrong. At the moment, his concern was over getting the job done, and getting the team back out safely afterward. Earlier, alone in his cabin aboard *Bellman*, he had allowed himself a few moments to consider the personal importance of the mission. *If they succeed, I've got it made at the Agency. If they blow it, I might as well submit my resignation right away; I'll be done anyway.* He had fought the urge to go ashore with the SEALs, take part in the assault on the terrorists, do what he could to help insure that it was successful. But that would have been an unforgivable indulgence. It was far more important for him to spend the time on *Bellman*, make sure the men ashore got any intelligence that came through and—even more important—make sure they were retrieved when the time came. Extraction might prove extremely difficult, even if they were totally successful decapitating the terrorist Hydra. Besides, he had forced himself to admit that he was not even close to qualified for this mission. *It's their pidgin, as the Brits say,* he had told himself.

Frank sat in his usual spot at the bow of the RPB, scanning the shore and water with binoculars. His hands had quit the trembling that had started during his smoking marathon the night before. Frank had smoked almost the entire pack, most of it in chain fashion. He still wasn't sure why, or at least couldn't admit that he did, not even to himself. He had smoked the last two cigarettes from the pack after a late breakfast, then had brushed his teeth and gargled. After that, he had not even felt an urge to smoke again. Good thing, he decided. I might need my wind before this job's over.

Rob found it unusually difficult to concentrate on watching his side. An edge of anger kept trying to dominate his thoughts, and he wasn't certain what he was angry about, or who it was directed at. His dislike for Harry Tombs had been instantaneous and nothing had happened to mitigate that, but Rob had made the necessary allowances; Tombs did, at least, seem to be competent. The terrorists? They were the enemy, but faceless and nameless, even though Rob had studied the photographs of the ten leaders expected to be at the meeting and gone through the names enough times that he could recite them from memory if necessary. The Navy? The Teams? His team mates? Rob shook his head, trying to force himself away from the distracting thoughts; emotion had no place on a mission. *Just mad at life, maybe,* he thought, and his eyes started sweeping the horizon again.

Beau paid attention to the job at hand, as always. He knew that his team mates considered his laid-back attitude a pose, and that was—when he dwelled on it, which wasn't often—a laugh. In realistic terms, there was no place else he would rather be than in the Navy, in the Teams. Sure, there might be fantasies of a glamorous life in professional sports or in acting, but those had always been fantasies. This was a life that Beau knew he was good at. *So maybe I don't live to a ripe old age. Maybe I wouldn't live so long fishing, or living on the streets back home. You take your chances.* He had dismissed the thought that just maybe, this was a mission that not everyone would come back from.

Ike was worried, but there was a difference. This time, he wasn't frightened, or nervous about the mission and how he might perform. He was worried because he couldn't completely submerge the tingling of excitement, *anticipation*, that he felt heading in for what would almost certainly be the most dangerous mission he had been on in his time in the SEALs. *I don't want to be a combat junkie,* he thought. He remembered one of the instructors at BUD/S who had seemed to get an almost sexual release from remembering and talking about his experiences in Grenada, Panama, and Iraq. *I don't want to get like him, ever!*

"The deception seems to be working," Tombs said in a loud whisper. "The police launch is tagging along, staying right with *Bellman*'s boat, about three quarters of a mile to the side. They're a good seven miles south of us now."

Beau's response was to open the throttle a little more, give the RPB an extra mile per hour. The boat was still two miles from shore. The villa where the summit meeting was to take place was thirty degrees off the port bow. The villa was marked by several lights in windows, and a small searchlight was playing over the ground on the shore side of the complex.

Something Tombs didn't mention, Frank thought, as he watched the operators moving the beam of light. We'll have to take that out with the first volley.

Frank turned his attention farther north, toward the landing area they had chosen, more than a half mile from the villa. The searchlight should be no problem getting ashore and up the slope to the area where they would go to ground to wait for the next sunset. There was no sign of movement, no lights, nothing but rock and a few scrubby trees and bushes close to the edge of the sea.

We'll have an hour and a half, maybe a little more, to find cover and get settled in, Frank thought, scanning higher on the rocky slope behind the narrow coastal ledge. After that, it'll start getting light. There were several possible locations. The last time *Bellman* had passed Port Sudan in daylight, Harry Tombs had taken a number of photographs with a massive telephoto lens. It was just a matter of getting to the spots they had seen on those photographs, and making certain that they were indeed suitable. It was hard to determine the depth of any of the holes from the flat pictures.

Frank shifted his search again, looking along the shore toward the villa. There might be a patrol on the near side, or the men in the sentry post at the northeast corner of the compound might be looking with binoculars, even their own night-vision gear. He bent forward a little more, though he was already nearly as low as he could get in the boat. If they were seen going in, there would be no point in trying to go forward with the mission. They would have to abort. If they could.

Two hundred yards from shore, the RPB moved past a projection of land that cut them off from direct observation of the ground in front of the villa. If they didn't see us before, they won't see us now, Frank decided. He scanned the shore directly in front of the boat, then lowered his binoculars and checked the safety on his Uzi. The next ten minutes will tell the first tale, he thought, whether we're going to have a chance.

Beau did not ease off on the throttle until the boat was within thirty yards of land, then he twisted it all of the way down to idle. The boat nosed against shore. Frank was first out, grabbing the painter to hold the boat steady while the rest of his team climbed out of the boat.

Tombs had taken the tiller from Beau. As soon as the last SEAL was ashore and Frank had pushed the RPB, starting it into a turn, Tombs put the engine in reverse and held the tiller over for a moment, then started the RPB forward again, away from the SEALs. There were no words of farewell.

The four SEALs went prone above the overhanging shore, clear of the mud at the edge of the sea. Although time was critical, Frank took five minutes to assure himself that they were not walking into a trap, that there were no hostile forces waiting to open fire. He also picked out the route he intended to take, scanning along it for any obvious difficulties.

Finally, he got to his feet and started moving forward, in what was nearly one fluid motion. He was conscious of all the weight hanging from his body, the extra burden it represented, but that could be borne. They were not going to make a twenty-mile hike or a six-mile jog.

The land they had to cross was empty. They might have been hundreds of miles from the nearest outpost of civilization instead of little more than half a mile. Even close to the edge of the sea, this was desert, rocky more than sandy, but with grit blowing on the breeze. An imaginative person might almost be able to think it was the Martian landscape rather than a part of Earth that had been inhabited for many thousands of years.

Frank moved as carefully as he could. A careless step, on a rock that might shift, could lead to a twisted ankle, or worse. And there was a chance—remote though it might be—that the Sudanese troops had put out listening devices against the possibility of intruders.

The others followed, spreading out but staying on the same line, two to three yards between men. Ike, Rob, Beau—every man focused entirely on the job at hand. They were professionals. There was no time for anything else, not if the mission was to be successful . . . if they were all to have a chance of getting out alive.

From the start, the trek was uphill, gently at first, then on an increasingly steep grade. Fifty yards from the water's edge, the slope was twenty degrees, and it got worse soon after. The switch from walking to climbing was almost imperceptible. It became convenient to occasionally use a hand on the rocks ahead and above to move. Then it became essential.

Frank had started to angle to the left before

that point. Going south would be more difficult the higher the SEALs got. And even starting as soon as he did, there came a point when Frank had to concede a few yards of altitude to find an easy route to get around a jutting outcropping of rock.

After twenty-five minutes, Frank sat down. He needed a break, a chance to take some of the weight off. Two minutes, he promised himself as the others also sat or squatted. *Just two minutes.* They could not afford to rest much longer than that, not before finding cover that would protect them through the day.

Frank did not need to consult his watch, but got on his feet a few seconds short of two minutes after he had stopped. Another sixty yards up, he thought, looking for the best route. Maybe a hundred yards horizontally. On the flat, it would have taken less than a minute, even loaded down with eighty or ninety pounds of gear. In the dark, on this slope, it might take all of the hour they had left before they had to start worrying about the first lightening of the sky in the east.

He took one more short rest—less than a minute—after they had covered slightly more than half of the remaining distance. His legs ached. The muscles on the backs of his calves and thighs felt as if they had been strained almost to the breaking point.

A few feet behind, Ike told himself, *It's still not as bad as Hell Week at BUD/S.* It was the fourth time that thought had intruded on his concentration. He felt as if he were drowning in sweat despite the breeze in his face, a breeze that had strengthened over the past ten minutes. When Frank got up and started moving again, Ike groaned mentally . . . but he got up and followed without complaint.

The last twenty minutes were almost entirely vertical. There was no doubt at all that *this* was mountain climbing. Handholds and footholds were readily available, but each had to be tested before anyone could put all of his weight on it. At the end of that stretch, there was a narrow, rising ledge, three to six feet wide, that led toward the areas that Lucan and Tombs had circled on the photographs.

"This will do," Frank said, after a cursory look inside the first hole. It was not really a cave. Part of the face of the hill had fallen, leaving an overhang above and a number of large fragments in front. It would shield the four men from observation except from one angle, from the air, and if a helicopter or airplane came anywhere near, they would have time to duck into better cover among the rubble in front of the gouge.

"Just look carefully before you sit or lay down," Frank added. "I don't know just what kinds of snakes we might run into, but you can bet your ass they'll be mean and poisonous."

"As if the snakes with feet aren't bad enough,"

Rob whispered, peering into the darkness of the hole, trying to see everywhere at once. "I don't like snakes."

"And, for God's sake, if you do see one, remember not to use a gun on it," Frank said. "Give it a chance to get out if you don't feel up to taking it with a blade."

The warning was enough to set all four men to poking very carefully about the limits of their hideout. Ten minutes of searching turning up nothing reptilian, which let them all breathe a little more easily.

"I'll take the first watch," Rob offered. Snakes were his weak point. His fear of them approached phobia. It had almost washed him out of one survival course the Teams had sent him on, in the jungle of Costa Rica.

"Okay, two hours," Frank said. "Wake the kid then. By the time he gets his time in, it'll be daylight." He paused. No one saw his grin in the darkness. "That's when the snakes start getting active."

"Very funny," Rob muttered.

Even without mention of snakes, Rob would have had no difficulty staying awake. The adrenaline rush of a mission guaranteed that. Perhaps if he had gone for two or three days without sleep it might have been difficult, but not for less. He lay down his XM18 and stripped off the bandoleers of projectiles as well as his canteens and the pack with his MREs. After that, he felt almost light enough to float away.

He moved outside the sheltered overhang and prowled around for a few minutes, carrying his M-16, looking for the best vantages and checking out the immediate vicinity for threats and possibilities. He was careful about exposing himself to view from below, and especially from the area of the villa. With Sudanese soldiers on site, someone might be searching with night-vision gear.

Routes in. Routes out. Zones of fire. Looking for those was a reflex. Know where the enemy might come at you from. Look for ways to evade the enemy or get in position to counterattack.

Once Rob was confident that he knew the layout, he got in position on the ledge and kept watch with binoculars, studying the disposition of forces in and around the villa. He was high enough to have a good view inside the courtyard walls. He saw five men come out of one of the secondary structures built into the wall, leave through the main gate, and relieve the fire team on duty at the nearest guard post. The men who were relieved went into the building the others had come out of.

There's a target to remember, Rob thought.

Frank was surprised to find himself waking just after sunrise—surprised because he had not expected to sleep, certainly not soundly enough that he had not wakened at every real or dreamed noise in the night. He pushed the night-vision goggles up off his eyes, then took them off and rubbed at his eyes for a moment. He stretched in place, then rolled over and got up, slowly. Ike was out on the ledge, his attention somewhere below. Rob was sitting on a rock under the overhang, looking around within the hideout, as if he were still uncertain that the SEALs were not sharing their hole with any snakes. Only Beau appeared to be still sleeping.

"The head's about ten yards south," Rob said when Frank got to his feet. "If you stay low, there's no chance of anyone seeing you from the villa."

"You get any sleep at all?" Frank asked.

"Not so's I could notice. You and your damn snakes."

"Sorry about that, but they are a danger here. Why not catch some shuteye now. The rest of us will make sure nothing crawls into your pants."

"Maybe later. I don't really feel the need yet."

"Suit yourself, but you'd better get some sleep today."

Frank went out on the ledge and stretched out next to Ike. "Any activity yet?" Frank asked.

"They changed the guards about twenty minutes ago," Ike whispered. He did not take the binoculars away from his eyes. "I think the first contingent of the day just arrived. Three men in an old British jeep—Land Rover. There's a boat patrolling two hundred yards offshore, running back and forth, about a mile past the villa either way. Two heavy machine guns on deck, a half dozen men in uniform visible."

"Police or navy?" Frank asked, looking out over the water for the boat. It was not in sight at the moment.

"Police, I think," Ike said. "Can't be sure, though."

"Right. Go give Beau a kick. Tell him it's his watch."

"I'm awake," Beau said. Frank turned his head. Guisborne had not moved.

"Then get out here," Frank said. "Take your watch. We've got a room with a view. Enjoy it. I'll relieve you."

The first Sudanese helicopter flew overhead an hour after sunrise, heading north from Port Sudan. The SEALs did not actually *see* the aircraft. As soon as they heard it, they pulled back into the best cover they could manage. The helicopter appeared to be following the ridgeline west of the overhang that sheltered the intruders. Ten minutes later, the sound returned, then faded away to the south.

It was fifty minutes later when it came back. That established the pattern. The helicopter passed over twice, ten or fifteen minutes apart, more or less each hour throughout the day. The actual interval varied. Activity on the ground increased as well. Patrols of ten to twelve soldiers followed the shoreline north from the villa for a mile, then moved inland to the last easy trail on mostly flat rock. They went south to a point just past the villa, then went back inside the courtyard. A few minutes later another squad—the SEALs *assumed* that the patrol duty rotated among squads—came out and made the same trek. A different group, only occasionally visible, patrolled south of the villa. That duty seemed to be divided between soldiers and the security police detail.

Different groups of people arrived at unpredictable intervals during the morning. Shortly before noon there was a major commotion in the courtyard and around it. Troops were rousted from the buildings where they were billeted, and formed up into ranks. A large Mercedes, preceded and followed by Land Rovers with machine gun–armed guards, drove into the courtyard. Several men, apparently officers, came to attention as a rear door on the Mercedes opened and a thin man dressed in a camouflage uniform got out.

Rob Rhodes was manning the binoculars at the time. "Hey, it looks like the big cheese just arrived. That has to be Landin." He passed the binoculars to Frank, but the chief didn't get a chance to verify the sighting. The helicopter was approaching again and the men had to retreat out of sight.

The ledge was shrouded in deep shadows more than two hours before sunset. After the heat of the morning and midday, shade gave at least an illusion of coolness for the men waiting for the coming of night. The rocks around them no longer seemed to be radiating more heat than they received, and there was an occasional hint of breeze around them.

All four SEALs had managed to get at least a little extra sleep, though the routine passages of the Sudanese military helicopter meant that no slumber went undisturbed for long.

"One little SAM," Rob muttered after one fly-by. "Why couldn't we have brought along one little SAM to take care of the odd buzzard?"

"Because we couldn't have settled for just one," Frank said. "We'd have wanted enough to take care of three or four fighters as well. Maybe a torpedo to eliminate their navy, too. If that thing's still buzzing around when we get ready to strike, keep your eyes open for a chance to pop it." He gestured at Rob's XM18. "It would make a pretty show."

Rob looked at the weapon. "Yeah, it would." He tried to calculate just how difficult the shot would be—whether it would be worth the effort. *Maybe,* he decided. It would depend on how fast the helicopter was moving, how close it was, altitude . . . and luck. On the plus side, any kind of hit was almost guaranteed to bring a small helicopter down.

Sleeping, watching. In between, the men cleaned their weapons to make certain no sand or dust would clog the action when the time came. They ate. They drank enough water to keep from getting dehydrated. Leg cramps could be a major distraction, and in the desert heat, they were all too possible.

The shadows moved toward the sea, across the villa, finally out over the water. Just after 1900 hours, several men came out of the main building of the villa in two groups. They walked around in the courtyard, stretching, looking at the sky, apparently talking among themselves—the groups separate. These werc not soldiers or security police, but the men who had come to the conference.

"One's the Hezbollah guy, with two of his guards, I guess," Beau said. He was the one on duty with the binoculars. "I think the other group's the Libyans, but I can't be sure. I can't see their faces."

"The only thing we have to be concerned with now is if any of the groups leave before we hit," Frank said. "We want all the chickens in the roost."

"Nobody moving for any of the cars," Beau said.

"Just stretching their legs after a long session of planning how to kill women and children," Rob suggested.

He moved back a couple of steps, deeper under the overhang, as he heard the helicopter coming south again. The others moved as well. This time, the helicopter was flying slowly along the shoreline instead of along the ridge. It was less than a thousand feet above the water, moving in a zigzag pattern. Looking for folks like us coming in, Beau thought. This was the best view the SEALs had had of the helicopter all day. They could see machine guns mounted in the side doors of the aircraft, uniformed men hunkering over the weapons, looking for targets.

"We're gonna have to deal with that, one way or t'other," Beau said.

"Looks that way," Frank conceded. "Just something else to remember when the time comes. At least there are no rocket pods on that chopper."

"There might be more than one of them," Ike said. "We don't know it's been the same bird flapping back and forth all day. Could be two or three, taking turns."

The helicopter moved out of sight to the south, past the villa, toward the city. The SEALs continued waiting.

Lights were on in many of the rooms of the villa. Outside, the soldiers had moved their searchlight to the shore side. The light was moving slowly across the water, out to about two hundred yards, looking for waterborne intruders. The earnestness of that search gave Frank a feeling of relief. They don't have any idea we're already here, he thought. They're watching for anyone coming in. It might give the team a few extra seconds of surprise when the attack started. Perhaps the first response of the forces guarding the villa would be to look for attack from the sea. That confusion would not last long, except by the wildest chance, but seconds could make the difference between success and failure ... between life and death. And the SEALs wanted every fragmentary assist they could get.

Except for the man on watch, the SEALs held off donning their night-vision goggles for as long as possible—as long as there was any remnant of daylight out on the Red Sea within their sight. The equipment was second nature for the SEALs—so much of their work was done in the dark—but there was something about the retreat to the green-glow world of infrared vision that gave the men pause. It was different, going from daylight to night rather than starting on a mission when it was already dark. Not a man in the team could have explained what that difference was, or why it affected them, but each of them felt it.

One by one, though, they slipped the night-vision gear over their heads and plunged into the world of green light and shadow. The time for action was approaching.

"We work our way down and to the right," Frank reminded the others as 2100 hours got near. "From the recon photos, it looks as if we'll have good cover until we get within two hundred yards of the villa. That's close enough for the XM18s. We'll spread out as much as we can without losing sight of each other, and I want all four of us popping the trigger at the same time when we start. When we do open up, Ike, you and I will concentrate on the troops and police guarding

the place. You handle the people on the right, I'll
take the left. The guard posts outside the villa, the
searchlight and machine guns, then we work on
that building inside on the south that they seem
to be using as a barracks. Rob and Beau, start
working on the main building right from the start.
Get your range and do as much damage as you
can. Go for windows and doors as much as possible, that's easier than trying to knock holes in
stone walls, even with the rounds we've got. Ike
and I will add our bit as soon as we can."

"What's the cut-off?" Rob asked. "When do we
stop worrying about blowing the hell out of that
compound and start worrying about getting our
asses out of harm's way?"

"We're going to have to play this by ear," Frank
said. "*Bellman* will see the first explosions and
know it's time to get ready to lend a hand. Once
we don't have to worry about radio silence, I'll
get on the horn and make sure Tombs knows
what's going on. Even if we knock out all the
security at the villa in the first few seconds we
can't count on having more than five minutes
before the Sudanese get more troops in. The helicopter, whatever they've got on the water, and
more. So we need to save some of the popcorn for
that."

"We supposed to go inside for a body count, or
to ID the targets?" Ike asked.

"Much as Tombs would like confirmation, we
only go through the villa if that looks like the

safest route home," Frank said. "Tombs can get his information wherever he's been getting it before. We're not going to try for fingerprints and pictures." *Wherever he's been getting it*: Frank had spent some time wondering about that. The intel had been so accurate that he suspected much of it had to be coming from ibn Landin's inner circle, someone who knew where and when the renegade millionaire was going to move. Maybe someone in the villa with him now, Frank thought. If he hasn't found a way to get himself out.

"There's the helicopter!" Ike whispered. "Out over the water again. Must be a half mile out." The others looked, saw the beam of the light the helicopter was shining on the surface of the Red Sea. "They're still looking for somebody coming in."

"Helicopter, police launch, and that searchlight on shore," Rob said. "Might make the assault easier for us, but it's gonna complicate the hell out of getting home."

There had been no synchronizing of watches. The attack had been planned to start at about 2130 hours, but the exact time remained up to Frank. He kept looking at his watch, let 2130 slip past. 2135. 2140. The team had been ready for a half hour. Everyone had slipped back into their field gear, donned the bandoleers of projectiles, web belts, and the rest of it. Their trash, the remnants of the meal packs they had eaten during the day, had been concealed under rocks; there wasn't enough loose dirt or sand close by to bury the garbage properly.

"Let's go." Frank got to his feet and started along the rough ledge leading south from their hideout. It was 2146 hours. He pushed his wristwatch farther up on his left arm so that the luminous dial could not give them away.

Ike was second out, followed by Rob and Beau. They had all looked over the first part of the trail they would follow during the day, knew where the obstacles were. But as soon as they were forty yards away, they were on ground they had not been able to see, feeling their way along the side of the rock-strewn slope. Frank moved slowly, stopping occasionally to look ahead, trying to find the best route. He did not want to get to a dead end and have to backtrack.

Somewhere out to sea, *Bellman* would—Frank assumed—be moving closer, getting into position to provide cover with its deck gun, and to launch boats to come in to pick up the SEALs. *Pompano* would be out there as well, perhaps just more than three miles out; the SDV was probably out of the DDS already, maybe no more than a few hundred yards offshore, waiting to find out if they would have to make the pickup. *Roosevelt* and the rest of the battle group were farther away, at least a hundred miles from Port Sudan, but it would not take fighters from the aircraft carrier long to get to the scene if they were needed, even if they weren't already in the air as part of the battle group's normal air cap.

It might get hairy, but we'll get out, one way or another, Frank thought. He needed the reassurance, and hoped that he wasn't lying to himself. By this time, a few minutes past 2200 hours, all of the battle group's assets should be on alert and watching for the first sign that the attack on shore had started.

Something moved near Frank's feet, scooting out of the way, under a rock. Frank did not see what it was, but had the impression that whatever the animal had been, it had moved on feet. Lizard or rat, something like that, he thought. Not a snake to spook the Farmer. The barest hint of a smile flitted across Frank's face and quickly vanished.

He kept moving.

It was just after 2230 hours when Frank decided they had reached the best location they were likely to find. He motioned for Ike to move past him, then gave Beau the signal to hold his place. The team spread out across thirty yards. They were near the bottom of the slope, behind the last cover to hide them from anyone looking out from the positions around the villa. From here, they would have to slide into firing position on hands and knees, perhaps even on bellies.

Frank waited until the others were as spread

out as he wanted, then started moving slowly toward their target. It was an awkward crawl—slightly downhill, around one large boulder and into position between two rocks that were each about the size of Volkswagen Beetles.

Give them a few more seconds to get ready, Frank told himself. His would be the first shot. As soon as the others heard the sound of that, they would pull the triggers on their projectile launchers. That first volley should hit in a tight bunch, and after that, they would work through the magazines as quickly as they could line up targets.

Frank took aim on the machine gun post at the northeast corner of the villa. He had the gun itself in sight, the slight motion of heads behind the waist-high barricade of sand bags about a hundred and seventy yards away. He adjusted his aim, then counted silently to three.

Now!

Frank pulled the trigger, felt the recoil, heard the sound of the shot. He moved the XM18 back into position and sent a second round on the same trajectory, before the first had a chance to reach the target, before he heard the reports of the other projectile launchers.

Total concentration. Barely controlled chaos. Fire and smoke. Noise, an all-out assault on ears and nerves. Frank concentrated as tightly as he had ever concentrated on anything as he moved his aim from one target to the next, methodically, being as efficient in his movements as possible.

He kept pulling the trigger until his XM18 clicked on an empty cylinder. It had been no more than seven or eight seconds since the first explosion.

Frank ducked back, opening the drum magazine as he moved, shaking the weapon to dump spent casings. He started pulling new projectiles from a bandoleer, shoving each into place. His fingers trembled a little as he reloaded. He was halfway through the task when he realized that all of the other XM18s had stopped firing as well. Everyone had to be reloading at the same time. He could hear gunshots from the villa, and around it, but the enemy didn't seem to know where the attackers were yet. The gunfire was ragged, uncoordinated. Blind.

When Frank finished reloading and lifted his head to look for targets again, he could see that the bombardment had already had considerable effect. There were several small fires burning inside the main building, and a larger blaze from the smaller building that the soldiers had been using as a barracks.

Frank was more selective about targets with the second magazine of projectiles. He looked for concentrations of soldiers or police, but sent most of the rounds into the villa's buildings. He used his radio to call Harry Tombs, and left that connection open. He had attention to spare for more of the team's surroundings as well, and spotted the approaching helicopter when it was still a half mile away, its searchlight feebly reaching out toward the hillside behind and above the SEALs, looking for targets from too far away.

"The helicopter!" Frank shouted, uncertain whether any of his men would hear his warning.

The helicopter had not quite reached the villa when it suddenly exploded. The range was too extreme for any of the XM18s to have reached the aircraft.

"One from the fleet," Tombs said over the radio. "You've got three Tomcats in range. They'll handle the gunboat too."

"Give them my thanks," Frank said, keying his transmitter just long enough for the sentence. It was time to reload his weapon again.

"Work your way toward shore, a hundred yards north of the villa," Tombs instructed as Frank filled the last chamber in the XM18. "Two whirly-birds coming in, one for pickup, one to ride shot-gun."

"Take us five or ten minutes," Frank said. "There's still a little opposition between us and the water."

"Ten minutes will work out fine," Tombs said. "We're getting great pictures. Doesn't seem to be anyone getting away from the villa."

"Any reinforcements on their way in?" Frank asked.

"Not close enough to worry about yet," Tombs said.

A grenade exploded fifty yards in front of Frank, close enough to make him duck, too far to be overly threatening. There were still soldiers ready to fight.

"Time to shag ass," Frank said. He was talking to himself, not over the radio.

"Ike!" he shouted. "Let's go!"

"Aye!" Ike shouted back. "I'm ready."

As soon as Ike reached Frank, the chief motioned him on toward the north. "We go out around that side of the villa. Our ride home is on the way in, with cover."

They picked up the other two men on the way, and kept moving. The SEALs did no firing once they started leaving their positions. There was still some gunfire behind them, but nothing that came close enough for any of them to notice. Several grenades went off, getting closer to the positions they had evacuated. Within the courtyard, there was a major explosion as the gas tank on one of the vehicles parked there cooked off. Thirty seconds later, a section of wall crumbled from the main building, falling into the courtyard, exposing the fires burning inside.

Hell on Earth, Rob thought, stopping for a second to look.

Once the team moved away from the cover of the scree and boulders at the base of the hill, a few of the villa's defenders spotted them. Automatic rifle fire came at the SEALs. They went to ground, turning to face the enemy. A dozen forty-millimeter projectiles slowed the rate of incoming fire for a few seconds, but not long enough. There were more men coming at them.

An explosion behind the SEALs dropped bits of stone among them. It was followed by another explosion, just seconds later.

"Hell, they've got a mortar working on us!" Rob shouted. "Must be coming from behind the main house."

"More men coming in from the south too," Ike said.

The villa was fully engulfed in flames now, fire spouting through doorways and windows, smoke curling around the eaves. One section of roof collapsed inward, sending a torrent of sparks up and out. Night had disappeared from the area. The fire was so bright, and hot, that the SEALs all pushed their night-vision goggles up onto foreheads. It was easier to see without them.

"Hey, Tombs, we're not going to be able to get down to the shore," Frank said into the radio— not quite a shout. "We're going to have to pull back, try to work our way north and west, away from all the shit here. They got their reinforcements in faster than we expected."

"Working on it already," Tombs said, almost calmly.

"Frank, look toward the main gate." That was Rob. A small group of men was moving away from the gate, due west, toward the slope about fifty yards south of where the SEALs had been forced down. "That's ibn Landin in the middle. I got a good look."

"Aw, shit," Frank said under his breath. He keyed his radio transmitter again. "The big cheese is making a break for the high ground, Tombs. Him and maybe a half dozen others. Looks like he's running, and not back toward the city."

"Can you get him?" Tombs asked.

"Get these other bastards off our backs and we'll try."

A dozen separate fires were burning in and around the villa, casting dancing shadows. The SEALs heard the popping sounds of ammunition being ignited by the flames. Twice they heard gasoline tanks explode. In the distance they heard the growing wail of sirens, pulsed tones moving closer.

"The helicopter crews have your position located," Tombs reported over the radio. "The gunship pilot suggests you move farther north, immediately."

Frank did not question Tombs. He simply got his men up, and started jogging. With so much of the ammunition for the XM18s already expended, the men all felt considerably lighter— more than could rationally be explained by the precise weight of that ammunition.

Twenty-five seconds after Tombs's warning, Frank and Ike spotted twin fiery streaks coming out of the darkness over the sea. Two missiles smashed into the main building of the villa and exploded inside. Through that noise, they heard the rapid stutter of a gatling gun, ripping across the level ground through the nearest group of Sudanese soldiers.

Although the SEALs were two hundred yards

from the rocket blasts, they all instinctively dove to the ground and covered their heads at the sound, before debris started to rain down around them.

"Come on. We've still got work to do!" Frank shouted, after just a couple of seconds. Lighter bits of debris were still coming down.

"They're heading straight for the top of the hill," Rob said. "Must be about a dozen of them now."

"That bastard must have planned an escape route," Frank said. The team was moving again, heading west now, climbing the slope again, hurrying as fast as they could. "A bolt hole, some kind of transportation."

The four men gave little attention to the scene behind them now, no more than an occasional glimpse—as often as not unintentional. Ike was the only one who saw the helicopter gunship explode, a hundred yards from shore, hit by a surface to air missile fired from somewhere in the vicinity of the burning villa.

The villa and the ground around it could have passed as some wildly morbid vision of the gates of Hell. Explosions and fires, dirty clouds illuminated from within, orange and red flames curling around each other. Tracer rounds streaking through the night, up and down. The defenders on the ground had not been destroyed, despite the mayhem that had been dropped on them. Beyond there were the sounds of distant sirens. More troops were approaching. Two helicopters came up from the south, and these were hostile, not friendly. Over the radio, Tombs relayed news that the Sudanese had scrambled two of their precious few MiG fighters.

Near the top of the slope, the SEALs had to stop for a moment, mostly to catch their breath. All turned to look back down toward the sea.

"Sweet Jesus," Rob whispered, his voice hoarse and labored. He was having trouble sucking in enough air. "How can anyone live through that?"

Frank lifted his head—a little. "Not our problem. We've still got ibn Landin to get. You see where they went?"

"No. Lost sight."

"They be seventy—eighty—yards south, maybe a bit higher than us," Beau said.

"Can't leave them above us," Frank said, pushing himself back to his feet. "Let's go."

The plateau was a rocky wasteland with virtually no living plant life that the SEALs could see. They had all donned their night-vision goggles again. Away from the flames, the night seemed darker than it ought to be.

Distance muted the noise behind the SEALs, dull thumps and thin cracks. They were able to hear the Sudanese helicopters coming in low over the plateau before they saw them. The helicopters were close before the lead bird turned on a searchlight and started moving it back and forth across the rocky terrain.

"What happened to the Tomcats that were supposed to keep off enemy choppers?" Rob asked.

"Too busy worrying about the MiGs," Frank

said. "We're going to have to take care of these birds ourselves."

"Are they after us or looking to pick up ibn Landin?" Rob asked.

"Either way, we've got to stop them," Frank said.

"I've only got one grenade left in my XM18," Ike said, "and I think that's incendiary."

"I've got two HE," Frank said, looking at the drum magazine of his projectile launcher. "Rob?"

"Zip."

"Beau?"

"Two, one frag, one HE."

"It'll have to do. Let's go. And keep your eyes open for the bastards on the ground." Frank got up and took the point, heading south.

He moved cautiously but fast, darting from one bit of cover to the next. The broken rock field atop the plateau gave plenty of protection. It was almost a maze. The SEALs moved a little farther inland, away from the precipice and—Frank hoped—a little farther from the group of armed men with ibn Landin. Take care of the choppers first, Frank told himself. We can worry about the men on the ground afterward. While he led his men south, he kept one eye on the helicopter he could see clearly, the one with the searchlight.

He almost didn't see the second helicopter before it was too late. That aircraft had circled around on the east. It came in low and fast, without lights. It was within two hundred yards before Frank saw it and yelled, "Hit the deck!" just as the helicopter's machine guns opened up. The gunfire was too accurate to be random. The gunner had to be operating with his own night-vision system.

Ike had been on the right flank. He was the man nearest the helicopter. For a couple of seconds, Ike could scarcely hear the sounds of gunfire over the pounding of his own heart. Bullets had come far too close for comfort. Ike was so pumped up that he didn't even realize that his right arm had been nicked by one of the slugs. There was no pain yet, just the first real gut-twisting fear he had ever experienced. A convulsive shudder. Ike sucked in a deep breath and pressed his eyes shut—just for an instant. When he opened his eyes again, he lifted up on one knee, bringing his XM18 up into firing position, tracking the blinking lights of the machine gun in the waist of the helicopter. The round was barely away before Ike dropped the launcher and swung his Uzi around into position.

The explosion seemed to catch him by surprise, a hundred feet up and little more than sixty yards away horizontally, as the incendiary round exploded inside the helicopter. Ike ducked, wrapping his arms around his head as flaming debris erupted from the aircraft.

Beau was the only SEAL who did not duck. As the glare of the explosion lit up the sky, he raised up, aiming his XM18 at the second helicopter, farther away. He pulled the trigger twice, as quickly as he could make aimed shots, before dropping behind a large boulder and rolling as far under its edge as he could. He felt something burn his back, but the feeling was transient. It was several minutes later before it returned, and he realized that he had been hit.

Frank ducked, moved around the side of a rock, away from the debris, then crawled forward, coming up to his knees just as Beau stopped moving. Neither of Beau's projectiles had hit the second helicopter. They fell back to the ground before detonating.

Frank fired one HE round, and waited—unwilling to use the last round unless it was necessary.

It wasn't. The first round hit the nose of the last helicopter and blew it out of the air. There was no fire, but the aircraft started to rotate under its rotor, spiraling into the rocks. The larger explosion didn't come until the helicopter hit the ground.

Frank started moving back, scooting along the ground. "Everyone okay?" he called in what amounted to a stage whisper.

"Yo," Rob said. "Hey, Beau's hurt."

"I be okay," Beau said.

Frank moved toward the voices. Beau had crawled back out from under the edge of the boulder. He was lying on his stomach, and Rob was bent over him.

"How bad?" Frank asked.

"Looks like somebody pressed a fucking iron against his back," Rob said. "Piece of wreckage from the first chopper, I guess. Looks nasty, but he'll live."

"I be okay," Beau repeated.

Ike reached the others. Frank looked up and saw the wet, sticky area on his right arm. "What happened to you, kid?" Frank asked.

"What?"

"Your arm." Frank pointed. Ike reached up with his left hand and touched the spot, then pulled his hand away and looked at the blood on it.

"Shit, I didn't even know. Can't be bad."

"Let me look," Frank said.

Beau moved around, sitting up, flexing his back and shoulders as if testing his limits.

"Just a scratch," Ike said as Frank leaned close to his wounded arm. "What about the bad guys? We've still got work to do."

"Yeah, man," Beau said, using his rifle as a prop to help him get to his feet. "Got to do them 'fore they do us. They be here, close. I kin smell 'em."

"You need a shot for pain?" Frank asked.

"Later."

"Leave the launchers here together," Frank whispered. "We get a chance, we'll retrieve them later."

Who's hunting who? Frank wondered, as he started moving again. He put Beau and Ike in the middle. Ike's wound was insignificant, but Frank didn't want to take chances with the young man. His nerves might be about shot, Frank thought. Let him look after Beau. That left Rob on rear-guard.

Frank had lost all track of time. He wasn't certain how many minutes had passed since they had first taken on the helicopters. Dealing with the aircraft and then the wounds had robbed the chief of the time. Glancing at his watch didn't help. It told him the current time, but not how much had passed.

Where are you, Landin? he asked in his head. Are you running to save your ass or coming after us? Were the helicopters your ace in the hole? Or do you have something else here?

The questions did not detract from Frank's alertness. He moved slowly, cautiously, stopping after almost every step, listening hard for any sounds that didn't belong. His eyes kept moving, scanning the terrain ahead and to either side. The barrel of his Uzi moved with his eyes, an unconscious mimicry that meant that if he did spot anything, the submachine gun would already be pointed in the general direction of any target.

Beau, second in line, was a little to Frank's left as well as three yards behind him. Beau moved with his teeth gritted against the growing pain of the burn on his back. When he eyes started to tear up he had to stop and rub the tears away—a few dangerous seconds of less than full attention. God, we got to get this over fast, he thought.

Ike's wound had started to sting, but it was only a minor irritant, more a wonder to the youngest member of the team than anything else. I got shot and didn't even feel it. That amazed him. He was a little to Frank's right, but only two steps behind

Beau, close enough to catch him if he started to fall. How can he keep going with that? Ike wondered. He had seen how severe the wound on Beau's back was. The burn went through the skin to the meat below.

Rob let himself drift farther back than he usually would have on rearguard, leaving more than ten yards between himself and the two men in the middle. He ranged a little more freely from side to side as well, looking for a better angle, looking for any extra edge to help him see their targets before the targets saw them . . . and started shooting first.

It was a near thing.

Rob saw—or thought he saw—a hint of movement off to his left, no more than thirty yards away. He shouted, "Down!" as he pivoted and opened fire with his M-16, just as at least six men started firing toward the SEALs. Rob dropped to the ground in what was almost slow motion, his finger riding the trigger of his rifle the whole way, spraying bullets across the muzzle flashes. He heard bullets whiz by, heard them chipping rock, felt splinters of rock against his face. He also heard someone scream—one of the terrorists.

By that time, the gunfire was general. The other SEALs were firing back.

Rob did not wait around. He started crawling away, back north, going as quickly as he could on hands and knees. There had been no orders, no communication at all with Frank. But with the two groups so close together, there was no time for that. Rob wanted to get an angle, flank the terrorists— get somewhere he could have a clear shot at them.

He needed five minutes to get into position. He climbed up on a rock, careful not to expose himself any sooner than he had to. He could see five men seventy yards away.

Ducks in a pond, he thought as he switched the selector on his rifle from automatic to single shot. He rested the barrel of the M-16 on the rock and lined up his first target. There was so much noise going on that the terrorists might never notice that one gun was shooting from ninety degrees away from the rest.

One bullet, one body. Rob fired quickly but accurately, working his way down the line. Four men went down before anyone even thought to look his way. The fifth man went down as he brought his AK-47 around to bear.

There were more of the enemy, out of Rob's view, but they were fully occupied by the other SEALs. Rob could make out the sound of the two Uzi submachine guns, combining to make a sound almost like a buzzsaw.

Then Rob heard a man start shouting in Arabic. Rob could not see him, so he missed the finale.

Frank had started trying to work his way around to the right, unaware that Rob was moving left. He was unable to get far. There was an open space, and the enemy had it marked too closely for him to make it across. Frank gave up the attempt. When he heard the report of single shots from an M-16 at some distance, he guessed what had happened, and worried less about his own ability to flank the enemy. He put a fresh magazine in his Uzi and worked to keep the terrorists pinned down.

Ammunition was getting short. Frank only had two more thirty-round magazines, so he was as sparing as he could be of it. A second single shot. A third. Frank knew how good Rob was with a rifle, even if the M-16 wasn't a usual sniper weapon.

Frank raised up a little higher than he had been, and got off a short burst at one of the men shooting at him. Got him! There seemed to be only two or three of the terrorists still firing.

He ducked back down and brought the radio to his mouth. "Tombs! You ready to get us the hell out of here?"

"Soon as you give the word it's safe to bring a chopper in, Chief."

"Getting close. Just a couple hostiles left here, I think."

"You get ibn Landin?"

Frank almost missed Tombs's question.

Bullets started hitting all around him, coming from his right—the south. Frank fell flat and twisted around, yelling for Ike and Beau to watch out as he moved.

Two men were running straight at Frank, firing their AK-47s on full automatic, screaming as they raced toward the SEALs. Frank started firing back, spraying across the two men. For impossibly long seconds, nothing seemed to touch the running men. Frank heard an M-16 firing past him from behind, also on full automatic—Beau. And Ike's Uzi joined in almost as quickly.

Still the two men came on, as if they were untouchable. They were within thirty feet of Frank before one of them fell. The other kept coming. Frank's magazine went empty. There was no time to reload. He dropped the Uzi and drew his pistol, but he knew he was not going to have time to get it up before the last terrorist—*ibn Landin himself,* Frank realized—got to him.

Frank could see the murderous rage on the Saudi terrorist's face, a hideous contortion of his features. He was screaming unintelligible words. Frank got up on his knees, ready to rise to tackle ibn Landin.

"Down, Chief!"

Frank dropped and Ike Jensen moved up level with him, firing point blank into the terrorist. Frank could see where a half dozen bullets hit, stitching a pattern across ibn Landin's chest. The man stumbled. The muzzle of his rifle drooped, then the weapon fell from his hands. Two bullet holes appeared in his face and ibn Landin stumbled again, then fell. He twitched several times, then his entire body was wracked by a massive spasm before he quit moving.

* * *

Half a minute or more passed before Frank realized that all the shooting had stopped. Slowly he got to his feet, never taking his eyes off the dead man not more than three yards away from him. It wasn't until he heard someone stumbling around behind him—noisily—that Frank turned.

Beau was doing the stumbling, a crooked hesitation step. His rifle dragged on the ground. His head was tilted back, as if he were studying the stars. "I got the last one," Beau said, his voice sounding dreamy. Then he collapsed, falling heavily to his knees. Before he could tip forward and fall on his face, Ike got to him and eased him more gently to the ground.

Frank reached for his radio again, but there was only wreckage left. "Kid, you still got the backup radio?"

Ike found it intact and handed it to the chief.

"How's Beau?" Frank said

"Been shot. Bullet in the side. I'll get pressure bandages on," Ike said.

"Farmboy?" Frank shouted.

"Yeah. Coming."

Frank keyed the transmitter. "Come and get us, Tombs."

POST-MISSION

"You did it. You really did it." Harry Tombs stood over the body the SEALs had brought back with them. The corpse was lying in the companionway at the aft end of *Bellman*'s superstructure. Beau and Ike were already being tended to, ready for transportation to the better medical facilities aboard the aircraft carrier.

"It is him, ibn Landin, isn't it?" Frank asked.

"It'll take a couple of days for a positive ID, but I don't think there's any doubt," Tombs said. "I've spend hours staring at photographs of him."

"Funny thing is, he could have gotten away again," Frank said. "If he hadn't tried to come after us, he could have survived, gone back into hiding."

"Maybe he was just too pissed off at what we'd done to think straight," Rob suggested. "We rained all over his little parade back there."

"Crazy, pissed off, or just too damned fanatic to stand seeing his plans destroyed," Tombs said. "Let's get him into a body bag so the helicopter can take him over to the carrier. They can keep the stiff on ice there until we get home."

"We going home now?" Ike asked.

Tombs nodded. "The job's finished. All but the celebrating."

"Too bad we don't get all that reward money the government was offering for this bastard," Rob said, giving the corpse a nudge with his toe. "Five million bucks."

Tombs chuckled. "I can't get that much for you, but I think the Agency will be able to cover the price of a damned good celebration and a month's leave to give you a chance to recover from the celebration." And there would be a little more. Tombs had discretionary funds at his disposal. I'm going to come off smelling like a million-dollar rose, he thought. I can spread a little of it around.

EPILOGUE

Two weeks had passed. The SEAL team had been airlifted directly to *Roosevelt*. Beau and Ike had spent three days in the ship's sickbay before the chief medical officer approved transferring them to a hospital ashore—at the American facility on the island of Diego Garcia. Frank and Rob had been "treated and released" but had made the trip with the others, as had Harry Tombs. Another four days passed before the team was flown back to the United States in an Air Force jet that refueled in flight.

The final debriefing had taken place at CIA headquarters in Langley, Virginia. Beau and Ike remained under medical attention for another week. Frank and Rob were returned to duty.

Frank's first action was to report to Lieutenant Holman's office. Holman's yeoman sent the chief straight in.

After the two men exchanged salutes, Holman came around the desk and shook Lucan's hand.

"I'm glad to see you all made it back, Chief," he said. "The Agency seems to think you did okay."

Frank grunted. "Nice of them to say so," he said, in what was nearly a growl.

"The press is going wild with speculation."

"I've seen some of it," Frank admitted. "We're not saying anything, right?"

"No comment across the line." Holman nodded and smiled. He went back to his chair and said, "Take a load off, Frank. If I had a bottle here, I'd offer you a drink."

"That's okay, Lieutenant. You can owe me." Frank sat and stretched out his legs.

"The White House has no comment. The CIA has no comment. The State Department has no comment. The Department of Defense has no comment." Holman leaned back in his chair and chuckled. Then he lit a cigarette. "The folks on the other side are sure commenting. They're bitching all over the place." He took a deep drag on his cigarette. "Beautiful, Frank. Worth the price of admission."

"Glad you think so, sir," Frank said, slightly annoyed by the skipper's exhuberance. Frank found no joy in the memories. Men had died, even if they were "the enemy."

"I'm not going to ask you to tell me anything you're not supposed to. I've just got one question to ask. How did the spook stack up?"

"Tombs?" Frank paused, weighing his answer. "He's a coldblooded bastard, but I've got to give him one thing. He took care of us."

In the end, that was really all that mattered.

SEALS

by H. Jay Riker

The face of war is rapidly changing, calling
America's soldiers into hellish regions where
conventional warriors dare not go.
This is the world of the SEALs.

SILVER STAR
76967-0/$6.99 US/$8.99 Can

PURPLE HEART
76969-7/$6.50 US/$8.99 Can

BRONZE STAR
76970-0/$5.99 US/$8.99 Can

NAVY CROSS
78555-2/$5.99 US/$7.99 Can

MEDAL OF HONOR
78556-0/$5.99 US/$7.99 Can

MARKS OF VALOR
78557-9/$5.99 US/$7.99 Can

IN HARM'S WAY
79507-8/$6.99 US/$9.99 Can